## *Love kills*

Lijena could scarcely believe that she was in bed with Davin Anane, the man who had kidnapped her and whom she had sworn to kill. Still, she was powerless against the voice whispering in her head.

"You love him," the voice commanded.

"I love you, Davin," she repeated in an emotionless tone.

Her hands urged him, and he came to her, his body matching her rhythms. She sighed, her lips and hands exploring, teasing.

The voice spoke again. "The dagger. Beside you. Take it. When his pleasure peaks—strike!"

His eyes closed in ecstasy, he didn't see Lijena as she reached for the dagger, lifted it high and thrust for his bared chest...

·SWORDS·OF·RAEMLLYN·

# TO DEMONS BOUND

## ROBERT E. VARDEMAN
## AND GEO. W. PROCTOR

ACE FANTASY BOOKS
NEW YORK

TO DEMONS BOUND

An Ace Fantasy Book / published by arrangement with
the authors

PRINTING HISTORY
Ace Original / March 1985

ISBN: 0-441-81464-6

Ace Fantasy Books are published by The Berkley Publishing Group,
200 Madison Avenue, New York, New York 10016.
PRINTED IN THE UNITED STATES OF AMERICA

For Kerry who has given me the best of all things and the worst, too ... *Bob*

For Mike Presley who weaves the spectrum with a brush ... *Geo*.

# UPPER AND LOWER RAEMLLYN

OCEANS OF KUMAR

SEA OF BUA

GULF OF QATERA

OCEANS OF KUMAR

| | | |
|---|---|---|
| 1. Kavindra | 16. Evara | 31. Melisa |
| 2. Kressia | 17. Salim | 32. Delu |
| 3. Sarngan | 18. Yaryne | 33. Jyotis |
| 4. Amayita | 19. Leticia | 34. Initha |
| 5. Bian | 20. Bistonia | 35. Zahar |
| 6. Cahri | 21. Harn | 36. Elkid |
| 7. Chavali | 22. Nawat | 37. Uhjayib |
| 8. Degoolah | 23. Vatusia | 38. Fayinah |
| 9. Garoda | 24. Rakell | 39. Pahl |
| 10. Jyn | 25. Solana | 40. Rattreh |
| 11. Meakham | 26. Faldin | 41. Ohnuhn |
| 12. Parrn | 27. Weysh | 42. Gatinah |
| 13. Qatirn | 28. Salnal | 43. Ahvayuh |
| 14. Orji | 29. Yow | 44. Nayati |
| 15. Iluska | 30. Litonya | |

# *chapter*
## 1

BLACK QAR, GOD OF DEATH, favored the night's shadows that veiled the streets of Raemllyn's cities. No more than an icy chill that wove within an unseasonably warm late autumn's eve, the Great Destroyer entered the avenues of Bistonia. She . . . he . . . it—Qar's sex was as varied as the profanities spat into the Death God's face by those whose lives the Black One claimed—hungered.

Outstretching an invisible finger of ice, Qar tapped the unblemished forehead of a young mother with child suckling at breast, then passed on.

The gently smiling woman tightened the arm cradling the frail bundle at her bosom. Her hand, supporting a tiny head too weak to lift its mouth to a nourishing nipple, worked inward with a steady and increasing pressure. With a motherly smile, she watched the red face of her infant daughter disappear in the whiteness of her milk-swollen pap. She hummed a soft, crooning lullaby until the miniature arms and legs wrapped within the warm constraint of a woolen blanket lay still and lifeless . . . then the horror of her act penetrated the icy numbness of her brain.

A mother's wail of anguish echoed through Bistonia's streets.

Qar smiled, appetite whetted. The Black One extended another finger.

Garrid of Salim, twenty years Bistonia's finest cobbler, eased from the cozy warmth of his wife's side to walk from their bed to his workbench. There he hefted a wooden mallet used for preparing uncured hides. Pleased with its weight, he returned to the bed. For a moment he stood above his wife. The mallet rose.

And fell.

Garrid the cobbler was hard pressed to explain the bloody hammer in his hands and the bodies of his wife and seven children when he was discovered by the city guards the next morning.

Qar moved on, once more lifting a finger. This time Death's frigid touch tapped the nape of the neck of Aylrah the Fleet, a minor purse-snatch in Bistonia's network of thieves, while he stood in the blackness of an alley near the Inn of the Winged Ram.

Aylrah had spent the better part of the eve trailing a young newcomer to the city, maneuvering, scheming. The rich weave of the young man's deep wine-red silk brocade vest, the full, unsoiled sleeves of his white silk blouse, the fine leather of his over-the-calf boots, and the weighty sway of a pouch tied to a broad, silver-buckled belt about his waist had first drawn Aylrah's attention.

The young man's manner of dress bespoke wealth and a money pouch fat with gold rather than copper. More than vest, silken shirt, boots, and silver-buckled belt, it was the pouch that mesmerized Aylrah.

That the raven-haired young man carried a sword and dagger upon that same belt from which the money pouch dangled was of little concern to the thief. Nor did he give more than a glance to the burly hulk of a man who walked beside his intended victim. After all, Aylrah was dubbed "the Fleet," and rightly so. For ten years he had artfully eluded the grasp of Bistonia's city guards and managed to live quite comfortably off the purses of others less agile than himself.

Aylrah's right hand dropped to his waist. A slender, finely honed knife slid from its sheath as the richly dressed man and his companion approached the alley. The blade rose high to pause at the top of its arc. An icy fire flowed within Aylrah's veins. With all the strength he could muster, he drove the pointed sliver of steel toward a vulnerably exposed back as his victim strolled past the dark alley, oblivious to Qar's servant.

"Aaarrggaa!" Agony gasped from Aylrah's pain-twisted lips.

The deadly blade hovered in midair, its needle point a hairbreadth from a wine-colored brocade vest.

The pain-accented cry spun Davin Anane around. The swarthy young man's hand poised—too late—on the hilt of his own silver dagger.

The danger had passed . . . for him!

"Friend Goran!" Davin Anane grinned widely. "What have you found this fine night?"

Though Aylrah's blade hovered at Davin's chest, it might as well have been embedded in granite for all the harm it could deliver now. Davin's friend and fellow freebooter Goran One-Eye held the scrawny thief at arm's length. The purse-snatch futilely kicked and struggled.

Against Goran, Aylrah's efforts availed him naught. The red-bearded giant's powerful arm bulged with the effort of keeping the would-be assassin's feet just inches off the ground, his sole grip around one bony wrist.

Abandoned by his legendary quickness, Aylrah desperately swung his left hand up to salvage the knife from his bloodless right.

Davin's own arm shot out with a speed that left Aylrah's jaw agape. The young adventurer snared the knife and sent it cartwheeling into the night. It clattered against the cobblestone street twenty yards distant.

A curious bypassing pedestrian, wrapped in the fur-lined cloak of a merchant, peered into the alley, saw the deadly tableau, and blanched. He turned and hurried on his way, muttering to himself about crime running rampant. In the city-state of Bistonia it was not wise to meddle in others' affairs, especially when those affairs all too often spelled death for the unwary.

"So you thought to rob me, eh, little one?" Davin eyed the thief with more humor than he might have shown on another occasion.

He and Goran had successfully completed a daring robbery of their own only a week before. Four days of hard riding had ensured their escape. For the past three days and glorious nights they had been enveloped in the wonders—and debaucheries—offered by Bistonia. As long as gold weighed nicely in his pouch and the city guards kept their distance, Davin Anane was willing to let bygones be bygones.

Not so Goran.

The massive mountain of muscle and bone relished a good fight almost as much as anything else life had to offer—a trait that had given Davin pause, and a shiver of fear, on more than one occasion. But then, of all men alive, only Davin knew Goran One-Eye's secret—the man was no man!

Rather, Goran was a Challing, a creature nine parts spirit for every one part physical.

Some claimed the Challings came from another space, drawn to this world by magicks so powerful that only a few mortals had ever heard the chants, much less mastered them. For Challings were changelings, entities capable of assuming the form of any living creature—or inanimate object.

Davin knew Goran's sorry tale of being ensorcelled by the demented mage Roan-Jafar and brought to this world for scurrilous deeds best left unmentioned. But Goran's anger at being sundered from his own realm gave him energies unknown to the summoning mage.

Goran had killed Roan-Jafar with the sorcerer's own knife, an act that had freed the Challing of his would-be master, but not of the gargantuan form to which he had been bound. Since that day, over five years in the past, Goran had journeyed the lands of Raemllyn in search of another possessing the sorcerous knowledge needed to free him from the bonds of human flesh.

To return to his own realm was all Goran sought from life—but that didn't prevent the hulking giant from enjoying a few of the more human pleasures encountered during that search. Although those *pleasures* were often beyond Davin's comprehension.

"I enjoy the feel of blood—another's blood—oozing between my fingers," Goran declared loudly.

More than bravado boomed in that resounding voice, a fact apparently all too crystal clear to the dangling thief, whose eyes grew saucer-wide. An instant later, sinews sprang forth on Goran's log-thick forearm as his bear-paw-sized hand squeezed vise-tight about Aylrah's wrist.

A heartbeat before the thief's wide eyes clamped shut and anguish tore from his throat, Davin heard the crush of bone.

"Do with him as you will." Davin refused to allow his friend's sanguinary diversion to dampen his own high spirits.

While he would have sent the thief scurrying with a well-placed boot to a bony backside, the cutpurse had earned whatever reward Goran decided to bestow upon him. *Indeed, mayhaps even more! The son of a mange-ridden Oraidian bitch meant to bury his blade hilt deep in my back!*

With a final glance at the helplessly dangling thief, Davin turned to leave. "I intend to spend my time in more . . . exciting pursuits."

"That wench Belatha, eh?" Goran peered at his friend through his one good eye.

The witch-fire burned brightly in it tonight, making

Davin shiver slightly. The sight of those demon sparks adance like light reflecting off the insides of an opal betold of Goran's magical powers on the wax. Davin wanted no part of his friend when this happened—Goran had scant control of prodigious energies at the best of times.

As for Goran's other eye, or darkened socket, it lay hidden beneath a fox-skin patch as fiery red as the Challing's magic-bound mane. How Goran had lost that orb provided something of a mystery for Davin because of the giant's propensity for cobbling together a new and even wilder yarn every time he was asked.

"Please, lords, I beseech you! Be kind to a poor man only trying to steal to support his sickly wife and seven malnourished bratlings," Aylrah squealed, obviously fearing for his life.

"Ah, a liar as well as a thief! I'll wager that this one is incapable of siring offspring. Two bists that he is shriveled and much too wormlike to properly render the services a woman requires of a man."

Davin waved away the proffered bet and shook his head, neither of which stopped Goran from reaching down with his free hand, gripping the thief's belt, yanking, and exposing his squirming plaything to the night.

"Ha! I was right! See, Davin, see? This rooster can no longer crow. It's no bigger than a joint of my thumb! And his jewels hang like sparrow peas in a dried husk!"

"Let him go play with himself, Goran. We've better things to do than badger this pathetic wight. Belatha awaits me at the inn. And didn't you mention a game of chance over on the Street of Five Winds you wished to attend this night?"

"That I had. And fat merchants who don't understand odds! A dozen or more are to be there. Tonight I turn this paltry stake into real wealth." Idly Goran discarded the thief as another might a crumpled sheet of foolscap.

The scrawny man slammed into a solid brick wall and

slid to the alley, clutching his broken wrist and glaring
at the Challing in giant's form. When Goran glanced his
way, the merest spark of hellfire burning in his one good
eye, Aylrah swallowed hard and scuttled toward the street,
thus depriving Qar of two souls that night, Davin Anane's—and his own.

"Ha-hiya!" Goran's bellowed laugh rolled resonant
and rich from the hidden depths of his barrel chest. "This
will be a good evening. Can you watch after yourself,
friend Davin? Or would you like me to hold it for you
while you're seducing lovely blonde Belatha?"

Davin ignored the Challing's coarse attempt at humor.
His thoughts preceded him to the side of a busty woman
with emerald eyes that smoldered and burned with ill-
suppressed passion.

"Let us not waste another moment in this Qar-damned
alleyway!" Without so much as a backward glance, Goran
One-Eye lumbered off, his mighty battle-ax swinging at
his hip.

Davin watched the Challing's retreat with a shake of
his head. Goran was incongruously out of place with the
gold-threaded finery of his satin breeches and the tightly stretched expanse of orange and burnt umber tunic
held at his waist by green *pletha*-snake hide.

Davin's attention returned to the two braziers ablaze
before him that marked the entrance to the Inn of the
Winged Ram. He edged aside the erotic image of cur-
vaceous Belatha that tauntingly wove into his mind.

That same alluring vision had almost cost him his life
but moments ago. Bistonia was a dangerous city for the
unsuspecting or the unwary—or the foolhardy! He had
been too intent on the unspoken promises he had seen
in Belatha's lingering gaze that afternoon to even notice
the purse-snatch tucked away in the alley's shadows. Any
street waif displayed more caution than that—especially
at night!

If he intended to collect those emerald-eyed promises,

and he *did* desire Belatha with all his heart, soul, and body—at least for this night—best that he pay less attention to his lust and more to his environs.

# chapter
## 2

DAVIN ANANE'S GAZE moved along the prosperous Street of Lungs. Nigh deserted now, it gave no hint of the bustling throngs that crowded it during the security of daylight. Nestled deep in the heartlands of Upper Raemllyn, Bistonia was hardly the commercial hub of the realm, or even a major kingdom. It did readily offer a variety of diversions to lighten Davin's purse. And there were ample avenues of fortune for one of enterprising wit and little regard for local laws of property.

Davin smiled as he hastened to a tiny courtyard a few paces distant and entered an elaborately contrived wrought-iron gate, depicting in its intricately worked pattern the epic of the ancient hero Kaga stealing the winged rams of the God Brykheedah. None had ever accused Davin Anane of a shortage of cunning or a respect for the law. Before Goran and he quit fair Bistonia, at least one opal merchant on the Street of Lungs would awake one morn to find his cache of gems deftly purloined in the silence of the night.

A quick glance about the courtyard revealed three tables occupied by wealthy merchants lost in discussion of profit. Two other small oil-lamp-lit tables were taken by four soldiers wearing the crest of Lerel, ruler of Bistonia. The guards paid Davin no heed. Their leering gazes were reserved for the serving wenches and the shapely turn of a calf or half-exposed bosom flirtingly revealed for their benefit.

The few tables secluded in cozy alcoves around the courtyard were cloaked in shadow. Davin could not tell if they were occupied or not—not that he had any intention of claiming one of the darkness-veiled tables. He didn't want his personal affairs openly aired. For too long he had lived by his wits. It never proved wise to allow strangers the merest hint of one's intentions, even when they were, on rare occasion, honorable.

Who he didn't see was Belatha!

*Has she found another this night?* Davin's brow furrowed.

She *had* mentioned the moneylenders who flocked to the inn every night. Had those emerald eyes sold their lusty promised to one with more weight to his purse?

His doubts evaporated as two very feminine arms encircled his waist from behind. There was one definite squeeze before enthusiastic hands spun him about. Before he could so much as utter a syllable of greeting, his arms filled with a squirming, warm, sensuous female intent on smothering him with kisses.

In the next instant, Belatha broke off the deeply passionate kiss and shoved him away with surprisingly strong arms to demand loudly, "How dare you?"

Davin's questioning frown concealed a hasty glance about the courtyard. Those at the tables were too engrossed in their own pursuits, be they gold or stolen gazes at plump breasts, to notice Belatha and him. His attention returned to the bountifully endowed blonde with the fiery eyes of emerald hue, although he was uncertain whether that flame stemmed from desire.

With hands planted firmly on hips, Belatha stomped a sandaled foot to the flagstone. "You promised to be here one grain of sand past sunset. Why, I've been waiting for . . . hours!"

Davin summoned up an expression of boyish innocence to mask a grin of amusement. The wickedly delicious smile on Belatha's full red lips told the true story. No matter when Davin had arrived, it wouldn't have been soon enough for this daughter of Bistonia.

*And I worried about losing her to some creaking, overage moneylender with bulging sacks of gold and silver bists and eagles!*

"You cannot know the half of it." To complement his pitiful expression, Davin solemnly lowered his voice to a whisper. "I was set upon by a thief—thieves! Fully a dozen! Armed with rapiers that sang in the air like venomous metallic snakes."

Belatha's eyes widened to emerald orbs ignited by the excitement of danger and admiration for the handsome young adventurer standing before her.

"I had but one thought as they backed me into an alley, intent on slicing my body into bloody ribbons." Davin milked the moment for all it was worth.

"What?" Belatha's voice was throaty with excitement. "What was the thought? Your life being relived? A mystical vision?"

"I thought only of you. I would be denied your precious company." Davin mustered all the sincerity he could to deliver that less than sincere line. "I yanked out my dagger and sword, slew the six on my right, and by the time I'd swirled to assault the six on my left, why, they'd turned tail and run like cravens!"

Belatha snorted in mock disgust, then laughed, realizing she was on the receiving end of a fully embellished, impromptu tall tale.

"I knew you tarried with that red-haired, thick-hided *lanka* you call a friend far too long. This but proves my case. You are beginning to lie as powerfully as he does!"

"I but told it the way it should have occurred, my lovely. Nothing—not even a full dozen brigands—could keep me away this night." Davin hooked an arm about

Belatha's slender waist, escorting her to a rough-hewed oak table.

The bench that accommodated them was as hard as Davin's firm-muscled thigh, which suggestively pressed against Belatha's softer, yielding one. Under the table came a feminine hand, moving slowly, seeking, finding. Davin sucked in a lungful of air as the hand methodically sought to transform him into a bull in rut.

He turned to the divine vision at his side. Belatha was no peasant, no tavern wench, no day worker. Nor was the frosty-haired temptress a mere courtesan, of that he was positive. Her skin was of the finest and smoothest. The hand on the table—and the one so delightfully employed beneath—had never toiled. They were untouched by blemish and work-hardening.

While she had never hinted that she was more than she appeared, Davin fantasized that she was a highborn lady of some manor, her lord old and haggard, the amorous fires long dead within his loins. Belatha now sought adventure elsewhere. She required a man to fill her nights, to give her the pleasures that had since fled the marital bed.

That was Davin's fantasy, a fantasy that only fanned his desire. The woman beside him was not woven from his imagination. Nor were her sensuously half-hooded emerald eyes, the small smile crinkling the corners of carmine-tinted lips, the soft flow of cheek and jawline, the delicately formed ear peeping out from beneath a cascade of lustrous golden hair.

Davin's arm tightened about Belatha's waist, drawing her closer so that his lips might teasingly brush that ear. He felt a shiver of excitement rush through his highborn lady disguised as a serving wench, a shiver that was transformed to a quivering when his tongue lightly toyed with her earlobe.

Belatha wiggled closer. Davin caught his breath as the hand stroking his thigh under the table pressed into his groin and squeezed eagerly.

"The Inn of the Winged Ram is famous for its mulled ale," she whispered in throaty little gasps. "I will get us some."

Before Davin could protest, the sleek Belatha slipped away, leaving her lover for the eve alone in momentary confusion.

Davin chuckled. Belatha wasn't a woman to rush things. She intended for him to stew in his own desires for a while, before fulfilling the promises of eyes and hand.

This was yet another reason for believing her a lady to the manner born rather than a scullery maid. Lower-born tended to take their pleasures lustily, quickly, without need for sexual intrigue. Beyond his own fantasy, Davin truly suspected Belatha of being more than she appeared—a consummate actress living out her own fantasy with him.

While the highborn ladies fascinated him, Davin rue-fully admitted that all women of beauty and wit awoke equal interest. Let Belatha play out her role; he would fuel the fires of fantasy and then show her how superb reality could be—with the right man.

Davin leaned back and turned toward the inn's open doorway. From within the main hall of the Winged Ram came a flood of dancing orange light cast by the burning logs in the stone fireplace. The blaze was for its cozy effect only. The lingering warmth of late autumn beguiled the world with a false promise. It was, after all, early winter. The first snow could be no more than weeks away.

Belatha abruptly appeared in the doorway, her slender form silhouetted by the light from inside.

Davin's preferences in women's clothing had always been for the thin and form-fitting. He was now presented with a special treat as he stared at the approaching blonde.

Belatha's loosely flowing skirt seemed to glow with

an inner radiance, giving shadowy hints of fine legs beneath. The light white cotton blouse she wore turned almost transparent, to present him with a glimpse of her breasts and the erect nipple topping each.

"I must tend to a few of the other patrons," she said when she reached Davin's side. Then, before his disappointment-pursed lips could utter their complaints, she pressed her mouth to his.

"The tidings are not all ill. The owner has sampled too much of his own wine this night and has taken to his bed like a common drunk. Ambika has promised to relieve me as soon as she has the old fool tucked away and snoring." Again her kiss silenced Davin. "Then the night will belong to us. That I promise, my Davin."

She turned toward the Winged Ram, then glanced back at the young freebooter. "Wait for me in the garden. You'll see my signal . . . and let no full dozen thieves delay you this time!"

Davin grunted while he watched Belatha's alluring form once more disappear within the inn. If this were but another ploy to fire his anticipation . . .

He shoved the thought away as easily as he pushed from the table. The delay was a small price to pay for all that Belatha promised, and the garden was but a few steps away, behind the Winged Ram.

He was leaning against the cold bole of an ancient oak when a single candle shone at last from a second-story window and a sash squeaked out a metallic protest as it opened.

"Davin?" Belatha's voice was a husky whisper.

"Coming," he answered, moving toward the flickering beacon.

"I hope not too soon." Belatha giggled, then, "Please be quiet, you mustn't awaken the patrons."

"I'll be as quiet as a thief." Davin gripped a thick vine of ivy, now turning brown in anticipation of the onslaught of winter storms, and pulled upward soundlessly. He moved like the night breeze, quiet, soft-touching, virtually unnoticed.

One quick heave at the window's ledge sent him through the opening and into Belatha's bedchamber.

And into one another's arms.

He enfolded the gorgeous daughter of Bistonia and drew her close. Her slender arms returned the embrace with equal enthusiasm.

Their kiss started with full-blown desire, and then the intensity mounted. The Winged Ram's courtyard had been too public for Davin. Now they were alone. There were no half glances or probing stares to restrain him. Davin allowed the total measure of his desire to wash through him and out his exploring fingertips to greet this voluptuous flower of Raemllyn.

"Beautiful," he murmured when their mouths parted.

That one word, then his lips sought—and found— the delicate lobe of her ear just a nuzzle beneath the frosty gold of satiny tresses. He nibbled ever so lightly, while his tongue occasionally flicked to taunt and caress.

"Ahhhh! Sweet bountiful Ediena!" Belatha's pelvis thrust forward and undulated in an edacious rhythm as she moaned to the Goddess of Love and Pleasure.

Davin Anane answered not with words but with actions. His teasing tongue and teeth continued their sensual assault even as his fingers found the string bow to Belatha's blouse at the base of her neck. A single tug and it fell free.

Rippling waves of goosepimply excitement tingled over Belatha's flesh in response to Davin's caressing touch. Gently he worked at the blouse's fabric, easing it over the creamy slope of the blonde's shoulders.

"No, my darling, allow me." Her palms flattened against his chest as she eased from his embrace. "It will be soooo much nicer this way . . . you'll *see.*"

A lighthearted laugh floated through the candle-lit room like the muted tinkling of silver bells. Belatha spun

away to stand before him. Her hands found the hem of
the blouse and in one fluid motion pulled the fabric upward, over her head, to toss it aside.

*See?* Davin did! Sleek, swaying cones thrusting outward in an unashamed invitation for mouth and hands.
*His mouth and hands!* He stepped forward.

Again the alluring daughter of Bistonia danced beyond
the reach of his outstretched fingertips.

With another chiming laugh, she tossed back her luxurious mane of frosty gold, an action that set her breasts
bobbing and jiggling in a most provocative dance. Her
eyes narrowed and a wickedly sensual smile touched the
corners of her ruby-blushed lips.

Having totally captured Davin's attention, her fingers
dipped to the bright red slash of her skirt and slowly
pulled. Like the veil covering some finely crafted sculp-
ture, the last of her clothing slid downward to gather at
her ankles, only to be kicked away to join the discarded
blouse on the floor.

Naked the golden-tressed beauty stood, allowing
Davin's gazing eyes to feast ... which they did! He
drank in the firm shape of those sleek, rounded calves,
the equally supple strength of satiny thighs that bore not
a single dimple of fat. He but glimpsed the downy triangle
of gold, perhaps a shade deeper than the hair cascading
like a cloud about her shoulders, bushed over her most
intimate of treasures before she coyly turned to present
the tight mounds of her backside.

Like some regal feline, she moved to the bed and
stretched out on her back. Her arms, long and slender,
reached out for the admiring Davin Anane.

"Do you like what you *see,* my darling ... my lord?"

"No, I don't like it." His voice contained a husky
resonance that hadn't been there a moment ago.

Confusion, mayhap a bit of hurt, tinted the emerald
eyes that stared up as Davin strolled to the side of the
bed to gaze down at the voluptuous woman who awaited

his attentions. With trembling hands, he pulled off his vest and threw it atop the pile of Belatha's clothing.

"I don't *like* it," he repeated as he yanked his shirt over his head. "I *love* it!"

Doubt evaporated from the temptress' eyes and her arms once more rose to him.

Although he ached to accept her invitation without delay, Davin could but shrug and silently curse the sorcerers of Raemllyn as he seated himself on the bed and tugged off his boots, then shed his tight-fitting breeches. Would that one of the weavers of magicks might create a spell that dissolved clothing at moments such as these! Clothing might protect the body from nature's elements, but the awkwardness of removal only hampered lovemaking.

Finally as naked as the lovely flower of Bistonia lying at his side, Davin Anane turned. He reached for the twin mounds of shimmering flesh that he had been so long denied. Quick hands darted up to snare his thick wrists and hold his fingertips a hairbreadth from the coral-hued nipples standing at attention for him.

"My lord, they are yours. I am yours—but not to touch with these," Belatha said in a low whisper that promised empires. "Your mouth! I want to feel your lips!"

He answered with a smile and a kiss firmly planted in the deep valley between her upthrusting breasts. While she hugged and caressed, he provided the attention she so desired with an enthusiasm that had her squirming beneath him when, at last, his lips and tongue left those mountainous delights to drift downward over the flat plain of her stomach, past the sensuous well of her navel, to the destination revealed by the wide parting of satiny thighs.

He abandoned the task given him only when her body writhed and quaked in full release atop the feather-down bed, and then but for one pleasure-gasping heartbeat

... just enough time to slide atop the quivering Belatha and unite them as man and woman with one urgent surge of his hips.

Belatha moaned loudly at his unexpected but welcome entrance. Her hands kneaded his rock-hard buttocks, desperately attempting to draw him deeper into the clutching heat of her body.

He held for a moment, soaking in the marvelous luxury of her before he lifted himself on his elbows. His back arched. And he moved, hips swinging in an ever-increasing rhythm that brought Belatha rushing to the pinnacle of ecstasy for a second time within mere minutes. He soared with her an instant later.

There were no lulling moments to savor the sleepy pleasure of their mutual release, no pause to sip from the jug of mulled wine which Belatha had brought from below and which now sat untouched on a small table beside the bed.

Belatha swarmed over him, stroking, biting, teasing, caressing, until he was again able to perform his pleasurable duties ... and again ... and for a fourth time. ... If Belatha had demanded another, he would have been ruined for life, but mercifully the blonde's passions were sated—for the time being.

Arrayed like spoons in a kitchen drawer they slept, groin pressed firmly against rounded behind, masculine arms safely harboring feminine form.

Davin Anane had no idea how long they slept before a battering ram slammed into the wall. Sleepy, mind still numbed by satiation, he half sat up in bed, his arm draped over a curving white hip.

"Wha'?" Davin dragged a hand across his face to wipe away his mental lassitude.

The battering ram thundered against the wall once again.

*No!* It wasn't a battering ram. And it wasn't the wall. *The door!*

Belatha stirred as someone or something crashed into the door for a third time. The barred door did not hold but exploded inward on its hinges.

Davin reacted instinctively, diving across Belatha's recumbent form in an attempt to reach his sheathed sword where it lay discarded atop a pile of rumpled clothing. Bedclothes tangled his legs and Belatha's stirring beneath cost him his less than solid balance. He fell. Like a marionette with strings severed, he tumbled onto the floor, feet entwined in muslin sheet.

Through eyes adaze with brightly flaring stars he saw unpolished boots rushing toward his head. Hands reached down for his sprawled form.

Arms beneath him, he pushed hard, lifted, and kicked in a vain attempt to free himself from the rudely grasping hands and reach his sheathed blade lying but a foot away.

Davin Anane did not see the jeweled sword pommel that swung downward. He only felt the exploding pain as it crashed into the back of his skull, and then just for an agonizing instant. The room swung around and around in wild, dazzling circles before vanishing behind a cloak darker than any night.

## chapter 3

THE DELUGE—a frigid shower pouring straight from the heart of Ianya, legendary realm of ice and snow—washed over Davin Anane in an unrelenting tidal wave. Sputtering and ashiver, he struggled upward through the darkness away from the floodwaters toward...

A hammer pounding throbbed at the back of his head. He still lived! Qar had yet to come and steal away with his soul to the moldering halls of Peyneeha, the Dark God's nether realm. He still lived!

But the damnable head-rattling pain! A testing hand rose to find a swollen lump the size of a *kelii*'s egg nesting at the base of his skull.

And the cold! Davin shivered with the realization that he lay as bare-assed naked as he had been when.... *The door! The boots!* Blurred memories wedged their way into his pain-befuddled head.

"Quit your faking! On your feet. Now! Or I'll have me lads skin you where you lie!" came words as cold as the icy water.

Davin fought to lift an eyelid. The light, dim as it was, burned through his skull to stab into the egg-sized lump on the back of his neck.

"What's going on?" he managed to mumble over a

tongue that felt like a well-used saddle blanket that hadn't been washed in years of hard racing.

"Leastways he didn't ask where he was!"

An approving cluck of the tongue sounded from across the room. "There's few men still alive who could forget being with the likes of *her*."

Davin got both eyes open and pushed to his knees amid the small lake puddled around him on the floor. A quick head count gave a total of five men—none he had ever seen before. All looked as big as Uhjayib gorillas from Lower Raemllyn. Each man equalled Goran One-Eye, at least in size. About their waists were slung dirks of the finest silver and gold, treasures that stood out against the coarse weave of their clothes. And their swords bore inlays of intricately worked silver and gold with rare gems studding the pommels. The men also looked quite capable of using those fine weapons grasped in their island-sized paws. Their faces betrayed no qualm about applying the bared blades on him—or even their own grandmothers.

Belatha stood naked, huddled against the wall. Her crossed and clutching arms did little to conceal her bountiful attributes from the intruders' leering gazes. Even in the dim light, Davin could see the gooseflesh ripple over her body. He could also hear the chatter of her teeth, whether from cold or from fear he couldn't tell.

Her own gaze was subserviently focused on the floor to avoid the intimately probing eyes. The humble pose did nothing to stop the men's lewd stares.

For the briefest of moments, Davin thought that therein lay the avenue to escape. While the brigands eyed Belatha's unclothed charms, he would try for his sword.

The thought died when he tensed, prepared to leap for his sheathed blade. All five swords jerked up to prick at his vulnerably exposed nakedness.

"Think only of pleasing us, scum. Otherwise it will be our extreme pleasure to puncture your worthless hide and let out all the juices." This came from the one at the center of the five.

"She's already drained his juices," snickered one of the others, bringing throaty laughter from his companions before they returned their covetous leers to Belatha.

Davin's eyes never left the man in the center, obviously the band's leader. He wore a tattered cavalry officer's jacket, replete with tarnished gold braid and a set of medals parading across his chest. Several sparkled with inset jewels, and all appeared most official. However, as much the uniform hinted at the city guard, Davin knew it was a lie.

This man was not a member of any military. He only strutted about wearing the garb.

"You like my uniform, eh?" the man demanded, noting Davin's interest in his threadbare apparel. "I am Jun, Captain of the Guard to our most gracious and noble Emperor Velden."

Davin shook his head, trying to clear it, and instantly regretted the effort. It felt as if his brains rattled noisily inside his skull. He closed his eyes, swallowed hard, felt cold shivers pass throughout his body, and tried to concentrate.

He made no sense out of any of this. There was no Emperor Velden, or none that Davin had ever heard about. He prided himself on keeping up with politics throughout Raemllyn. In his chosen profession as thief *extraordinaire* and cavalier, it behooved him to know who valued property the most highly—and to what limits they would go to protect it. Most such security rested on the back of local city-states. In Bistonia, thievery was punished severely by Lord Lerel, ruler of the city-state.

The mere thought of Lerel sent adrenaline pumping through Davin's arteries. He knew little enough about Lerel, other than that the man was called the Weasel— in hushed tones—and that he was the first to bring troops and succor to Zarek Yannis as that treacherous usurper fought High King Bedrich the Fair. Lerel's arrival had allowed Yannis to slaughter Bedrich the Fair on the battlefield of Kressia and assume the Velvet Throne of Raemllyn.

Davin cared little for the tides of Raemllyn's politics. Who claimed what throne by what right was of no concern to him—except for the riches they amassed. But with Zarek Yannis he would one day make an exception, if the opportunity ever presented itself. He had a very private debt to collect from the usurper king—one best paid with Yannis's head!

"The Emperor awaits you, swine," Jun said as his gaze moved from Davin to Belatha. He then turned to his companions with a shake of his ugly head. "There's no time, men."

It was obvious what he referred to by the expression on his face. Rapine was an accepted consequence of defeat in Bistonia. Jun's reluctance to claim his rightful booty was a concession to the power of this mysterious Emperor Velden. That power—to sway decisions as important as rape—confused Davin even more.

Even if Lord Lerel allowed another to rule Bistonia in his stead, Yannis would never permit it. The prerogatives of a high king were great, and Zarek Yannis jealously guarded them all.

"Dress." Jun's attention returned to the naked man on the floor at his feet.

Amid proddings from cold steel blades honed to nigh on invisible edges, Davin did as he was told. When he at last moved toward the door under the direction of those same blades, he cast a single glance—an apology—at Belatha.

The woman cowered down, huddling in upon herself, ignoring his gesture. Davin shrugged. Whatever was going on, she would be safe now. He knew that *he* and not the lovely blonde was the root cause.

Jun's fellow gorillas roughly shoved him through the

broken door and down the highly polished steps leading
to the inn's common room. Where once men had joked
and laughed and the fire had blazed merrily in the stone
fireplace, now came only ghostly echoes and the cold
dread that he might never again see it or share the warm
delights offered by Belatha.

"Into the street," came Jun's quiet command.

Davin looked around, for once in his life wishing to
see a squad of city guards. The street lay deserted. He
glanced above and checked the constellations, determin-
ing the time to be about an hour before dawn. The War-
dog still chevied the tail of the Pard, but the Lesser Rat
and its companion the Armored Knight had already vanished under the horizon. The Glory of the Morning had
yet to burst upon the sky as harbinger of a new day.

That was if the Sitala, those ancient Gods of Fate,
intended there be a new day for Davin Anane: a thought
the young adventurer did not relish pondering, yet a
possibility he could not ignore. The Sitala might very
well have designed to lead him into cold Qar's embrace.

Davin glanced back to the five and their bare blades.
Who or what they were—or the purpose for which they
had so rudely disturbed his cozy sleep—or what plans
they had in mind for him still remained shrouded.

*Who?* The oldest and only son of the House of Anane
desperately shifted through the faces and names within
his throbbing head in search of a clue to their identity
and that of Jun's Emperor Velden. He found nothing,
not even an inkling of why this was happening to him.
He had no enemies in Bistonia. How could he? He had
first set foot in the city only three days ago.

*Who? By Yehseen's great jewels, who?*

He thrust the question from his aching brain. At the
moment, *who* didn't matter. Staying alive did! And if he
intended to keep himself off the business end of those
five swords, he had to keep his wits about him.

A moment's indecision or inattention from his captors

was all he needed. A simple distraction would open an
avenue of escape for him. While he was weaponless, he
still had his feet and legs. Both were well trained for
fleet flight—a fact to which guards in at least ten Raemllyn cities could attest.

Perhaps the same thought had occurred to the self-
styled captain of the Emperor's Guard, for Jun allowed
his captive no such chance. Davin was blindfolded with
yellow silk permeated with the bitter smell of stale onions
and garlic.

"So you will be more appreciative of the sight of His
Majesty the Emperor Velden," Jun explained, then ordered two of his subordinates to take the freebooter's
arms.

Davin bit back the reply forming on his lips. The men
and their unsheathed swords remained too close for flip-
pancies. If he was to continue living, he had to appear
docile and beaten, at least until the viselike hands so
securely gripping his arms relaxed enough for him to tear
away the blindfold and run.

All sense of direction failed him as they led him through
the early morning streets of Bistonia. At first he tried to
draw a mental chart of their progress, but the twistings
and turnings, intentional or not, confused him to the point
where he no longer knew north from west. The only real
hint of direction came when he heard rusted metal hinges
grating open. The gust of vile stench rising from the
room left his throat agag and his empty stomach threatening to upheave.

"Inside," commanded Jun, shoving his captive forward.

Davin groped out blindly for support and found none.
He tumbled headfirst down a flight of cold stone steps.
Slime and decaying organic matter made the steps all the
more slippery. Any attempt to slow his downward tumble
only hastened his slither through the reeking ooze.

A steel post, hard and unyielding, slammed into his

left shoulder to end the downward careening abruptly. He gasped, unable to contain the pain as his shoulder throbbed in counterpoint to his head.

The odors of an open sewer clogged his nostrils and set his belly churning uneasily once again. Choking down the bile, he managed to right himself enough to sit, back against the post. Rusty chains clanged balefully next to his ears; he pictured the situation in his mind: a retaining post and chain railing . . . then a precipitous drop down into the sluggishly flowing excrement from an entire city.

Heavy footfalls, squishing and sucking in the muck, sounded on the stairs above him. Carefully they maneuvered down the flight of slime-covered stone he had descended in mere seconds on his belly.

Jun's rough hands pulled him to shaky feet. "This way, scum."

"We're in the sewers!" Davin's words came thick with disgust. "Is this where your vaunted Emperor Velden rules? Over rats and sewer crawlers?"

The flat of a sword blade landed solidly on the back of Davin's knees and sent him sprawling in the malodorous ooze for a second time.

"Loosen your tongue again, and I'll cut it from your foul mouth!" Jun's threat was harsh and hissing, leaving no doubt he would not hesitate to do just that. "Now get up. We've wasted enough time with you!"

Davin had known better than to speak. Silently he cursed his damnable pride. Had it not been for that unbending pride, he would not be here now—wherever in Qar's Hell *here* was! He would be safe and secure in his homeland of Jyotis. Bedrich, the murdered High King of Raemllyn, had first instilled that pride in the breast of a young child—and first wounded it.

But it had been Lord Berenicis, young ruler of Jyotis, who was called "Blackheart," that fired and tempered Davin's pride, forging it into a weapon that Berenicis used to bring the House of Anane down about the head of his young adversary and eventually send Davin fleeing

Jyotis with a price on his head.

Rebellious pride would gain him naught here, blindfolded and lost in the sewers of Bistonia. Wit and cunning were his only weapons. He had to use them and not his tongue. Davin, heir to the House of Anane, was no longer. He was simply Davin Anane, thief and adventurer—and survivor!

If the Sitala had so deemed, he would have the time to repay Jun and his cohorts for the Bistonian hospitality they had shown him. When—not if—that time came, he would be ready. Until then...

Davin, drawing in a steadying breath, pushed himself from the slime-covered stone. He stood with back straight and moved forward. Muck sloshed over his brightly polished boots, ooze dripped onto him from above, and his arms brushed stone walls caked with the effluence of ages while he marched in front of Jun's swordpoint. Thus he continued for half the sand of an hour's glass before ordered to stop.

Ahead came the sound of rusty hinges creaking as they opened. This time Davin was spared the rush of a fetid blast that assaulted his senses. His nose *did* wrinkle; incense burned nearby. Heavy and perfumy it hung in the air, veiling the sewer fumes.

Or was there something else beneath the thick cloak of incense?

Blindly he stepped forward. His nostrils flared as he tested the air. Beneath the masking incense came a different odor, a softer one, warmer and more comfortable. The smell of *man!* Men lived here, free from the noisome rush of filth just a few feet away.

The texture of the floor under his boots turned springy. Davin guessed a carpet graced the floor. He also sensed a vastness about him that hinted at a room larger than most above ground. Of sounds there were few, and those were muted, as if sound-deadening tapestries covered the walls.

Rough hands grasped the side of his head. Fingers

awkwardly fumbled with the knotted silk blinding his eyes, before simply yanking the onion-reeking cloth free.

Davin blinked. Soft light bathed the immense room stretching before him; a perpetual light, he realized as his eyes blinked once more in amazement. The light radiated from phosphorescent mosses that dangled from a lofty ceiling, a nature-made light for men who dwelt deep beneath the streets of Bistonia.

A smile of self-satisfaction touched the lips of Davin of Jyotis. He had guessed correctly! A thick carpet, lush, deep-piled, and once expensive before slime-coated boots had trod on it, spread across the stone floor.

Particolored tapestries decorated walls. Again the tarnished elegance screamed forth. The once rich hangings had turned dingy from the sewer gases that leaked through the portal into this room. In every corner burned censers pumping forth heavy clouds of smell-deadening incense: jasmine, Davin noted, his nose atwitch beneath the musky assault.

As amazing as the wealth—or what had once been wealth—was the very structure of the room itself. The entire chamber had been expertly hewn from the living bedrock of Bistonia. Years of toil had gone into its careful fashioning. The intricate carved figures adorning the rock, the false pillars etched into the granite were the work of generations of skilled artisans—craftsmen that Davin suspected had long faded from the memories of those who inhabited the city above.

Like everything else, the finely hewed rock betrayed a worn and abused aspect. The bright rock that must have once gleamed under the glowing mosses now cast back a dimmer reflection, only a hint of former glories. Life beneath the surface and amid the sewers tainted everything.

"On your knees, swine. Show proper obeisance to the Emperor," Jun ordered.

Heavy hands on his shoulders forced Davin to kneel.

Another hand pushed his head forward. He resisted at
first, then relaxed. The time to fight had yet to come.
Let them enjoy their brief dominance. Soon enough they'd
pay for their insolence—if the Sitala so deemed.

Soft footsteps from the right and the whishing of tapestries brushing a rock-carved doorway drew Davin's
attention. His eyes strained to catch sight of the underground Emperor.

"All rise," came the imperious command.

Davin sucked in another steadying breath and rose to
his knees. With pulse apound, his eyes rolled upward
and he gazed upon His Magnificence—the Emperor Velden.

# *chapter*

## 4

MAN-RAT WAS THE ONLY WORD that flashed in Davin
Anane's mind.

A smallish, round-shouldered man, who bore a definite resemblance to a rat rather than a human, waddled
across the chamber and placed a well-padded backside
on a replica of the High King's Velvet Throne. A thin
claw—the long unkept nails on that hand gave it the
appearance of a claw—raked through thin, greasy hair
while the Emperor Velden's tiny, deep-set eyes darted
about like those of a cornered rat. The sharp nose and
strong overbite accentuated the image Davin formed of
this man scuttling about on all fours, battling other sewer
vermin for the finest piece of offal for dinner.

There the parallel ended.

No rat ever had such finery. Yards of gold cloth formed
Velden's billowing tunic and breeches; a soft oyster-
white velvet cape spun about the man's shoulders and
draped to the floor, where it turned gray with sludge
along the hem. Suspended from his belt of golden links
hung a sheath; the hilt of the dagger within was encrusted
with enough precious stones to make Davin's agile mind
begin appraising. A minor fortune reposed in that dagger
alone, and a more immense one to maintain this underground empire.

"Emperor Velden," Davin said, bowing low again, trying to keep both words and action from appearing too mocking.

"My captain of the guard Jun has retrieved the proper man, I see," Velden said, ignoring Davin's greeting. Louder, with a clap of his small hands, Velden called, "Bring me Aylrah."

Behind him, Davin heard steps retreating—but not enough. At least four men, not counting Velden, remained in the throne room. Escaping the chamber would not be sufficient, Davin realized. He'd have to traverse the sewers and find the steps to the surface, something not likely to be done easily. The twists and turns once in the sewers had confused him as surely as the meanderings above in Bistonia's less noxious streets.

A drapery to the left of Velden's throne parted. Davin's eyes narrowed when he saw the man who strolled into the audience chamber.

"You recognize my faithful retainer Aylrah, I see." Velden smiled a smile that turned his lips more feral than ratlike.

"I seldom forget a sneak thief who tries to stab me in the back."

Aylrah was the same thief whom Goran had saved him from earlier. Wrist heavily bandaged and hung in a sling about his neck, the little thief cowered away, then gained the courage to step forward.

"He's the one, my liege. The very same!"

"Yes, and we thank you for your information. Here, faithful Aylrah. A reward for your diligence and attention to our majestic needs." Velden tossed a bag of gold bists to Aylrah, who clumsily dropped the bag. The golden coins rolled across the floor, sending the diminutive thief groping with his one good hand to retrieve the treasure.

"You might think my empire small and insignificant." Velden's gaze returned to the Jyotian. "But you are wrong. Most wrong. I am Emperor of all Bistonia's thieves. To us they, those above, pay homage—and taxes."

"Another word for extortion," Davin muttered under his breath.

Even as the ratlike man spoke, he judged his chances for escape. When one guard passed in front of another, he acted with the swiftness of lightning striking.

Davin sprang forward, one hand reaching for Velden's thin throat while the other groped for the jeweled dagger hanging at the man's belt.

The attack failed as quickly as it began. Only Davin's swift reflexes saved him from disaster as he fell forward. His legs had buckled under him just as a mewling infant attempting unsteady first steps might fail. He barely succeeded in getting hands outthrust to prevent his face from smashing into the carpeting.

Emperor Velden laughed maliciously while Jun hauled the fallen man to his feet by his collar, then jerked him away from the Emperor of Thieves.

"No one approaches my throne without my leave," Velden said proudly. "It is only a minor spell of no real import, but on occasion it proves useful."

Davin felt needles dancing along his calves as circulation returned to his deadened muscles. In a few seconds he stood without need of Jun's supporting hand.

"How did you get a mage to cast the spell? They jealously guard such." The only times Davin had encountered a tangle-foot spell had been in vaults laden with chests of gold bists and sacks of precious stones. Mages notoriously refused to cast such magicks, save for exorbitant fees. He doubted Velden had agreed to any such fee.

"It proves invaluable in preventing petty pilfering from the sorcerers of Bistonia," came the proud answer. "In return the mages perform small feats, such as this one."

Velden grinned broadly, reached beside his throne, and held aloft a crown of white gold and ethium. He placed it upon his brow; the magically excited ethium cast a bright glow over his face, a halo floating inches above the man's head.

"A nice touch, don't you think? But one such as your-self might not be impressed with trinkets."

Davin eyed Velden suspiciously. He had been brought here for a reason. He wished the man would cut the circumlocution and get to that reason. The sooner the tribute was paid, the sooner Davin returned to the sunlit streets of Bistonia and the warm embraces of Belatha.

"Why did you bring me here?"

"You are the Davin Anane who, with Goran One-Eye, robbed the Harn Spring Festival of the prize money? About six months ago?"

"Rob? You must have me confused with someone else." Davin sounded as indignant as he could. "You mistake me for one of your own subjects!"

"I think not. Goran One-Eye is a distinctive character. You and he stole the prize money in broad daylight, a most daring maneuver. The city guard of Harn sought you for days thereafter, but you eluded them in some clever fashion. One day you must tell me how."

"I have been to Harn and know the city well enough," Davin admitted. "But steal prize money?" He shrugged, seeing what reaction Velden showed.

The Emperor of Bistonia's thieves' facial expression remained unchanged. Davin's lie had been received for what it was.

"I offer you the rare opportunity to preserve a life. These days one is so often denied the altruistic outlets that were available in old times, don't you agree? Society is in such a bad way, I think." Velden's smile was barren of even the slightest trace of humor.

"You said I could save a life? What did you mean?"

"A life hangs in the balance, yes. Goran One-Eye attracted much attention when he came into one of my establishments, the Brass Cock. He wanted to gamble, he said. And gamble he did. Betting wildly, he began to lose. How absurd of him to accuse my employees of cheating. That giant intimidated one of the dealers, in-sulting him by saying we used magically endowed cards.

How ridiculous. Who could get a mage to perform such an act of dishonesty?" Velden chuckled, again without mirth.

Davin considered the tangle-foot spell only the merest hint of the magicks Velden commanded.

"Yes, how ridiculous. What happened to Goran?"

"Alas," Velden went on, as if not hearing Davin, "your companion slew two of my employees. Loyal men they were. Of some tenure in my service, also."

"You want me to pay a fine for Goran's release, is that it?" It was Davin's turn to laugh — with all the false bravado he could muster. "Let the red fool rot in your sewers."

"A fine? Come, come, a life cannot be bartered for money. What gold bist is worth a life? Show me a palmful of gems that equals the lowliest of lives. I fear Goran One-Eye has been sentenced to die for his misadventures at the Brass Cock."

"Then why tell me? What can I do?" Davin shrugged to maintain his air of disinterest.

"That is simple. Perform a task—a simple one for a man of your daring and wit—and Goran's sentence is commuted and his life spared."

Davin waited for Velden to continue. Whatever he wanted, it wouldn't be simple. Of that, Davin of Jyotis was certain.

"You know the city of Harn well. Your escape from the Harnish Spring Festival proves that." Velden leaned to the edge of his throne and stared at his captive.

"I have spent some time in Harn," Davin admitted again, more cautiously this time. Most of his efforts prior to the theft had gone into learning the city streets and choosing the proper escape routes.

"Then you have heard of Tadzi." For the first time, Velden showed real emotion. His eyes narrowed to slits, his fists balled, then gripped the ornately carved armrests, and he bent forward, his crown tipping slightly and causing the halo to go askew.

Davin swallowed hard. He *had* heard of Tadzi. The man ruled the Thieves' Guild of Harn with an iron fist. Getting away from the Harnish city guard had been easy compared with eluding Tadzi's men. Tadzi was like a master horseman. A slight variance caused a light flick of the reins. A more serious deviation brought forth the whip. Any show of real independence spelled certain death.

Davin Anane knew the master of the Harn Thieves' Guild all too well, at least by reputation.

"Tadzi has kidnapped my niece Lijena. The exchange is a simple one: her life for your friend's." Velden's voice calmed a degree as he sought to regain his composure.

Davin puzzled over this odd request on the part of the Emperor of Bistonia's thieves. There was no honor among thieves, but the rivalry between Tadzi and Velden ought not to amount to much either. The city-states were far enough distant that what happened in one scarcely affected the other.

"If your niece is so precious to you, why not call forth your own captain of the guard to rescue her? Or better yet, mount an army, invade Harn, and free her!"

Velden laughed harshly.

"While I *could* lead my followers to Harn, we would be conspicuous and in open confrontation with Tadzi. Many men would be killed," Velden explained. "I am a fair and gentle ruler, unlike Tadzi. I could not live with such blood on my hands. My lovely Lijena is worth the sacrifice, but . . ." His voice trailed off.

"But your men wouldn't follow you—or go on their own," Davin finished. "So you expect me to risk my neck for Goran to bring your niece back."

Velden nodded and said, "That is succinct. Steal her back and I commute your friend's death sentence."

Davin considered letting Goran embrace Qar. It would serve the Challing right for getting into a game with magically controlled cards. Yet there was a debt to be

repaid. Goran had saved him during that robbery in Harn
and gotten a freely given promise to find a mage powerful enough to send the Challing back to his own world.
And only the night before, Goran had again saved him
from certain death at the hands of Velden's sneak thief,
Aylrah.

He owed Goran One-Eye much.

"I wish to speak with him. Otherwise, how do I know
he is not already dead?"

"We should embark on this venture with mutual trust,
my good friend," Velden replied, doing his best to appear
hurt by the suggestion.

"I am *not* your good friend," snapped Davin.

He instantly regretted his tone when Jun slammed a
meaty fist into the back of his skull. Stars spun in crazy
constellations; the guard had unerringly struck the same
spot his sword pommel had found earlier.

"Show him the condemned," ordered Velden.

Jun grabbed Davin's elbow. Thumb and forefinger
pressed the nerve at the joint. Jangles of pain lanced into
the Jyotian's shoulder; Davin went willingly with the
guard captain.

Yanking aside a tapestry to the left of the chamber,
Jun and his nerve-squeezing grip escorted Davin down
a corridor rudely slashed through the bedrock until they
came to an iron door. Only then did the ill-dressed captain
release Velden's "guest" to fumble a key from a coat
pocket. He glanced at Davin, shook his head slightly,
then opened the door.

A hasty appraisal of the corridor they'd just traversed
convinced Davin of the futility of an escape attempt. A
dozen armed men stood, eyes narrowed belligerently,
waiting for just such a bid for freedom.

With a shrug, Davin entered the dark cell. His stomach
churned violently. The stench surpassed even that of the
open sewers.

Worst of all was Goran. Bound in chains, the Challing

in human form dangled from the ceiling. Manacles cut cruelly into his wrists; thin rivulets of blood trickled down the giant's brawny forearms and biceps. The torturous kisses of white-hot branding irons had left their marks on his flesh. Oozing blood-encrusted scabs marred both arms and legs.

Some of the scabs moved! Again Davin blanched, barely able to contain his heaving stomach. At least half the scabs weren't! They were leeches applied to the Goran's vulnerably exposed flesh!

His toes barely brushing the stone floor, Goran swung around. His one good eye peered out blearily. For an overly long moment the Challing simply stared at Davin with no hint of recognition in that orb normally sparked with witch-fire.

"Ah, Davin." Goran's voice was a mere whisper. His face betrayed the strain required to pronounce those few sounds. "At last you've come. Did Belatha tire you so?"

"What have you gotten yourself into?" Davin hastily examined the chains and decided there was no way of opening the locks in the time he'd be allowed with the redheaded giant. A lockpick, which he didn't have, would be required.

"The damned cards. They were ensorcelled. But I finished two of them. Their days of cheating are only memory." The trace of a smile touched the Challing's parched lips.

"And Velden has sentenced you to death unless I retrieve his niece." Davin attempted to conceal his helplessness, with little success.

"So, blast you, fetch her for the man! Women fawn over you. Draw her into your web and pull her back to her rightful place. Child's play for Davin Anane of Jyotis! Aaaggg!" Goran jerked his head toward his friend, an action that drove the manacles deeper into his wrists.

"Tadzi kidnapped her," Davin said softly.

The giant didn't reply. His gaze rolled downward with

the full weight of that pronouncement. Davin went to him and rested a hand on a shoulder. The barely suppressed quaking told the tale.

"I'll get her, don't fear," Davin assured his friend as Jun returned and motioned the Jyotian from the cell.

Davin had nothing more to say to Goran. The words would have sounded hollow if he had urged his friend to patience. He simply gave the Challing's shoulder one last squeeze and left him there dangling in the darkness like some side of beef awaiting the butcher.

Back in Emperor Velden's audience chamber, Davin fought to keep calm. What Velden had already done to Goran demanded revenge. He knew, however, the penalty for speaking out now. Both he and Goran One-Eye would perish unless he fulfilled the Emperor's task.

"Your friend still lives," said Velden without preamble. "Rescue my Lijena and he will continue his misbegotten existence."

"Tadzi is no fool. He'll know you'll try to regain your niece."

"That is why I have chosen one as daring as you, Davin Anane. Your companion is my insurance you will comply. But I fear that Tadzi plans dastardly things for Lijena," Velden continued.

Davin went cold all over. Velden's words carried hidden meaning—meaning important to the would-be rescuer.

"To ensure swiftness in your mission, you have two weeks from this moment to return with my niece." The pronouncement came coolly, almost casually.

"Two weeks!" cried Davin. "That's not possible. It's a three-day ride to Harn."

"Two, if you ride hard."

"What you ask is impossible. Can't be done."

"First we shall draw and quarter your friend. This takes the better part of an hour. My executioner is most expert; Goran will survive this parting of his limbs. We

shall then boil the still-living sections in acid. Perhaps a
flaying to start things off, then the drawing and quartering." Velden rested his chin on one long-fingered hand,
then shook his head in mock indecision. "No, no, that
won't do at all. We must keep this simple. Just the
drawing, quartering, and boiling in acid." His voice
turned hard as he added, "In two weeks."

"But if I'm delayed . . ."

"Don't allow any delay. If you have not returned with
my niece in this time span, I will be forced to think that
you have fled like a craven or have been killed. In either
case, the red-maned one will sleep with Qar that night."

"I want to start immediately," said Davin, feeling
defeated before the task had been begun.

"A wise choice. Jun, see him to the surface. Blindfolded! Jun will discuss the exchange arrangements with
you as you depart."

Emperor Velden leaned back in his throne and smiled
wickedly, pleased with the little surprise he was sending
his arch-rival Tadzi. Should Anane fail, what would it
matter? Tadzi could never trace the freebooter back to
the Empire of the Underground.

Velden threw his head back and laughed raucously,
the tapestries in his tawdry audience chamber absorbing
the sounds.

Davin stared into the sewer opening down which
Jun and his companions had disappeared. There was a
scurry of feet from below, then nothing. Davin shook
his head, then glanced above. Fingers of golden pink
announced Raemllyn's rising sun in the east. The first
day of his quest began, whether or not he was prepared.

*Nor do I have any guarantee that Velden is not slitting
Goran's throat at this very moment.* The situation was
not to his liking, but there was nothing he could do about
it. He either rode to Harn and rescued Velden's niece
and hoped the ruler of Bistonia's thieves would hold up

his side of the bargain, or simply left Bistonia and his friend to Velden.

He couldn't do the latter. So he had a simple choice: ride to Harn and risk the possibility that Velden would kill Goran before his return. Davin pushed the unsavory thought from his mind. He had to believe Velden's word, it was all he had.

Meanwhile he wasted time pondering things over which he had no control. He needed to be on his way as quickly as possible, and before he could begin, he needed a mount . . . one he hoped to steal before the sun's full face burned in the sky.

# chapter
## 5

HOT BREATH, transformed to mist in the morning cold, billowed in panicked snorts from widely flared nostrils. Jet-lacquered forehooves pranced uneasily as though prepared to rear high without further provocation. In an abrupt lurch, the dapple-gray mare shied nervously from the approaching mounted guard. The mare's rider clutched tightly at long strands of blue-gray mane to maintain her precarious balance in the saddle.

"Ho, Presko, give way! The chill has awakened Orria's spirits this morn. She's as high-strung as a new foal turned to pasture—ready to kick up her heels and race the wind," the gray's rider called out to halt the guard. The fur-robed woman then leaned forward to stroke the broad dappled neck soothingly and whisper gently to alertly perked ears, "Soon, my Orria, you will have your head and run before Minima's chilled breath to your heart's content."

"My lady Lijena, I *am* sorry," the burly, bearded guard apologized. "The gate is narrow, and our lord Tadzi has ordered that one of us always precede you."

Lijena made no attempt to disguise a snort of contemptuous disgust. "Lord Tadzi can take you and all his guards and . . ."

41

She swallowed the remaining words; curses were of no avail against Tadzi or the small army of armed guards with which Harn's Lord of the Thieves' Guild surrounded himself—and her. In Lord Tadzi's palace, freedom was a word that had no meaning.

Through aquamarine eyes tinted with a muting shade of woe, she glanced over a shoulder at the immense estate that stretched behind her. Crisp golds and yellows, fiery reds and burning oranges splattered over the countryside to mingle with the dark hues of evergreens—the Goddess Jalya's herald of beauty that warned of the coming dreariness of winter. The magnificent panorama, for as far as Lijena could see, was the sole property of Lord Tadzi—a full eight hundred acres of the lushest territory in sprawling Harn.

All was securely walled to a height of twelve feet with the finest of stones from Norgg Province!

Lijena's gaze shifted to the encompassing barricade. Rumors told of fifteen hundred slaves who had lost their lives mining the fabulously expensive stone, battling treacherous mountains, ice and snow, and myriad creatures lurking in that realm of perpetual hoarfrost to bring such opulence to Raemllyn's heartlands.

From deep within the heart of the Norggstone came a suffusing warmth and an opalescent sheen that captivated both heart and mind—a treasure any sacrifice justified, wise men agreed. After all, what were the lives of mere slaves when one could bathe in the glow of such beauty?

To Lijena the barrier of Norggstone was simply a wall, nothing more, nothing less.

The Palace Tadzi provided the perfect centerpiece for such an impressive periphery. Eight stories high, with massive columns thrice the thickness of a man fronting the entryway, and a façade of the purest ebony, Lord Tadzi's palatine repose had required forty years to construct and the wealth of a dozen poor city-states—or several rich ones.

For Lijena it was but a prison . . . a prison of silks and gold, to be certain, but no less a prison than had the edifice been built of cold gray stone with iron bars set in each window. Not stale bread crusts and water but the finest delicacies and wines were her daily fare. Nor did hooded men in sweat-stained jerkins tend her in some dark subterranean cell. Her jail was a suite of silk- and tapestry-adorned chambers, serviced by a minor troop of handmaidens who scurried about at her beck and call. Her slightest whim, no matter how ludicrous or trivial, was instantly fulfilled. There were few in all of Raemllyn who would not kill their own mother and their mother's mother to spend only one day amid such elegant luxury.

She was kept in a magnificent style unheard of, even by the royal family. High King Bedrich himself had never enjoyed the delicacies from far-off countries served her nor slept in a bed with sheets so fine—warmed prior to her retiring by a half-dozen girls so that they would not chill her delicate flesh.

Velvet-covered though they were, the chains confining Lijena were forged of tempered steel links. Her skin crawled at the thought of spending even one more minute within those walls. Yet there was no escape from her prison of splendor—she had explored all avenues and found Tadzi's guard waiting in each.

Only these morning rides offered a reprieve from the walls of the Palace Tadzi, and then for such a few precious, fleeting moments. And those moments were no more than an illusion of freedom. There was no freedom when she was encompassed by guards, and Presko and his men always surrounded her when she rode.

". . . There are dangers, my lady," Presko continued. "Lord Tadzi but ensures your safety. Should any harm befall . . ."

"Tadzi would kill me with his kindness! I am not one of the Lord's orchids from the jungles of Lower Raemllyn that he keeps locked away in his glass hothouses! I do not require such close and intimate attention!"

Lijena's anger melted into a watery shiver of apprehension. The sergeant of guards' expression bespoke more than his words. He obviously *did* consider her fragile and needing great nurturing. That he desired to be the one to furnish the "close and intimate attention" was also obvious from the hungry glint in his dark eyes.

*I would mate with a pig first!* The thought of Presko's grubby paws upon her body sent another tremor of revulsion down her spine, although she had nothing to fear from Presko or any of Tadzi's men. They feared their lord far too much to risk his wrath with even so much as a gaze that lingered an instant more than what was considered polite.

*Amrik, are you not returned to Bistonia? Have you not learned that I am captive here in Harn?* Lijena's mind reached out, calling to one whose sheltering embrace she yearned to hide within.

Her silent pleas were as fruitless as her numerous escape attempts. Amrik Tohon now tarried in Leticia, a city-state that lay beside the River Faor northeast of Bistonia. He would not return to his home for three days hence.

*Then, Lord Tadzi, we'll see if your walls and guards can hold me!* Lijena's breast swelled at the thought of daring young Amrik come to rescue her from Tadzi's prison.

"There be brigands about, my lady," Presko protested.

The sergeant's voice oozed with such gravity that Lijena was unable to restrain a laugh of contempt. *Of all people to worry about thieves and cutpurses and other scum...*

Tadzi set his thieves to protect her from other thieves. It was a jest worthy of Zarek Yannis's court fools!

She hugged a lush, deeply layered oyster-white *sartha* fur robe about her sleek shoulders and returned her attention to the gate ahead and the road beyond. Thinking of Amrik and his strong arms only made the situation worse. She could but bide her time until he came and freed her.

*Until then, I have Orria! And she will serve as best she can!* Unable to break the sense of desperation encasing her heart, Lijena let her silver-spurred boots nudge Orria's dappled flanks.

The gray needed no further encouragement. The mare bowed her broad neck against bit and rein and trotted through the open gate at a pace that was soon transformed into a rhythmic canter, then a full, flighty gallop.

The feel of Orria's straining muscles beneath her brought the needed reprise from captivity. Lijena's mind blocked out the hooves that pounded behind, and she lost herself in delicious fantasy. She was free as the pair of hawks that winged through the cloudless sky above. There was no wall of Norggstone, no Tadzi, no palace prison—only the countryside, Orria, and herself. And they raced the wind, the very breath of the Goddess Minima.

Lijena laughed aloud in defiance of Tadzi and all his confining chains. The wind, strong airy fingers, tugged at her long frosty-blonde mane, sending it astream like some proud banner unfurled.

"My lady, not so fast!" cried Presko from the head of the four heavily armed guards he led.

Lijena glanced over a *sartha*-fur-adorned shoulder to see the sergeant spur his horse to greater effort. The steed strained and snorted huge plumes of silvery breath into the chilly early morning air.

And the four who rode on his heels? How well she knew their faces—had come to know them during these weeks. There was Breatt, who gambled heavily and might be bought for a few silver eagles, but she had no confidence in his prowess or courage.

Nor did she believe that Marvensko the Large, ponderous in his leather armor and with massive shield dangling on right arm, would provide more than a moment's diversion for a real warrior. The man drank to excess, wenched at every opportunity, and carried half again too much weight in softness around the middle.

On the remaining two Lijena had often pondered. They seemed inseparable, more like brothers than many she knew. Cens and Portrevnio practiced their sword work together, ate together, rode together, and, for all Lijena knew, shared the same bed. But were her life at risk, Cens and Portrevnio were the ones she'd most prefer to have before her, swinging sword or mace.

"Sergeant," she called, allowing Orria to continue the breakneck pace, "I will ride again this afternoon."

"Were it mine to command, I would order the grooms to prepare the horses for the afternoon," Presko answered as his mount drew beside the dappled gray. "But Lord Tadzi's express orders are that you are to ride but every other day."

*"Lord Tadzi!* Are those the only words known to you!"

Lijena fumed as she set booted feet firmly in the silver-rimmed stirrups. At least Tadzi permitted her to ride astraddle rather than sidesaddle, although that was but a small consolation—it wasn't Orria she wanted, but freedom, her home, and Amrik Tohon.

For a second time she tried to lose her thoughts in the rhythmic strides of the magnificent gray as the mare bounded forward. She found no escape. Reality pressed about her, cruelly smothering the illusion of freedom.

*To be home! To be nestled securely in Amrik's arms!*

Tears welled from the corners of her aquamarine eyes and trickled down her cheeks. The wind whipped the salty droplets to pull them coldly across her face. Lijena cocked her head to one side and allowed her tears to soak into the warm depths of the *sartha* fur where none might see them.

*Fool!*

Davin Anane reprimanded himself for the foolish race

of his pulse as he caught sight of the approaching riders.
Anticipation, not fear, brought the pounding to his temples.

Because of that anticipation, he berated himself. Now
was not the time to allow his groin to befuddle a clear
head. Lijena was not some tavern wench to be wooed
and won for a night's tumbling among sleeping silks.
She was the ransom that would free Goran from his cell
within Velden's sewer kingdom where he hung chained
and battered—dying, for all Davin knew.

Chide himself as he did, Davin could not evade the
spell Lijena's beauty wove. Long and frosty, her blonde
hair rippled in the wind as she rode toward where he lay
concealed in a dense clump of evergreen cherry holly.
His gaze traced the contours of her slender figure, apparent even beneath the elephantine bulk of white furs.

Davin realized in that instant, as he had the first time
he had spied on Lijena and her ever-present guards, why
Velden was using such tactics to regain his niece—though
how such a beautiful creature could be related by blood
to the ratlike Emperor of Bistonia's underground taxed
Davin's powers of imagination.

As Lijena and her armed escort reached the forest's
edge, their pace slowed to an easy walk, and they moved
past his position to enter the wood on a westward road
that eventually led to the city-state Hyian.

Davin edged free of the cloaking leaves of waxy green
and, in a half crouch, silently moved on a path parallel
to the road, using the dense underbrush to shield him
from the guards' wary eyes. He moved on foot through
the Harnish wood in part because a man alone was easier
concealed than one on horseback. Besides, he had sold
his stolen mount immediately upon arriving in Harn for
a paltry few silver eagles. Harn was an expensive city,
and when the time came, he would again steal the mounts
he required.

Glimpses of Lijena's beauty, rather than tortured visions of Goran One-Eye, now gave impetus to his feet and his active mind that appraised the forest, questing for a solution to the problem he faced.

Individually, the soldiers guarding the captive niece of Bistonia's Emperor of Thieves would have presented little problem for Davin's sword arm. Together, they appeared formidable. He ruled out a direct attack. One sword against five, as well as the battle-axes slung on the guards' hips, would be a simple case of suicide, and Davin Anane had no desire to seek such a quick and ugly end to his young life.

If there had been more time, he would have considered bribery, knowing that a palm well greased with gold or silver could often accomplish feats tempered steel could not. Time, however, was the one thing he did not have. What little remained to him grew shorter with each passing heartbeat.

*The forest has to be it!* There was a panicked desperation to his thoughts and the darting of his eyes as he searched the wood for overlooked detail. *There has to be something here. There has to be!*

Twice before during his six days in Harn, he had witnessed Lijena's morning ride—and it always followed the same route. From the west gate of the Palace Tadzi the party galloped straight ahead and rode a league on the wooded road to Hyian. While there were several places where an ambush might be accomplished, he was but one against five. Such an ambuscade had little chance of succeeding.

*There have to be other ways.*

Rather, there *ought* to have been; there weren't. He had spent much of his time in Harn circling Tadzi's estate, probing for weaknesses, looking for a bolt-hole in which to hide, a postern gate left untended.

Even a hint at easy entry evaded him.

Nor had long discussions with Harnish merchants, who supplied the vast estate, given him much hope of success in breaching the walls. Tadzi, like a man possessed, dwelt in constant fear of enemies penetrating his defenses. Merchants were contracted to deliver food-stuffs and other supplies only to the side gate. From there Tadzi's personal servants reloaded the goods and freighted them into the household.

One goat cheese seller Davin had spoken to, however, claimed to have been inside the mansion.

"Aye, 'twas five years back," the man had said as he thoughtfully picked his black teeth with a splinter from a chair leg.

"How'd you come to be so lucky?" Davin asked.

"'Lucky' you call it. Ha! Anything but luck was in-volved." He shook his head, all wise, all knowing. "Pure accident it was. I delivered the cheese, and a smelly lot it was, too."

Davin didn't have to be told that. The entire store—and its proprietor—reeked.

"A lackey came out with a serving wench. The two of them wanted to . . . eh . . . you understand?" He made an obscene gesture and grinned broadly at Davin's expression. "So the servant boy lets me drive me rig up to the side of the house whiles the two of them went at it in back."

"Must have been an experience, such wealth, such finery." Davin prodded constantly to keep the man talk-ing about the layout of the house.

"That it was, that it was." He ruminated a while longer and finally said, "Never saw a place with more guards. All armed for the righteous fight. Everywhere! And Tadzi himself knew the instant I came in. Spells! Everywhere filthy magicks!"

"Guard spells as well as human soldiers?"

"That's what I said, young'n. I told a friend about the place, the pearls as large as my fist, the lapis lazuli doors, the gold cutlery I saw in the kitchen. Why, that fool upped and tried to steal from Tadzi. The lord let him live."

"For how long?" Davin was getting the feel of how

Tadzi—and Velden—thought and worked.

"Well-nigh a week. Heard his screams long after his body died, though. Tadzi fed him to the demons, and they kept after his soul for another week. Poor stupid Neeko."

The conversation, along with his excursions around the twelve-foot wall encircling the estate, convinced Davin of the futility of a rescue attempt within the Palace Tadzi or its surrounding grounds. Soldiery, ward spells, and demons held by diabolical magicks protected Tadzi from the outside world and any rival wishing him harm.

*Black Qar take you, Velden! Why do you pressure me with time so short? There is a way. I know there is. But . . . how? How?*

The Jyotian wanted nothing more than to have Goran beside him for this escapade. The pair of them might make quick work of the five guards riding protection for Lijena. Goran One-Eye by himself could make quick work of them—leaving Davin to attend the fair Lijena on the ride back to Bistonia.

Alas, that was impossible. Goran dangled by chains in Velden's torture chamber, awaiting the searing branding irons and the sharp flensing knives that would strip meat from bone in the most agonizing manner possible.

*Just like you, One-Eye. When I need you the most, you're off somewhere else enjoying a holiday at another's expense.*

The grim humor did nothing to alleviate Davin's spirits. The task remained . . . dangerous, bordering on suicidal. And the forest refused to reveal any hint as to how he might accomplish that task.

On silent feet Davin kept pace with Lijena and her guards, all the way to a shallow ford across the River Kukis. He watched the soldiers turn the dapple-gray around for the return the the Palace Taszi, then ride eastward.

Rather than retrace his path, Davin climbed into the

limbs of a lofty pine and there, precariously perched in a deep V notch, gazed after the disappearing party.

*Two days ... two days ...* He mulled over the time remaining before Lijena and her guards once again rode into the forest. Davin shuddered. Already ten days had passed. Waiting two more left only a pair remaining of the fourteen Velden had allotted for Goran's time in this world.

"Two days' ride to Bistonia, with all of Tadzi's hell-hounds on my tail. And with *her* slowing me down," he mumbled aloud, while his gaze darkly surveyed the autumn-colored forest about him. "These damned trees are packed as thick as ..."

Davin's words faded, lost in the seed of a thought that sprang fresh. *These trees!* He searched the boles around him. *Yes, by Yehseen's potent jewels, it just might be possible!*

A self-satisfied smile played at the corners of the young adventurer's lips as he carefully picked his way down the pine and darted eastward toward the gates of Harn. There were supplies to purchase and preparations to make, and damned little time!

# *chapter*
# 6

THE CRISP AUTUMN AIR gave life to fragrances wafting through the Harnish bazaar. Exotic aromas of pungent spices from the tropical realms of Lower Raemllyn, the musky odors of textile dyes from merchants' shops, the tantalizing hint of smoked meats and sausages asizzle, the earthy smells of livestock crowded in rickety pens of branch and rope mingled in the afternoon chill to suffuse the marketplace with olfactory intrigue.

Likewise autumn brought a burst of color from the Harnites that rivaled the magnificent hues cloaking the ancient forest that surrounded their city. Robed in radiant reds and yellows, sea blues and royal purples, vibrant pinks and rich greens, the throng that moved through the bazaar like a ceaselessly shifting kaleidoscope flaunted its multicolored garb in the face of approaching winter. Soon the Goddess Jalya would dull the dazzling spectrum of cloth with the browns, grays, and blacks of heavy woolen and fur cloaks.

Also, the chilly air intensified sound so that it came sharp and clear as crystal. The laughter of street urchins running helter-skelter through the shops and tents rang like a chorus of tinkling glass bells. Merchants called in singsong voices to bypassers, enticing them to view wares.

Beggars, acrutch and apatch, each wailed his own aria of woe and misfortune accompanied by the rattle of copper coins within tin cups. The dutiful haggling of seller and buyer, the coo of dove, the crackle of chicken, the squawk of goose, the grunt of pig, the din of hammer on anvil played counterpoint to one another, rising in a cacophony that engulfed and rolled back onto the bazaar.

Davin Anane neither smelled, saw, nor heard any of this. Instead he leaned cross-armed and -legged against a corner post of a potter's tent. His gaze and attention focused on a merchant's shop no more than a score of strides before him. So he had stood since his return from his reconnaissance into the Harnish wood that morn.

Neither thoughts of Goran One-Eye nor thoughts of the most desirable Lijena froze him thus, although both were constant in his mind. Instead the lightness of his money pouch left him motionless like a man petrified by some sorcerous spell. While his limbs lacked animation, his mind raced.

His pouch's few bists had been spent on half a stone's weight of jerked venison; an equal share of *gorp,* that mainstay of Raemllyn travelers, made of ground meal, dried berries, nuts, and honey; two sturdily sown wineskins, filled one third wine and two water; and a stone of oats. All of these were the supplies needed for two riders and mounts set on a nonstop journey back to Bistonia to reunite niece with uncle and save the hide of a Challing in man's form.

Davin grimaced. The return journey had to be made in a mere forty-eight hours, while it had taken him a full four days to ride from Bistonia to Harn. That was, of course, *if* he could free Lijena when she next ventured onto the road to Hyian two mornings hence.

The Jyotian's hand dropped to the razor-honed ax slung on his right hip. His bists had also gone for its purchase and grinding.

Whether his rescue plan would bear fruit rested in part

on his ability as a woodsman, and on whether hands
grown soft could endure the blisters the ax's handle would
raise. The freebooter's life he had led since fleeing his
homeland had brought little demand for hard manual
labor. After all, he reasoned, why break one's back when
riches abound for one with a quick mind and light fingers?

The lion's share of his purse had gone for six nights'
lodging in one of Harn's finer inns and the new suit of
clothing he now wore.

While others might have considered the soft doeskin
jerkin and breeches mere vanity or the squandering of
direly needed funds, not so Davin Anane. His fine garb
was a simple matter of camouflage; wine-hued silk brocade was very discernible, and very out of place, when
one sought to conceal oneself within the wilds.

All this left Davin with one major purchase, only a
few coppers within his money pouch, his eyes locked on
the merchant shop across the bazaar, and his mind scheming.

The shop he stared upon was that of a binding merchant who dealt in silken threads, twines of all sizes,
hemp ropes from delicate little garrotes to weaves as thick
as a man's forearm, chains of gold and iron, and even
anchor cable for the barges that sailed the River Kukis.

During the four hours Davin had watched the shop
and the customers who came and went, he had drawn
the simple conclusion that the rotund merchant within
had not gathered such a wealth of flesh because he lacked
brains. The man was shrewd and relentless when it came
to bargaining.

The merchant did have two weaknesses: every hour
and a half he left his shop to stroll up the street and share
a pipe bowl with a local purveyor of *mylo* weed; and a
less than quick-witted young, pimply-faced clerk.

So when the fat-rolling merchant next abandoned his
wares for a relaxed smoke, Davin hastened into the shop
and called out, "Good day to you, my son."

"Good day to you, too, sir," answered the puzzled clerk, who could have been no more than two years short of Davin's age.

The perplexed expression on the clerk's pocked face left Davin in no doubt that the youth was on the line just waiting to be reeled in.

"My son, are there any special prices on . . . anchor cable?" the Jyotian asked as he hefted a few heavy links.

"Master Merchant Tabim don't allow no special pricings," the pimply one replied and then, after a ponderous pause, questioned, "And what is it that makes you call me your son?"

Davin was hard-pressed to confine the self-satisfied grin that sought to wash across his face. *That's it, my lad, bite down again—plant the hook deep and solid!*

Instead of laughing aloud at the ease of his ruse, Davin arched a brow over a sorrowful eye. "Why, you are my son. All are my sons, except for those who be my daughters," said Davin in a grave voice. "But you do not recognize me, do you?"

A tousled head of blanched straw shook. The eyes beneath were dull and stupid.

This was far easier than Davin had originally imagined. He almost wished for Master Merchant Tabim's return. What use was plying a trade expertly—in Davin's case, theft—with none to appreciate the result?

"I am a monk of the Rumdumullite order."

"You? A monk? You're not wearing no robes or nothing like I seen others do," the clerk answered, his face darkening with increased befuddlement with each passing heartbeat.

"My son, that is why I have chosen your fine shop," Davin said, his voice lowering an octave.

"We don't make no robes here. Only rope." The clerk scratched at his head.

"And that is an important part of a monk's habit. Witness." Davin's eyes darted from side to side as he

searched the cluttered shop and found a thickness of rope
perfectly suited to his purpose. He walked to the snake-
like coils, lifted the end, and wrapped a loop about his
midsection.

"Now," Davin continued as he turned back to the
youth, "imagine that I wear a coarse brown robe. A belt
is required to keep it from flapping in the wind. So rope
goes around in a fashion like this."

He cinched another turn or two of the rope around his
waist.

"You want to buy rope to use as belts? Why not go
to the tannery and use thongs? That's cheaper by a goodly
amount. That you hold there in your hand is the finest,
strongest rope in the store."

"Truly, I did note its diminutive size and extraordinary
strength, my son. This is why your master's shop has
been chosen." He pulled another few turns of rope around
him and set it securely into place. "See? How fine we
shall look with rope such as this gracing our middles."

"You look like a mummy . . . uh, er . . . my father."
The clerk stared wide-eyed as Davin wrapped two more
loops about his midriff.

"My son, there is no need to address one of the Hum-
drumullite order by that title, unless you believe."

Davin paraded around the store, trailing rope behind.
In a perfectly casual gesture, he jerked and pulled and
turned, and the rope moved from coil to waist, hardly a
sound being made the while. He esimated fully fifty feet
now circled him. Just a bit more and he'd have all he
needed.

"That's not the name you said before." The clerk's
pimply face screwed up in a parody of concentration.

In reality, Davin did not remember what name he had
used for his mythical religious order.

"That is part of our tenet," he said, summoning up
his most pedantic tones.

He cleared his throat as if to start a sermon, which

caused the young clerk to look as if he had swallowed an emetic. Davin returned to the counter, pulling even more rope around him as he talked.

"We are not allowed to mention the name of the order twice in one day, so we must perforce alter it slightly each time. It is the gods' will, my son."

"But if you change the name each time, how do you know what order you *really* belong to?" The young man's face screwed up tightly as he obviously delved for an answer far beyond his limited grasp.

"Ahhh! That is a profound philosophical question. I am surprised that one not of our order has even considered it. It is the sort of deep thinking reserved normally for our most prized theologians," Davin said with all the sincerity and awe he could muster and still retain a straight face. "Are you a free man? Are you willing to give up all worldly possessions, all wealth no matter how small, all intercourse with those of the opposite sex, food except for cold gruel and salt water? Are you prepared to do all that and devote your full time to religious issues? My son, you will make a perfect Sumtumullite monk!"

"A monk? Me? Give up fair Lutecia and my job and any chance I have of ever being like Master Tabim? Insanity! What do you think I am?" The youth's head rolled from side to side.

"I think you are a very rude clerk. How dare you malign my sacred and profane religious order!"

Davin played the charade for all it was worth. His rage mounted. He shouted and ranted, and when his voice rolled like thunder within the confines of the small shop, he began throwing things at the poor clerk. The youth abandoned the hope of defending himself with flailing arms and ducked behind the small counter when Davin found individual links of anchor chain and pitched those in the clerk's general direction.

"Stop it!" cried the benighted youth. "Leave instantly or I must go for my master!"

"Do and be damned to burn in the lowest of Hells. How dare you so impudently insult my religious beliefs?"

Davin punctuated each sentence with a well-tossed link. Every time the clerk dropped back and hid behind the counter, Davin added a few more turns of rope to his booty. He grinned at the girth now gracing his mid-section and wondered if this was how it felt to be fat.

It was certainly what it was like to feel clever!

Another length of chain sent the clerk scurrying for the back door. The instant he made his move, Davin spun and coiled the last few feet of rope he needed around his waist. A quick flash of his dagger severed the length.

Then, as if he had all the time in the world, he went to the front door and yelled after the clerk, "I shall never return to this store, mark my words! Nor will any of my religious order!"

He swung his cloak out and around his body to hide the thick rope and walked leisurely into the bazaar to lose himself among the colorful throng. Here and there he noticed a curious lift of an eye to question the strangely proportioned man who strolled toward Harn's west gates. These he gave no mind, for his thoughts wandered to the use he had for the rope wrapped about his slim belly and all the preparations that had to be accomplished within an excruciatingly short time—if he was to save the lovely Lijena from Harn's King of Thieves and free his companion Goran One-Eye from Bistonia's counterpart.

# chapter
## 7

DAVIN SAT ASTRADDLE a limb as thick as a man's arm with his back to the rough bark of an oak trunk. A satisfied smile upturned his mouth when he cast an admiring eye on his handiwork. Goran would have been proud of such a diabolical device.

*Well . . . mayhaps not diabolical,* he admitted while methodically giving the network of four ropes one last going over, *but definitely effective—if the Sitala so ordain!*

Two lengths of the purloined rope held the simple device, and a third served as its release mechanism. The fourth length was securely bound to a pine limb across the Hyian Road; it was the Jyotian's means of descent from his high perch.

While he readily admitted that swinging downward into the fray with sword bared contained a pleasing touch of the melodramatic, it also held an element of surprise. When one man faced five, anything that might tip the scales in favor of the one, even for the briefest of moments, could well mean the difference between success—or death!

The clip of hoof on stone drew Davin's attention eastward along the road below. He ignored the racing of his heart as he carefully stood atop the broad limb and freed the deadly length of his longsword. Embedding the tip of the blade in the gnarled bark so that the weapon stood near and ready for his hand, he crouched on the branch like a panther awaiting its prey.

The steady clop-a-clop of hooves echoed nearer. Davin peered through the multihued canopy of leaves, searching for a glint of morning sunlight on plate armor or a glimpse of Lijena's white *sartha* furs. He saw neither, only heard the approaching sound of twenty-four hooves.

Then, through a small break in the brilliant reds and golds, he saw them: five armed guards and their single prisoner.

Coiling the end of his descent rope several times about his left arm, he held it firmly while he reached out and grasped the release rope with his right hand. All the while his pulse trebled its tempo.

*Insanity!* Doubt darkened his mind. *By Yehseen's angry staff, there's no way this can work. Only a fool . . .*

The time for scheming and doubting passed. Below the freebooter's lofty perch passed Lijena and the sergeant of the small troop, then another soldier, a corpulent beast of a fellow whom Davin saw as posing no problem to his blade. The remaining three rode in a cluster.

"Aieeee!" His cry rolled from chest and throat.

Simultaneously he yanked the release rope. The single slipknot holding it to the oak came free with a twang like the release of some monstrous bowstring. The rope wrenched from his hand and snaked high into the trees.

From even higher came the crushing sound of limb and branch.

In the simplicity of his hastily constructed device lay its beauty, and its strength. From a branch twenty hands above him rope ran upward into the leafy heights. A bushy pine across the road held a similiar length, also stretching upward. Both were attached to a freshly cut log strung high between the two trees and neatly hidden among the dense branches. The selfsame log now arced downward like the swing of some forest giant's child.

Ponderously the log plummeted forth from the cloaking autumn leaves. One guard turned in surprise at Davin's cry and froze with horror at the sight of death descending.

Not even the man's scream of agony could drown the awful sound as the log crashed solidly into his chest. Wet and asquish came death, accompanied by the brittle snap and crack of bones shattered to mere fragments.

Momentum unimpeded, the log carried its victim outward and into the horse of the next guard, who bent to avoid the crushing impact—and failed. The log slammed into his horse, his leg trapped between his dead companion and horseflesh. His anguished screams wailed as bones were ground to fine meal and flesh shredded.

And still the log swung in its deadly arc.

The third rider had an instant longer than the others to react. He threw up his arms and dived from his mount even as the murderous log crushed an equine skull.

Davin Anane but glimpsed the effectiveness of rope-borne log. A smile uplifted the corners of his mouth as he wrenched sword from limb and launched himself toward the remaining guards below.

Not steel aglint in the morning sun but the Jyotian's widely stretched legs met the saucer-round eyes of the fat guard whose head jerked around to find the source of a second blood-chilling cry—legs that clamped vise-tight about the man's beefy neck.

With a dexterous twisting of his lithe body, Davin snapped the man's spine and sent his corpse hurtling to the ground. Another adroit twist dropped the only son of the House of Anane into the guard's now-vacant saddle. In the next instant he snared the horse's reins in his left hand. His longsword swung high as he turned to meet the attack of the remaining warrior.

No attack came! The sergeant and his ward raced deeper into the wood.

"Jajhana's dried paps!" Davin profaned the Goddess

of Chance and Fortune as his heels dug into the horse's
flanks to send it in pursuit.

He'd hoped the sergeant would display a streak of
foolish heroics rather than prudent action. Apparently
Tadzi had instilled within the man the notion that Lijena's
continued captivity rode higher than personal honor.

Bent low to the bay's neck, Davin swung his sword
back, its flat popping the horse's rump. Again and again
he used the unyielding whip. To have reduced five to
one and then lose his prize . . . He refused to consider the
possibility. The sergeant would not escape!

Davin smiled as he rounded a bend in the Hyian Road.
There, no more than a furlong ahead, rode the armor-
clad sergeant, and four lengths behind—Lijena.

Even without Velden's goadings, Davin would have
rescued one so lovely. Her frosty blonde hair flowed like
a river of white gold in the morning sunlight, and in spite
of all provocation, she had not panicked. She rode with
jaw set firmly, courageously. Nor did he see a trace of
fear on her face when she glanced behind to judge his
approach.

Davin's heels spurred inward, matching the rhythm
of the whipping flat of his blade. As long as he remained
on the sergeant's heels, the man wouldn't have time to
consider reining into the forest to escape.

And fleeing down the middle of Hyian Road was
exactly where the Jyotian wanted this last guard when
he reached the ford across the River Kukis. There Davin
had stretched his one last advantage: the last portion of
the rope taken from the merchant Tabim's shop.

The din of crashing armor, a startled cry, and flailing
arms and legs as he tumbled from his saddle to the ground
announced the guard's introduction to that rope, which
was tautly stretched between two trees chest-high across
the road just at the river's edge. The sergeant, like a
turtle on its back, struggled to sit up, weighed down by
his heavy armor.

Lijena jerked back on her reins, bringing her dapple-gray to a halt amid flying stones and dirt. Her timely reaction saved her from being deposited on the ground beside her would-be protector.

"Do not fight it," Davin called out to the unseated guard as he drew his own mount to a halt. "Simply allow me to rescue the fair lady, and we'll be on our way. Your lord need not know how easy it was."

"Ride on, my lady!" cried Presko. "Go! Ride and get the commander of the guards. I'll hold this one off. The others won't be able to get by me."

"Others?" said Davin, in mock surprise. "There are no others. Just I."

Lijena remained motionless, her befuddled gaze shifting between the still-struggling sergeant and her self-proclaimed rescuer from the treetops.

"You've come for me?" she asked. "Who sent you?"

Davin didn't have time to answer. The sergeant rolled onto his belly and pushed to his feet. A broadsword flashed wickedly in the light filtering through the trees as it came free from a hard leather scabbard. Presko raised its tip toward the attacker who had single-handedly defeated his troop of four.

"A lovely spot for a battle," Davin said to the approaching warrior, "but I fear I'll have to rob you of the chance."

He reined the stolen bay to the right and warily circled around the sergeant. His nonchalant acceptance of Presko's challenge and his underestimation of the man's devotion to duty—or fear of Tadzi—cost him dearly.

In the blinking of an eye, fully weighted with plate armor, Presko roared like a great brown bear and charged. His blade flashed, whistling as it lashed out in a blow that ended when it cleanly cleaved the bay's right foreleg just above the knee.

A terrible scream of equine agony echoed in Davin Anane's ears as he threw himself from the saddle. He

hit the ground in a roll to avoid being pinned beneath
the falling horse. And only quicker reflexes saved him
from having his hair parted by Presko's massive blade
as it sang downward.

He rolled again; cold steel buried itself in the soft
earth not a hand's breadth from his head. He rolled once
more, this time to his feet with longsword leveled against
a renewed attack.

"I have no quarrel with you, friend," Davin said. His
sword point danced small circles in the air.

Presko, broad blade clutched in gauntleted hands and
eyes narrowed, advanced.

"Wait, Presko. We must talk with him. Perhaps this
isn't as it seems. This might be—" Lijena's plea ended
in a startled cry.

The dapple-gray had reared, frightened by sunlight
glinting off the sergeant's sword. Lijena tumbled backward from the saddle and fell heavily to the ground. She
didn't move, but lay as still as death itself.

Davin's gaze darted to the fallen daughter of Bistonia.
There beneath the white-gold cascade of her hair lay a
stone as large as a *kelii*'s egg.

"You've killed her, you scum-eating pig!" shrieked
Presko. The man lumbered forward, his blade slashing
out in a vicious arc.

Davin didn't try to parry. He jumped back, almost
losing his footing as he did so.

The blade whished around, and the fight would have
ended there had Davin been in a position to lunge. By
the time he recovered his balance, Presko was on him
again. The sergeant's anger had now turned to cold, hard
determination.

"You'll die for this. As surely as Lord Tadzi will flay
me alive for allowing this to happen, you'll die!"

Davin's strong wrist turned aside the blow and left
him an opening for a riposte directly to Presko's neck.
Something stayed his hand.

"She's not dead, friend," he said, trying to slow the

attack. "She is still alive. See her breast rise and fall?"

The pronouncement brought little comfort to Presko's slitted eyes. They now glared with burning rage. He swung high his broadsword to slash downward at the intruder from Jyotis. Davin parried and backstepped. Presko's blade danced upward in a deadly arc, to be met by another parry. Again, again, and again the armored sergeant swung, his might behind each blow. His strength was the bloodlust, for he attacked like a berserker.

Davin Anane never considered mounting an attack of his own, but struggled to ward off each of the weighty blows. He dodged from side to side, ducked, and retreated. Still Presko came. And still Davin danced away from the deadly singing blade, biding his time, for even the berserker strength fades.

"You tire," Davin said softly with no trace of taunt in his tone. Unlike his Challing friend, Goran One-Eye, he found no pleasure in maiming or killing. Rather he would win this by his wits than by his sword. "Let us parley. Lijena wished it so. You heard her before she was thrown. Let us tend her, then settle our differences."

Words were of no avail. Presko redoubled his attack, forcing Davin backward. Step by step, he retreated toward the River Kukis, then into it. The water sloshed around his ankles, gurgled to mid-calf, and finally trickled over the tops of his high boots. With tireless energy the sergeant of the guard pressed on, his blade seemingly as light as a mere feather in his hands.

If it weren't enough to contend with that slashing blade, Davin now found himself hard pressed to retain his footing on waterworn rocks as treacherously slick as glass. Time and again he barely dodged the honed tip of Presko's broadsword, only to nearly manage to lose himself in the river's current. Slowly the Jyotian's instinct for survival replaced cool reason.

He retreated steadily, purposely allowing Presko to beat down his guard as he feigned exhaustion. The sergeant took the bait. Every step brought the water creeping higher and higher, until it swirled about the berserker's thighs.

This was exactly what Davin Anane wanted. It would be only a matter of time until the glass-slippery stones beneath their feet took their toll. To hasten that collection, the young adventurer abruptly let his guard down completely.

With a growl rolling deep from his throat, Presko wrenched his sword high above his head, fully intent on swinging it down and carving Davin's head in twain. It was that very motion which cost Tadzi's sergeant his balance. Presko's feet slid out from under him, and he went down heavily—and sank.

Only bubbles rose from beneath the water, to be carried away by the swift current. Then there was only the current. With a shrug, Davin turned and waded toward the shore. Plate armor had its purposes; swimming wasn't one of them. Presko had drowned, weighted down by his fine, shiny suit.

Davin Anane reached the bank and flopped on dry ground. He lay there several moments gathering his breath before sitting to empty his boots of water. Then he rose and went to Lijena's side. Deft thief's fingers explored the knot on the back of her skull. She moaned at the touch but seemed none the worse for the fall and the knock to her head.

"Lijena," he said softly, "it's time to return to Bistonia and your beloved uncle."

He made no attempt to disguise the sarcasm in his voice. Returning Lijena to her uncle was the last thing he wanted to do with one so lovely. Yet Goran One-Eye remained in Emperor Velden's clutches—a duty that demanded his attention.

*Mayhap,* he thought with a sigh as he lifted her limp form, *there'll be time for us on another day.*

The snap of twig and rustle of dry leaves came from the left.

Davin, arms filled with unconscious woman, turned. Standing there, spear in hand, was the third guard—the one who had barely avoided the log.

"Cens is crippled," the guard said in a curiously monotone voice.

The life was gone from the man's eyes. A finger of ice tapped at the base of Davin's spine. This was a killing machine set in motion by a master artisan and not easily waylaid or destroyed.

"The lady is severely injured. We must get her to Harn immediately or she'll die," Davin said, hoping to divert the man's attention.

"I am Portrevnio. Cens is my . . . my . . ." The man's voice was as lifeless as his steel-gray eyes. "His leg is crushed to pulp. You did that to him."

Davin loathed facing a determined fighter armed with a spear. His opponent had reach on him by at least an arm's length, and perhaps more. The razor-edged spear tip could both slash and jab, and should he somehow manage to dance from under the point, he still had the shaft of the weapon to contend with. A practiced weaponsman used the haft as a quarterstaff. Davin had no doubt this Portrevnio was practiced in his chosen weapon—a weapon that was at once dagger, sword, and staff.

"He is in terrible pain. You shall die for what you did to him." Portrevnio advanced, spear tip lowering so that it aimed directly between the Jyotian's eyes.

"Your lord might want to question me." Davin sought to delay the warrior just long enough to lower the still-unconscious Lijena back to the ground.

"Tadzi hired us to protect that bitch," said the advancing soldier, his eyes coldly glaring at Davin, reflecting only the hunger for blood. "He said nothing about questioning those who attacked his guards."

The first thrust came just as Davin deposited Lijena on the road, and it struck for a target lower than the face.

Davin adroitly parried the spear and allowed the point to slip past his right ear. Before he could thrust for the soldier's neck, the haft of the spear swung around and smartly rapped his left knee.

Davin dropped, his leg suddenly numb. Through pain-watering eyes he saw Portrevnio thrust again. He drove his sword directly upward and perpendicular to the ground, deflecting the spear's wickedly pointed head—by scant inches.

"Die now, die, damn you, die!" Seething hate brimmed from Portrevnio's snarled lips.

Tadzi's remaining guard thrust for a third time.

Davin parried and rolled—not quick enough! The tip of the spear raked across his side, cutting through fine doeskin and flesh. Heat blazed along the growing red stripe, then wetness marred his side as blood sluggishly flowed from the razor-thin wound.

"Can I buy her from you? Is she so important?" Davin tried to regain his feet. His left leg, still numb, refused to support his weight.

"Qar take the bitch! It's you I want—for what you did to my Cens!" Portrevnio lifted his spear and moved in for the kill, ready to pin Davin to the ground beneath him.

"Cens!" The faceless name formed as a curse on Davin's lips—but gave birth to a glimmer of hope. Whoever this Cens was, he was more than just a friend to Portrevnio. Davin stared at a spot behind the spearman. "No! Cens! No! Your leg can't stand it!"

Portrevnio halted, uncertain. Then he turned. It was all the time Davin needed. He freed his dirk, grasped its needle-pointed blade, and hurled it at the soldier's vulnerable back.

With a fleshy thud, it struck deep and true.

"Cens?" The name came from Portrevnio's lips—then a long, pained grasp.

For a heartbeat that stretched into an eternity, Tadzi's soldier just stood there as though the impaling blade were no more than a beesting. Then his hands released the spear haft and awkwardly groped at his back, trying to free the dirk. The hilt evaded him, even as he fell face down in the dirt of the Hyian Road and the last breath of life escaped his lungs.

"Close," whispered Davin, trying to quiet the trip-hammering of his heart. "Too damned close. Black Qar, I'll not be yours this day. Someday, yes, but not this one."

Limping slightly, trying to stanch the flow of blood from his side, Davin returned to kneel beside Lijena. The color had returned to her face and she moaned softly now. But his best efforts wouldn't revive her.

"Staying here isn't going to gain me a thing. And Goran still hangs by his wrists in Velden's torture chamber. Time to ride, my lady, time to ride."

Davin hefted the woman's limp form and carried her to where the dapple-gray mare contentedly cropped at the grass.

"You don't know or care about the death and injury that has occurred this day, do you, old nag?" Davin said soothingly to the horse. The animal whinnied, then returned her attention to the grass.

"Would that I had your ignorance."

He grabbed the reins, then hoisted Lijena across the horse's back. She dangled, head on one side and feet on the other.

"Not the finest way for a lady to ride, but you'll appreciate it when we return to Bistonia. Your uncle's preparing a fine homecoming for you, I'm sure."

Davin Anane then captured the horse on which Presko had ridden and mounted. Leading Lijena's gray, he headed northward into the forest, intending to skirt Harn and then ride eastward to Bistonia.

"Such a fine homecoming it will be, too. You and your ratlike uncle and me with my one-eyed friend. What a combination!"

# chapter
## 8

A BLACKSMITH RAN AMOK inside Lijena's feverish skull.
Heavy and hard his sledgelike hammer rose and fell bang-
ing and clanging against the top of her head with blows
so mighty they reverberated downward to collide with
the jelly of her brain. Each and every individual stroke
of that powerful mallet brought a wince, and this movement left her stomach achurn. She weakly clutched at
her midriff and was immediately rewarded with intense
pain arrowing into her guts.

In that moment, Lijena realized that she had died, and
Black Qar himself . . . herself . . . itself personally tended
her with all the torments of the lowest levels of Peyneeha,
the realm men called Hell. There was no other explanation for the agony visiting itself upon her body.

"You stir." The words roared in her ears.

She fought, determined to make the Great Destroyer's
task as difficult as possible. Not easily would she give
up her life to the greedy God of the Underworld.

"No," she muttered, regretting even this small defiance. Her tongue lay wrapped in cotton and betrayed her
with its thickness. Better that some minor demon cut it
out so that she'd never be able to display her weaknesses.
"Go away. I defy you!"

"There, there," came words more soothing.

Confused by Death's gentle fashion, Lijena struggled to place the fragmented pieces in a coherent image. The effort only brought a renewed clanging from the demon smith who dwelt in her head, which, in turn, sent fresh waves of nausea trembling through her stomach. Better not to concentrate and thus aggravate the pain in head and body.

"You'll be just fine in a day or two, after you're returned to Bistonia and find a safe place in your uncle's care."

She detected a deep sigh punctuating Qar's soft words.

"Would that we might remain on the trail for a few days."

Again another wistful sigh, indicating that such was not dictated by the five Fates.

Lijena forced leaden eyelids open, blinked as light assaulted pupil and brain, then squinted at the flames that came from a small campfire not a pace away. *Campfire?* The quiet blaze was not the sulfurous inferno of Peyneeha's pits.

She blinked again, accepting the confused awakening of her senses. She lay on her side, that much was certain. And she faced the campfire with the warmth of its flickering yellow tongues bathing her cheeks. The tantalizing aroma of burning *morda* wood tickled her nostrils with the assurance that she indeed lived rather than stood condemned to Qar's flaming dungeons.

*But where am I? And who possesses such a tender voice?*

The warm pillow beneath her head shifted. Lijena's eyes widened in mild shock. *It's not a pillow . . . but someone's lap! The person speaking?*

She questioned no further, but closed her eyes and snuggled against the security of that comforting thigh. One with such a gentle voice could not possibly mean her harm.

The simple movement reawoke the needles of pain in her belly. Surreptitiously her fingertips pressed gingerly at her stomach. She was heavily bruised across the abdomen, as if she'd been severely beaten!

By the man in whose lap she lay? That made no sense. Why should he tend her if he had so brutally beaten her? And who was *he?*

She ignored the mad blacksmith in her skull and the protesting wince of her midriff and rolled to her back. A blanket of diamond-bright stars dotted the black velvet sky above. A blurred white oval obscured the glimmering array. Reluctantly she focused on the fuzzy whiteness, sharpening the image to that of a handsome young face.

"You return to the land of the living, my lady. I had thought you lost to me for the rest of the journey." A dazzling smile radiated down upon her.

The hint of a smile touched Lijena's lips, only to be abruptly transformed into a bestial snarl. *The forest!* Memories of the morning attack deluged her head, drowning the hammering smith within. *This man . . .*

She sat bolt upright. Her fingers curled into claws to fend off any attack.

*"You!"* The word came venomously. "You're the man in the forest. The one who killed the guards and tried to kidnap me!"

"Succeeded in kidnapping you," Davin Anane corrected with no small amount of satisfaction. "For all the work I went through, you might at least have the courtesy to thank me. I could have very well lost my life this morn!"

*"Thank* you!" she cried in disbelief. "You, a common cutpurse, a . . . a *kidnapper!"*

"A cutpurse I may be, but there's nothing common about me," he said with some edge to his voice.

"Who are you to steal me away from Lord Tadzi? Don't you know of his power, of his anger, once aroused? He'll stop at nothing to get me back—and to kill you for this horrible affront."

"I am Davin Anane," he said with a flourish of his arms, a gesture that took more energy than he wished to admit. The day's ride had been long and hard. He had run the horses for fully half the sands of an hourglass, then walked them for an equal time, hour after hour, all day, stopping only thrice to allow their mounts a drink. To have ridden them harder would have been disastrous; they would have died of exhaustion, leaving him afoot with an unconscious woman.

"As for Tadzi, I'm certain Harn's Lord of Thieves has men scouring the woods for us. But then I have ridden down many a stream this day to conceal our trail. His cutthroats will bother us not." Davin gestured again and grinned widely at Lijena.

If he'd been standing, Lijena realized he would have bowed as though in the High King's court. She barely repressed the smile that sought to spread across her face. *All things considered, he's not a bad-looking sort . . . for a brigand.*

"I take it you know who I am."

"That, my lady, is true. But you have nothing to fear from me. I have been sent by your uncle to rescue you."

"My uncle? I don't understand." Lijena wasn't certain what this man—this Davin Anane—had said. The buzz was still heavy inside her skull.

"He commissioned me to rescue you from Tadzi . . . which I have done." Davin's chest swelled proudly. "Now we must return—in less than two days."

She detected a grim tone to his last pronouncement, but his smile was wide, so she edged the hint of disquiet aside.

"I'm afraid I still don't understand."

Was this beauty without brains? Davin stared at Lijena, unable to hide his exasperation. After all, he had explained the rescue thrice, but he tried a fourth. "The Emperor Velden sent me. You uncle. Remember him?"

"Velden!" Lijena's mind reeled in disbelief and horror. "Velden is my father's bitterest enemy!"

Deep furrows ran across Davin's brow. For an instant she saw puzzlement on his face, then his expression darkened, his eyes narrowed, and he stared at her. Lijena tensed, prepared for . . . for what she wasn't certain. Velden was cunning, and his men had to be equally endowed with that low animal intelligence.

"It is my turn not to understand. Are you saying that Velden *isn't* your uncle?" Davin spoke in a voice deep and cool.

"Of course he isn't. He and my father have fought for years. The idea is ridiculous." Lijena's eyes remained locked to his . . . waiting for the worst.

"Then who is your father?"

"Chesmu Farleigh." Lijena watched his expression darken. "He heads Bistonia's Merchantry Guild. By uniting them some years ago, he led the merchants in their fight against Velden. It was my father who drove Velden into the sewers, and for that Velden has never forgiven him."

"I can imagine," said Davin, unable to disguise his disgust. The Sitala, those five capricious Gods of Fate, toyed with him—as did Velden! "Then you don't even have an uncle?"

"Of course I do. You kidnapped me from his custody. Tadzi is my uncle," Lijena replied with certainty. "My father sent me to Harn against my will."

"Then Tadzi *was* holding you prisoner?"

Relief touched her captor's handsome face. Lijena studied him carefully, noting the fine lines around the eyes. This one was young, but he'd had many cares in his short life. Still, they gave him an air of authority, of command without being overly dictatorial. Other lines around his lips showed the quickness of his smile, the richness of his laughter. He was a man she might have enjoyed meeting in some other fashion, at some other time, in some other place.

"At least I have rescued you, even if it was for all the

wrong reasons. Is there some family dispute? Tadzi attempts to extort money from his brother?"

"Nothing of the sort," Lijena said. "Tadzi is doing my father a favor, though it is no favor to me. My father was called to Kavindra on business."

Davin tensed at the mention of Raemllyn's capital, a reaction that doubled Lijena's fear. *Might this brigand be a rebel, also?*

"Go on," he demanded with a tilt of his head.

Lijena swallowed and shivered a little. The chilling breeze blowing through the shadow-cloaked forest sought out her bones to suck away body heat. She moved closer to the fire, but not to Davin.

"My father feared, and rightly, that his departure would allow me the opportunity to elope with Amrik." Lijena read the question on Davin's face. "Amrik Tohon is my intended."

"So all Farleigh did by sending you to Tadzi is prevent you from marrying a man of whom he does not approve."

"So he thinks, as does my Uncle Tadzi," she admitted. "But while *I* might elope and marry Amrik, *he* would never marry me in such an improper fashion. He is the *most* honorable of men in all Bistonia."

The wistful sigh that ended her reply made Davin smile. Obviously she had fought against this Amrik Tohon's misguided honor, and all to no avail.

"Amrik Tohon is a fool," said Davin.

"What? How dare you say that! You don't even know him. He is kind and sweet and treats me always as a lady." Lijena's aquamarine eyes fired with sparks of anger.

"Had I been given the chance to elope with you, I'd have taken it in a flash. Faster."

His leer, his tone, which bespoke bedding rather than wedding, drove home again exactly who this man was, and what he had done to bring her here—wherever *here* was.

Lijena felt a shiver of gooseflesh at the way the flickering light from the campfire gave him a demonic appearance. How could she have seen beauty in such a face but moments before? Heavy shadows cast upward against the planes of his face transformed his dark eyes into pools opening onto infinity. And the muscles that rippled beneath his tunic, and his wicked sword that leaned against the tree beside him . . . He appeared capable of any foul deed.

"What do you intend doing with me?" she asked over the fearful quiver of her lower lip.

"For the time being, nothing except this."

Davin leaned back toward his sword. Lijena's eyes widened in horror, and her heart raced at a maddening pace. *He's going to kill me!*

"Here, take this." He tossed her a tiny pouch withdrawn from a satchel next to his blade.

She caught the leather bag and stared at it in relief and confusion. "What is it?"

"It's a new invention we Jyotians have taken to using. It's called food. You put it in your mouth, chew it a while, then swallow. Quite an interesting sensation."

"There's no need for sarcasm," she snapped to conceal her befuddlement.

"Eat!"

She opened the pouch of jerked venison and took out a thick slice lacking the green mold she faintly saw gracing the other pieces. Daintily Lijena began gnawing. She found the smoky favor pleasing, a fact she'd never admit—not to the likes of this Davin Anane.

"Here. A wineskin."

"I know what it is," she said. "There's no need to treat me like a child."

Davin merely shrugged, then rose and turned from the fire.

"Where are you going?" Her eyes went round and wide as she glanced at the dark forest about her.

*Better the predatory animals than this two-legged*

*beast,* she thought. But the idea of his going—leaving her alone—bothered her strangely.

"I've got to think this out," he said. "Don't stray too far. There are direwolves about. I saw their tracks earlier in the day. They'd eat your like for supper and wonder where the rest of the meal was."

"You're not frightening me," she lied with a flare of false bravado. She'd seen the traveling shows where men were pitted against a direwolf. The bets always heavily favored the wolf—for a reason. It seldom lost.

Davin walked but a stride or two beyond the fire's glow. Lijena watched his dark form as he obviously wrestled with whatever problem confronted him.

For her part, she saw no problem at all. He had made a mistake. Now that he had been put right that Velden was her mortal enemy, he had no choice but to release her. While she would have preferred to return to Bistonia and Amrik's arms, Tadzi was not a bad second choice.

So would have been Davin's course, were there not other circumstances: those circumstances being one Raemllyn-stranded Challing who bore the name Goran One-Eye, and the subterranean dungeon in which he was chained.

*And there is Lord Tadzi,* Davin mulled. *Lijena's father may be a merchant, but Tadzi's ways of transacting business would allow no profit margin for this son of Anane!*

"Mount up." He had but one choice, one duty to fulfill. He turned back to the campfire. "We have many leagues to go this night if we are to reach Bistonia by midnight tomorrow."

"My uncle's in Harn! You're returning to him, aren't you? There was a mistake. Velden lied to you. You've got no choice but—"

"Mount up. I said we ride for Bistonia."

Tears of frustration and rage welled in Lijena's eyes. Salty tracks soon ran across dusty cheeks and dried, leaving mud in their wake.

"He'll give you gold, silver, whatever you want. Tadzi

is rich. So is my father. You *must* return me to him.
You must!"

Davin started to speak, then stopped. Silently he gestured for her to mount her horse.

"Velden will torture me. He . . . he'll rape me and then
torture me! He'll stop at nothing to gain his revenge on
my father. Don't let this happen. Please, Davin! Please!"

She dropped to her knees in the soft forest carpeting
and gripped his arm, tugging him downward. He jerked
away angrily.

"Stop the crying and get on your horse. If you don't,
I'll tie you across it like I did before."

Lijena reacted in shock. That was why her midsection
hurt so. She'd been bouncing all day long, her stomach
taking the full force of the bouncing horse.

"You wouldn't!"

When he didn't answer, she looked up into his cold
dark eyes. This was not the callow youth she'd assumed
earlier. This was a man hardened by the world. Whatever
Velden had promised him was more valuable than anything she might offer, even using Tadzi's extensive fortune as the standard.

"The blood feud between Velden and Farleigh is no
concern of mine," Davin said with no trace of emotion
in his voice.

Lijena saw a flicker of doubt in those dark eyes—for
a fleeting moment. Whatever hold Velden had on Davin
strengthened even as she pleaded. Her offers of gold and
silver held no sway over this man of Jyotis.

*Something . . . there has to be something! I have to
convince him—*

She caught herself in mid-thought. There was something!

"I can make it your business," she said in a low voice
choked with emotion.

Trembling with doubt, she stood, her sea-blue eyes
rolling to Davin. Uncertain fingers rose to the gold chain

about her neck from which her *sartha* fur robe dangled, and unclasped the chain. The rich fur fell from her shoulders to the ground.

"Don't," Davin commanded.

But his eyes betrayed him. In spite of his order to mount and ride, he wanted to see to what extent she would go to stop him. Lijena read it all in his eyes, his face, his body.

She had no desire to offer herself to him in this fashion, but her father had always said that the world was cruel, and the bargains set were not often entirely to one's liking.

And she dared not allow herself to be taken to Velden. Anything—*anything at all*—she could do to prevent it, she would.

"What I am offering you far transcends mere worldly riches. I offer you paradise," she said, voice none too steady, but her intent more than clear.

She unfastened the pearl clasps on her blouse. One after another the buttons slipped free, to reveal a titillating glimpse of honey-cream skin beneath. Lijena gave a final quick tug and the blouse opened, unveiling firm, high-placed young breasts.

In the dim light cast by the campfire, she saw his eyes focused on the uplifted cones of her breasts, saw the labored heaving of his chest and the growing indication of his arousal. She hated herself for doing this, yet what else could she do? Her life hung in the balance.

An inviting smile moved over the fullness of her lips as Davin slowly walked to where her robe lay on the ground. He moved like a wooden toy with carved gears and steel spring. Will had fled. She had him totally captivated by her bared charms.

He reached down and gripped the collar of the *sartha* robe. With a dexterous spin, he sent the robe sailing through the air and about her shoulders.

"Get dressed. We ride in one minute or I tie you across

your saddle again." A hint of a rude smile danced on his lips.

Startled, sputtering indignantly, Lijena did as she was told.

"Amrik will cut your heart out for this," she promised grimly.

"For not raping his fiancée?" asked Davin with a laugh and a shake of his head.

"You'll not get away with this!"

"There's no one left to stop me," Davin pointed out.

Lijena proved him wrong!

Her slender hand had found a poniard sheathed at her waist. In his haste to depart the scene of her abduction, Davin had failed to search her. The blade and the death it carried were the "paradise" she had intended to deliver him to the moment he had embraced her. Now there was no time for subtleties.

Lijena jerked the blade free, held it in her hand, point down, and ran for Davin, aiming for the center of his back.

The mere whispered hiss of tempered steel against leather sheath spun Davin Anane around. His arm snaked out and blocked the attack, deflecting the blade so that it harmlessly passed to his right. He twisted, caught her wrist, and forced her to her knees. Either she dropped the knife or he broke her wrist. The knife dropped to the forest floor.

"You're full of surprises," he said, looking down at her. "I had not expected such an attack. Is that one you learned from your uncle? Or did your father teach you to stab men in the back?"

"Only kidnappers," she raged.

Then Lijena softened her tone. Davin was too strong for her. There had to be other ways, and this seemed the instant to try once again.

"You've conquered," she said, her hands moving in more gentle ways now. "Take that reward which is due

the conqueror. Take it and return me to Bistonia!" She
started to open her blouse again.

Inexplicable rage blossomed on Davin's face. For a
heart-stopping instant, Lijena thought he would strike
her. Instead, he grabbed her wrist and pulled her to her
feet.

"Slut," he hissed through clenched teeth.

With a deft twist, he spun her around and caught her
other wrist. Bringing them together and easily holding
them in one hand, he said, "Can you ride with hands
tied behind your back?"

"No," she said. "I'd fall off if I couldn't use the reins
to control Orria."

"Orria? Your mare? She's got more sense than her
mistress. And more than I possess, that I'll grant."

"What do you mean?"

"I'll not tie your hands behind your back."

Lijena slumped at the news. He spun her around and
recaptured the one wrist he'd let free. "But I am going
to tie your wrists in front."

"Animal. You beast. You inhuman—"

"And I shall be forced to gag you if you can't control
your outbursts."

Lijena subsided, silently vowing to put an end to this
miserable man's life by her own hand when opportunity
presented itself. He helped her mount and they rode silently through the dark forest, heading toward Bistonia
and Emperor Velden's revenge.

# chapter
## 9

DAVIN ANANE SAT ON HIS HAUNCHES, back against the trunk of a gnarled *morda* tree; one hand rested lightly on the hilt of his longsword. While others' feet would have paced nervously as midnight approached, it was Davin's eyes that ceaselessly traced and retraced the small glade outside the walls of Bistonia.

He glanced at Lijena, sitting bound an arm's length to his left, to the horses tied to a sapling on the right, gratefully resting after their wild and demanding journey, and, finally, to the constellations wheeling above.

No more than a few minutes remained before the appointed hour of the exchange if the starry positions were to be trusted. *With Jajhana's grace, I'll soon be finished with this sorry venture!* The Jyotian's gaze skirted the circular glade for the thousandth time that eve. He was no gambler, and the Goddess of Chance and Fortune was not known for smiling on mere mortals.

"Something awry?" Lijena's tone dripped bitter sarcasm. "Has the misbegotten hero erred ... *again?*"

"Quiet!" he snapped menacingly.

Davin recoiled inwardly, his arm tensed, and he realized how close he was to striking a helpless woman. The tension refused to leave his body or mind. In spite

of all his scouting of the area, the simple fact remained:
he was one, and Velden's men were a multitude. He had
no guarantee that a small army of Bistonia's cutthroats
wouldn't descend on him in the next heartbeat.

Worst was the racing of his mind. The events of the
past two weeks had come too fast: Goran kidnapped and
held . . . Harn and the Palace Tadzi . . . the fight on the
Hyian Road . . . the realization he had been duped by the
Bistonian thief king . . . the two-day, breakneck flight to
this glade . . . his desire for Lijena, who had been inno-
cently ensnared in a brutal plot of vengeance . . . his own
guilt for what he must now do—everything blurred in a
mind-dazing maelstrom. His thoughts were not thoughts
at all, but nagging doubts that gnawed at him.

He wanted nothing more in the world than to be done
with the exchange, find an inn where he might sleep for
a week, eat voraciously for another week, then take a
club to Goran's thick skull for getting them in such a
mess for a third.

His gaze shifted back to Lijena and the hate reflected
in her gem-blue eyes. It would take more than a week
or even four to cleanse the dirt from his hands. To be
certain, his was the life of a freebooter and cutpurse, but
he only stole from those who could well afford to support
his expensive tastes.

He was born the only son of the Jyotian House of
Anane, and although he often boasted a total disregard
for what wise men called honor, he could not escape
concepts engrained into him since birth. There was no
honor in what he did to Lijena—nor could he avoid his
duty to his Challing friend.

*May the Sitala be damned to Qar's fiery pits for the
capricious games they play with my life!* He cursed the
five Fates that ruled the inhabitants of Raemllyn—and
himself.

Quick fingers, a quick sword, and a quick mind were
his pride. Now that brain sifted thoughts as slowly as

treacle. He ought to have been able to rescue Goran and save Lijena from Velden's treachery. But he had no schemes—no brilliant plans of derring-do.

An overly held breath pushed past his lips as a helpless sigh. In the end, he knew he would exchange Lijena for Goran One-Eye, then ride from Bistonia like some alley mongrel with its tail tucked between its legs. Velden would get his prize, the Challing in man's form would be free, and he would eventually learn to live with himself and his shame.

Only Lijena would lose—and there was nothing he could do to prevent that.

His eyes continued on their path. The glade was well chosen for the rendezvous. The forest afforded dense cover, and the isolation guaranteed no spying eyes and ears. A dozen different paths existed for a hasty retreat, should one party double-cross the other.

Davin Anane inhaled deeply; the faint fragrances of pine, sandalwood, and *morda* wafted into his nostrils. Night sounds croaked and creaked and barked and whispered as a gentle breeze stirred from the direction of the city. With it came faint sounds of nocturnal revelers and the effluvia of Bistonia.

His nose wrinkled. A different odor—that of open sewers!

Davin's hand tightened on his sword as three bulky thieves emerged from a tangle of undergrowth. They marched across the open patch with Captain Jun in the lead. Once again Davin's gaze was drawn to the fine weapons they wore: daggers of gold and silver, with sheaths to match . . . and the swords! He had only seen such worn by Raemllyn's royalty. But then, if one is a thief, one does not have to pay for such riches—only have fingers quick enough to claim them.

"You're prompt," Jun said without preamble. He glanced at Lijena. "And you have successfully completed the mission Emperor Velden assigned you." He motioned his companions toward the glaring woman.

The ringing song of steel against sheath abruptly halted the two. Davin stood between them and his captive, sword leveled and ready.

"Rebellion in the ranks?" Jun arched an eyebrow, but there was no surprise in his voice.

"Bring Goran, *then* we exchange," Davin replied with frost in his words.

"You can trust Emperor Velden. He is a monarch true to his word," Jun assured the Jyotian with a flourish of his right arm.

Davin snorted and glanced at Lijena. Silent pleas had replaced the hatred in her eyes. He turned back to the captain of Velden's guard.

"Your Emperor's concept of *truth* is as serpentine as a *pletha*'s path. Bring Goran, allow me to examine his condition, then we shall see about this trade."

A startled gasp jerked Davin's head around and brought a lodging thickness to his throat. The rising second moon cast a silvery glow over his bound captive. Her hair came alive with frosty color that took on a life of its own. The planes of her face cast shadows that enhanced an already considerable beauty. Her eyes widened, frightened and vulnerable, like the eyes of a doe cornered by hounds. To barter such a woman was a crime worse than any Davin had thus far committed.

"You exchange me for another?" asked Lijena, her voice incredulous and, at the same time, an accusation. "You can't do it! Velden will have no mercy! He'll—"

"Silence, bitch," snapped Jun, a wickedly pleased smile playing across his lips when Lijena's plea was choked by a piteous gasp. He raised a coat sleeve and pompously polished the medals dangling from his chest. "The Emperor foresaw such a request."

Jun motioned, and one of the thieves drifted to the left and merged with the darkness.

Davin strained, listening to the man's retreat until

night sounds drowned out his clumsy passage through the underbrush.

"How long do we wait?"

"Patience," said Captain Jun, obviously enjoying Davin's discomfort. "One would think you've never dealt in slaves before."

"You . . . a . . . a *slaver?*" cried Lijena. "I should have known!"

"Believe what you wish. It's no concern of mine." Davin lied, and then lied again, telling himself the hurt and fear in Lijena's eyes were also of no matter to him.

"A slaver!" She spat at him. "And you sell me to the highest bidder."

"Actually," Jun replied, "the bid was not all that high. In fact, it was quite paltry."

The captain of Velden's guard jerked as the tip of Davin's sword danced toward his chest. A small golden disk fell to the ground.

The startled fear on Jun's face was replaced by an expression of mock amusement when he stooped to retrieve the severed medal. "That was for meritorious service at the Battle of Kressia."

"You must have shined Lord Lerel's boots well!" Davin was unable to repress his sarcasm. Even one as lowly as Zarek Yannis' henchman Lerel would never consider taking such as Jun into his service. "Or was it for stealing water from a man dying of thirst? That is more your style."

Jun laughed harshly, then tapped Davin on the chest. "You press your luck, boy. Emperor Velden said nothing about what condition you and your friend were to be in when we ride back to the city."

Davin swung his sword again, this time guiding the tip so that it stopped just short of Jun's upper lip. He twisted the blade slightly and left a red weal across Jun's cheek. The captain of thieves was reaching for his own blade when the pounding of horses' hooves echoed across the clearing.

"Go on, hurry and kill each other," urged Lijena.

"Silence, slut," snapped Jun, his hand easing from his sword. "Your time will come, that I promise."

Jun angrily swung about and motioned for the riders to approach. "Here," he said, "is your oversized, gambling fool of a friend. Examine him as you will. He still lives, if only barely."

What Velden's emissary said was true. Goran lay draped over the back of a plow horse, probably the only creature Bistonia's thieves could steal that was large enough to carry his massive weight. But his was not dead weight, for he stirred, moaned, and opened his one good eye to peer at Davin.

"Don't let 'em force you, lad," Goran said. "They're devious. They lie. Oh, how they lie to a man."

The changeling from a realm beyond man's slumped; only his heavy chest rose and fell to indicate life remained.

Davin winced as he stared at the visible evidence of the tortures his friend had been forced to endure these last two weeks. The ugly welts on his wrists flowed with ichorous slime. The crisscross pattern of whip marks on the Challing's back were infected—or infested. Some rippled just under the skin, indicating that cutter worms fed on living flesh and drank from blood flowing in his veins.

"Satisfied?" Jun stood with arms crossed.

"Satisfied that you and Velden are scum."

"Take her." Jun nodded toward Lijena.

Davin's sword arm tensed as he watched the two drag Tadzi's niece to her feet. She bolted—a single stride before grasping arms cut short her escape. Struggle as she might, it was to no avail. Jun's fellow thieves hauled her kicking, spitting, and cursing toward the plow horse.

Davin turned his head from the scene and slammed his sword into its sheath.

"Good boy. Don't tempt the Fates." A smug smile touched Jun's lips. "This time Emperor Velden has been merciful. The next time you enter his kingdom, the penalties might be more than you care to pay."

"The burden of payment this time exceeds all fairness," said Davin, glancing back at Lijena.

Again he tensed and held himself as the two threw Lijena to the ground. They left her there just long enough to pull Goran unceremoniously from the horse and leave him a huge moaning pile in the dirt.

In the next instant, Lijena replaced the Challing, thrown over the plow horse like some sack of potatoes. They made no effort to let her ride with dignity.

"Davin Anane, hear me!" she screamed. "You will pay for what you do this night! Pay with your life! And I shall be the one who exacts the payment. By all the Gods of Raemllyn, I promise you this!"

Her curses and Jun's evil laugh of amusement echoed in Davin's head for minutes after the thieves had collected their ransom and disappeared into the night's blackness.

"Good riddance," Davin muttered when he at last found the strength to move, but his heart spoke differently.

He walked to where Goran still lay in the dirt and helped his friend sit. "You're none the better for this, I see. How long did they torture you?"

"Constantly. I had it for breakfast and dinner. For midday they fed me whatever insects crawled through the chamber. I'm not sure that wasn't worse than the whips and branding irons. I actually came to develop quite a taste for cockroaches."

Davin shuddered.

"But you have rescued me, my friend. That is a debt I owe you. Or are we even now? I can never remember. Perhaps we are equal. I did save you from the backstabber in the alleys of Bistonia."

"He was one of Velden's thieves."

"It surprises me naught to learn that. Now, friend Davin, lend me an arm so that I can get off this ground.

It is cold and wet and reminds me too much of my apartments for the last fourteen days."

Goran's weakness startled Davin as he brought the teetering giant to his feet and half carried him to Lijena's dapple-gray. Goran managed to get foot into stirrup but required Davin's shoulder applied to rump to heave his bulk into the saddle.

The hair on the nape of Davin's neck bristled as he mounted his own horse and rode beside his friend. The torn wounds about Goran's wrists no longer dripped blood and pus! Instead they looked clean as though they had been carefully bathed. Davin's eyes widened. The flesh itself was no longer shredded and mangled by the cruel bite of manacles. As he stared, new flesh grew and closed wounds that had been festering but moments ago!

Easing his horse back a stride, Davin glanced at his friend's whip-frayed back. The crisscross pattern of bloody lash marks faded as he watched! An icy finger tapped at the base of Davin's spine and sent chills up his back. He had never seen Goran sustain more than mere scratches in battle, wounds, he admitted, that healed unnaturally fast. He had never expected this! He often forgot that Goran was a Challing and not a man. Never again. This dramatic demonstration proved the flaming-haired giant was not born of any woman in this world, but in a realm where magicks reigned.

They had been asaddle less than an hour, riding eastward toward the kingdom of Leticia, when Goran broke out in a raucous and bawdy song. The Challing's wrist now revealed flesh, baby-smooth flesh—gone, too, were the inflamed whip bites on his back!

But neither the night nor Goran held Davin's thoughts. It was with his conscience he wrestled. He had done what had to be done. Yet Lijena was an innocent in this raging battle of wills. The true warring came between Chesmu Farleigh and Velden. She was only a pawn manipulated.

Davin Anane cared little for being the one to move the pawn on the board. A pawn's pawn—that was all he had been, doing Velden's will and nothing else.

One day he would find himself the self-styled Emperor Velden and make him pay for this. One day. He fingered the pommel of his sword and spurred his mount toward Leticia.

# *chapter* $10$

"BLINDFOLD HER! We wouldn't want her to shriek pre-
maturely with joy when she sees her luxurious quarters.
That is a pleasure best left to the Emperor." This came
with a mocking sneer from the pompous one with the
medals strewn across his chest.

"When my Uncle Tadzi hears of this, your pleasures
will be those of blinded, legless eunuchs!"

Lijena desperately played the only *ragha* card she
held—Taunting Fear. These men had no fear of her father.
Even if Chesmu Farleigh were in Bistonia and not in
faraway Kavindra to the south, the threat of his revenge
would not stay their hands. But Tadzi was of their ilk,
and Velden feared the ruler of the Harnish Thieves' Guild.
Tadzi understood treachery and deceit; but could rescue
her from Velden—if he learned the identity of her true
abductor.

*When he learns!* Lijena bolstered her uncertain courage. Then she would see to it that the first put to torture
was the black-haired man of Jyotis called Davin Anane.
She would personally administer the blood leeches to
that one's eyes.

But it was to her own eyes she now tended.

Jun snorted a malicious chuckle and lifted a blindfold

to her face. Lijena's head jerked from side to side to
evade the cloaking cloth—to no avail. With hands still
bound behind her, she was unable to fend away the soiled,
garlic-reeking rag.

The world, already dark and sinister, now dropped
away totally. Rough hands rudely shoved her forward.
She staggered rather than walked, colliding face first with
slime-coated walls. Her guards made no effort to guide
her, only laughed with each of her nose-punishing con-
tacts with their subterranean world.

Underfoot came the soft crunching of freshly rotting
vegetables. Odors of decay and filth assaulted her nostrils; her skin crawled, and demonic phantasmas darted
through her mind. All the while she bit at her lower lip
and kept her silence, robbing Velden's cutthroats even
of the small measure of delight they would take from her
startled and fearful cries.

"Down." Jun's voice came from behind.

A heavy hand between the shoulder blades sent her
forward in a tumble. She reached out to break her fall—
but Davin Anane's securely knotted rope held her hands
in a taut grip. Her fall ended abruptly as she flopped
painfully onto the slime-covered stone steps of a Bistonian sewer. Her cry and a sudden deluge of tears brought
a fresh chorus of laughter from Jun and his crew of
brigands.

*By Yehseen, the Father of all Gods, I* will *make Davin
pay dearly for this!* Her thoughts raged as she tried to
dry the flood of tears. *His life will be mine for at least
a month before I send him to Qar's fiery dungeons!*

Jun and his men let her struggle to her knees before
they jerked her to her feet and shoved her forward again.
Twisting, turning, she wandered blindfolded through
Velden's underground empire. Around her came the
squeaking of rats and the scratch of tiny clawed paws as
the sewer-fed vermin scurried away from the approach
of man.

Viselike hands clamped atop her shoulders to bring her to a slippery halt on the slime-caked rock underfoot. Chains clanked and a heavy bolt was drawn back; metal against rusted metal screeched, and unoiled hinges protested. Again a hand slammed between her shoulder blades, sending her face down on the floor.

To Lijena's surprise only a thin layer of scum coated the flagstones. She writhed to her side and struggled to her knees while Jun and his men laughed anew at her distress.

The male laughter was replaced by a cackling she couldn't identify.

"Who's there?" Lijena cocked her head from side to side.

It didn't help; the cackling grew closer.

She was lost, completely helpless, and adrift in the darkness. Tears welled anew as reality's weight pressed down on her bent shoulders. No one knew she was here, not her father or Tadzi or her beloved Amrik. No one except the knave Davin Anane! And he would tell no one of how he had delivered her into Velden's hands. She was alone, abandoned, at the mercy of a man who had no concept of mercy.

An unseen hand yanked her blindfold free!

Lijena gasped and wished it had remained. The scene that greeted her eyes was far worse than anything she had imagined. A skeleton hung from iron rings and chains on one wall of the tiny chamber. Only piles of excrement ornamented the floors, and then there were the five!

Five women, clothed in filthy loincloths and each weighing three times her own weight, huddled in the far corner of the chamber. Their voices hissed like vipers as they whispered among themselves, occasionally pointed at her, tittered, and went back to their muted discussion of her fate.

Lijena attempted to get her feet under her but the slime and filth turned the floor glass-slick. Time and again she managed to plant the sole of a doeskin boot only to have it fly out from beneath her when she tried to rise, sending her belly down in the grime. Finally recognizing the fruitlessness of her efforts, she pushed herself to a cold, damp stone wall and sat there with its firmness against her back. And she waited, frightened eyes locked on the blubber-laden five.

Those aquamarine eyes widened. The whispering abruptly stopped and five heads turned to her. The women pushed to their feet, standing in half crouches as they cautiously formed a semicircle. Their hands, like twisted talons, were held before them. A wicked smile moved over each of their faces, revealing broken yellowed teeth and dark gaps that no longer held teeth.

"Gold. Do you want gold?" Her voice was a thin, watery quaver.

The women's grins widened, and they advanced.

"My father, my uncle, they're both rich. They'll give you anything you want. Just let me go!"

They came even closer, their unfettered, pendulous breasts swaying to and fro with each slip-slide movement of their bare feet on filth-coated stone.

"Back," Lijena muttered, the courage gone from her.

The five stalked forward without pause or even a glance among themselves. Screeches like the cries of a descending flock of harpies filled the chamber, drowning Lijena's own scream of terror. Then they were on her. Their taloned hands ripped and tore, rending her fine garments and leaving bloody streaks behind in their haste to strip her naked. Their filthy fingers probed and touched and degraded until Lijena's screams melted into shuddering sobs.

Then the humiliation began in earnest.

"Can this be the proud young bitch offspring of my enemy, Chesmu Farleigh? Or is this some piece of trash procured on the streets of Bistonia?"

Lijena's eyes opened, and her neck craned toward the door to the chamber. A shiver, like an icy blast from legendary Ianya, worked along her spine. Was it a man . . . or a gigantic rat in the robe of a man that coldly glared down at her through beady little eyes?

"Velden?" A questioning whisper moved past her lips.

"Have her cleansed and brought to my chambers." The rodent-man ignored her and turned to two men behind him. "The stench of her is unbearable."

"Neither my father nor my uncle is likely to pay well for damaged goods," she managed to mutter as the possibilities of what awaited her within those chambers penetrated her dazed brain.

Velden's head jerked around, and he laughed without humor. "You make me sound like a common kidnapper. What need do I have for ransom money? My loyal subjects provide me with vast hoards of gold and jewels and other riches. For you I have other plans. Come. Allow me to show you!"

He turned and strolled away, snapping his fingers as he departed. The two who awaited their Emperor rushed into the chamber and wrenched her to her feet. Through dim subterranean corridors they dragged her. Briefly they paused in a Y junction of three passageways. There six women, these dressed in simple robes, waited with buckets and sponges. In turn, each stepped forward and emptied ice-cold water atop her head, then roughly scrubbed the slime and filth from her nakedness. Then the guards dragged her forward once more.

When they stopped again, Lijena had no doubt she stood within Velden's chambers—bedchambers. The tawdry glory of Velden's empire was evident throughout the immense room cut from the bedrock beneath Bistonia. Every place the man had tried to lend an air of richness and regalness, he had only added a parody of it. In a sudden rush of defiance, she told him so.

"Fine words from one naked and shivering," Velden

answered with an amused smile from the thronelike chair
in which he lounged.

Lijena tried not to flinch under the scrutiny of those
squinting little eyes. Her defiance fled as quickly as it
had flared. Gooseflesh rippled over her naked limbs; she
trembled, unable to contain her fear.

"If ransom isn't your motive, what then?" She finally
found her voice again.

"Are you so curious? Good! Many would prefer not
to know." A pleased smile grew on the lips of Bistonia's
Emperor of Thieves. "I like the idea of telling you. But
you mustn't misinterpret my intentions. I merely said
your father and uncle would never be asked for ransom.
But you will fetch a pretty price, mark my words on
that."

"I don't understand." A sinking sensation filled the
pit of her stomach, telling her she did understand, but
she wanted to keep Velden talking. She needed time—
time to think, to delay this rat-man.

Velden leaned back, hooked a scrawny leg over a
padded armrest, and steepled fingers on his rounded belly.
He gestured to a woman standing to his left, who trotted
forward to serve him wine from the jug she held. His
gloating eyes never left the naked prisoner who stood
before him.

"Nelek Kahl." The name rolled off his tongue like
honeyed wine. "I will sell you to the slaver Kahl, who
will break your spirit and require of you the most dis-
gusting things your feeble mind can conceive. That will
be your fate until the last day of your miserable life."

Velden idly sipped from his cup.

"No," Lijena said weakly. Hope fled at the mention
of Kahl's name. The man was notorious throughout all
of Raemllyn.

"Oh yes," said Velden, warming to the topic. "He
will teach you the proper ways, and until then I shall
begin your instruction."

He rose, hands fumbling to release a belt around his paunchy middle. His robe fell open; Lijena's skin crawled anew. With scrawny arms and legs, he looked like some giant insect advancing on her.

"You'll have no pleasure from me, scum!" Lijena whirled and grabbed a vase from a nearby table. She smashed it against one tapestry-hung wall. Quick hands grabbed a sharp-edged piece and held it against her own wrist. "Come any closer, and I'll kill myself. Never will I submit to you. Never!"

Velden's only answer was a mocking laugh. Then Lijena discovered the truth of the matter. Four of his men had silently entered the room behind her. One casually batted the shard from her hand. Another's thick arm encircled her throat. The other two each captured and held one of her naked legs. Before she realized what had occurred, she was being carried helpless to the table from which she'd seized the vase.

"Yes, there is fine. For the moment." Velden rose and continued shedding his soiled robes. "I shall have her on the table."

It was there he took her, first his laughter and then bestial grunts of lust mingling with her cries. And when he had spent himself, he pushed from her spread-eagle body and gathered his robes from the floor. In shock, and through tears of shame and degradation, Lijena stared up at the Emperor of Thieves. Silently she etched Velden's name beneath that of Davin Anane on the list she carried in her mind. For his brutal use of her, the ratlike man would one day die—slowly, ever so slowly.

Velden turned as he adjusted his broad belt across his bloated belly. With a nod, he said to the guards who still held her atop the table, "For your services, each of you may have her. Once.

"You will learn what it is to be a slave." Velden now spoke to the daughter of his most hated enemy. "Oh yes, you will learn. There are four days remaining until Kahl arrives. In that time I will do my best to show you!"

With that he turned and walked through the doors of his bedchamber, his laughter growing as Lijena's scream once more echoed around him. To be certain, he would have preferred the agony of her father, Chesmu, but that also would be his in time. What pleasure he would savor while he watched Chesmu's horror and shame as he described in minute detail all the sufferings he had heaped upon Farleigh's daughter, how he had degraded Chesmu's only offspring and heir.

*The torturer's blades, machines, and irons can but kill a man,* Velden thought with great relish. *With what I now do to the daughter—I will break the father, shatter his soul!*

Velden's laughter rang down the corridors of his underground kingdom. *And when I have destroyed his spirit, drained every ounce of his willpower—I shall kill him.*

## chapter

# *11*

LIJENA'S HAND TREMBLED FEARFULLY as she worked the tin spoon against the rock wall of her cell. Slowly, methodically, like a tinker at his wheel, she ground the end of the long handle against the stone. Upward two inches, then down the same path, and she halted. Her gaze, like that of some terrified animal, darted about the dim-lit granite chamber, with her heart racing out of control.

No one came in answer to the grating sound. She allowed herself a sly smile and dragged the handle up and down the rock again before testing it with a thumb. Her smile cautiously widened. It was far from being the needle tip of a dirk, but there was a point! That was more than she'd had when she began her...

...*When I began* ... *began* ... Her thoughts drifted in a confusing cloud of smoky cotton. She couldn't remember when she had begun, or even when she had been brought to Velden's subterranean hell.

Eyes still adart, she shoved the spoon tip against the rock. *Four days,* she recalled her tormentor saying. *Four days until I'm sold to Nelek Kahl!* But what portion of that time had passed? In a sunless realm, perpetually lit by torch and glowing moss, there was no natural procession of day and night, only eternal dusk.

99

To aid in her lost perception of time, there was the Dragonroote Velden had secreted in her water. Long used by mages and wizards to open their minds to the alternate corridors of the cosmos, the herb played on the mind of its user, dilating time so that a single minute might stretch to days or months.

And there *was* Dragonroote in her water bucket; she had learned that her first day. Velden had allowed just enough time for the herb to take effect before he had sent four other guards to visit her within her new cell. A lifetime passed before their blows subdued her, and another to sate their lusts.

After that she had tried to deny herself water and failed miserably. Water was all she had to fill her constantly gnawing stomach—that was, unless she wanted to force down her throat the bug-swimming soup she was served twice a day. That was a task she had been unable to do, not even to lift a spoonful of the foul-smelling liquid to her lips.

*Surely less than four days have passed,* she assured herself. She had heard tales of men who ate insects and rats when they had gone without food for a week, driven insane by hunger. While she could not deny the constant pain knotting her gut, her stomach still churned at the mere thought of partaking of such unsavory fare.

She worked the spoon against the wall again, as her gaze traveled over the small cell. The tiny chamber was clean; no trace of slime lay on the bare stone. In one corner sat her water bucket and soup bowl; in the opposite, another bucket for excrement. Except for the cot on which she sat, the stone chamber held no furniture.

A bitter, humorless smile twisted her lips. The clean stone, slop bucket, and cot were not for her comfort but for Velden's. Bistonia's Emperor of Thieves no longer brought her to his bedchamber for his amusement, but took his pleasure upon the cot with its straw-filled mattress.

Trembling fingers gingerly tested her stomach. She winced at the tenderness of flesh and muscle, a reminder of the futility of resisting Velden's demands. In reply to her one display of rebellion, Jun had beaten her, carefully directing his blows to her midriff at Velden's command.

"We must not mar her face." Velden's voice echoed in her mind. "Nelek Kahl pays little for wenches with black eyes and bruised cheeks."

From those blows she had learned subservience. No longer did she rage against those who came to her cell. She simply gave her body for their use, whether on her back or her knees. Deliberately she played the charade of a broken woman; from all outward appearance she had become a slave. Even Velden accepted the transformation, for he had come without guard on his last two visits.

Her body might be theirs, at least for the time being, but her mind remained unfettered!

She ground the spoon handle against the stone with a decided relish. Let Velden continue coming to her. Soon she would be ready for him! The thought of those ratlike eyes wide in surprise as she buried the makeshift knife in his bloated belly, his incomprehension as Qar sucked life from his body...

*Footsteps!*

She heard the sound of boot on stone. Temples apound and mouth suddenly dry, she shoved her precious spoon beneath the mattress and turned to the open entrance of the cell.

To be certain, although no door or bars barricaded that threshold, she could not pass to the other side. Magicks guarded the passage—a spell that set each cell of her body afire with searing pain at her approach.

Then Jun with his coat of stolen medals stood in the entrance. Leering, he stepped toward her, and she awaited him, all the while reminding herself that the blood of Chesmu Farleigh and his brother Tadzi flowed in her veins—that the time of her vengeance drew near.

When the captain of Velden's guard eventually left, she cleaned herself of him with water from the bucket and once again pulled the spoon from beneath the mattress. By the time weariness overtook her and she curled naked on the cot, the honed spoon handle drew a drop of blood from her thumb when she tested its sharpness.

She smiled; she would be prepared for the Emperor of the Bistonian underworld when he came again—and it wasn't pleasure she would be giving him.

Jun's rough hand on her bare shoulder and curt voice brought Lijena from her listless sleep. Her eyes blinked open and she stared up at Velden's captain of the guard.

"Up off your lazy arse!" Jun reached out and entangled a hand in her hair to help her to her feet. "The Emperor wants you in his chamber—clean and smelling like a rose!"

He nodded to six women standing behind him, each with sponge and bucket. Lijena shivered, remembering her first icy encounter with the six. However, she offered no protest, only walked to the middle of the room and awaited the freezing deluge.

None came! There *was* warm water and soap for her body and hair—and a soothing rinse of perfumed water. The women's hands had gentled since first they met. She almost imagined herself back in Tadzi's palace as they rubbed her dry with soft cloths, then lightly massaged her body with a pleasant musk oil. Then they were about her hair, toweling and brushing it dry until it cascaded soft and shining about her shoulders.

And there was food! Steaming sausages, roasted apples, and fresh-baked bread were served her on clean wooden plates. Cautiously she cut into the first plump link, expecting to find it acrawl with cockroaches. There was only meat—real meat! The fork was too cumbersome; she used her fingers to shove the food into her mouth.

"Aye, that should stop your stomach from rumbling!" Jun chuckled as he watched her clean the plate and lick the grease from her fingers. "You wouldn't want to offend the Emperor. That belly of yours would sound like a thunderstorm echoing off the walls of his chamber!"

He laughed, but she didn't hear him. Every cell of her body had gone rigid. *His chamber!* Her eyes darted to her mattress.

Jun had said it before, but now it penetrated. *Velden wants me in his chamber!* And there was no way she could get to her sharply honed spoon! Her plans for the Emperor of Bistonia's thieves, her slow methodical grinding of the spoon—it was for naught, unless she could get to the cot!

It was a desperate thought that died when Jun's hand grasped her shoulder and shoved her to the doorway. She balked, cringing from the fiery magicks guarding the threshold. With an amused laugh, Jun shoved her again. Lijena stumbled through the entrance. There wasn't the slightest sensation of warmth, let alone searing fires.

"Stupid bitch, the spell hasn't been there since the second day!" Jun grinned with relish as he nudged her along a moss-illuminated corridor.

Lijena's eyes narrowed and her head spun. The door had been open to her! She could have just walked from her cell! *Slave* . . . It echoed in her mind. Velden and his captain had taken more from her in this short time than she had thought. The door had been open—and she had been afraid to test it!

*They'll pay dearly for this! I'll see them in . . .*

Her rage dissipated, and she admitted the lies she used to bolster herself. What could she do to either Jun or his Emperor? Her hand-crafted spoon-knife lay useless beneath the straw of her cot, and there was no hope of rescue. Who could rescue her? Only the swine Davin

Anane knew of her captivity.

How she had deluded herself with the illusion of a free mind! The unguarded door to the cell proved that not even her mind belonged to her. Velden had accomplished this task: he had created a slave in mind and body.

She shivered, suddenly aware of her nakedness, her vulnerability. Tears misted the aquamarine of her eyes as she accepted the shame Velden heaped on her shoulders. Lijena, daughter of the House of Farleigh, was no longer, and in her stead stood a pleasure slave who answered her master's summons.

How childish all her scheming seemed now, how utterly useless. There would be no spike of sharpened tin for Velden's gut, no escape, no life as she had once known. She would serve as required, and when hunger grew unbearable, she would learn to eat gruel and enjoy the crunch of insects between her teeth.

So it was, the fate the Sitala had cast weighing her shoulders, that Lijena entered the chambers of Emperor Velden. With neck bent and gaze subserviently cast on the floor, she stood naked before him, no longer caring what new degradations awaited her, accepting the burden cruel gods had placed upon her back to bend her knees.

"Leave . . . all of you. Leave me alone with her. She offers no danger to my person," Lijena heard Velden command, but her eyes did not lift.

A scurry of feet came from about the room as guards and servants obeyed. Heavy doors to the bedchamber closed behind Lijena, and there was only silence and the sound of her own breathing.

"The women did well. There's a certain beauty in the Farleigh line. My women have succeeded in bringing a bit of it to the surface. Of course, compared to your mother, you are a mousy thing." Velden paused with a sigh. "Ah, Leet, you were as wondrous as the Goddess Ediena herself. Such a waste! You could have brought

the gold of the High King's own coffers on the auction
block!"

Lijena shivered. Leet, her mother, had died five years
ago at Velden's own hand, her throat slit from ear to ear
as she tended her rose garden.

"I do not expect the daughter to bring such a fortune,
but I believe Nelek Kahl will be favorably impressed by
your charms." Again Velden paused and sighed. "I would
partake of those charms one last time were Kahl's arrival
not so near. Instead I will comfort myself with a fresh
goblet of wine. There's a jug on the table beside you."

Without question, Lijena turned and walked to the
table. She lifted the earthen jug, surprised by its heft—
a weight she could soon accustom herself to.

*No!*

She railed against the Sitala! Her mother's death was
preferable to the yoke of a slave. Raemllyn's gods might
deny her freedom, but Dark Qar always waited. *Better
to welcome the Great Destroyer's cold embrace than
those of Velden and Nelek Kahl!*

Lijena's eyes cautiously crept upward, guided by the
strength of one who has accepted the inevitability of
death. Velden leaned back in his thronelike chair. A
spidery hand poked from the folds of his robes, holding
forth a golden goblet to be filled.

Like an obedient slave, Lijena crossed the chamber
at his command. She shifted the heavy jug to one side
as though to balance it on a hip to pour, abruptly jerked
it outward—and with the full weight of her body behind
her wide swing slammed it into the side of Velden's
head!

Thick, heavy earthen pottery cracked, then shattered.
Wine flew through the air in a deep purple spray! Lijena,
breast heaving, staggered back on legs abruptly gone
watery.

Velden's beady, dark rat's eyes went saucer-wide and
bulged like those of an insect. His mouth twisted open

to call his guards, but only a wet gurgle escaped those lips. His eyes went even wider, and his hands crept up to his throat, then jerked away.

There, firmly embedded in his scrawny neck like an oversized triangular dagger, was a shard of the brightly lacquered earthenware. A gash ran crimson from his left ear, across a neatly severed jugular vein, marking the course of the broken piece of pottery from impact to where it finally lodged, cutting vocal cords as it sank deep into his throat.

Velden's confused expression transformed to one of sheer panic as he recognized the mortal nature of his wound. With both hands gripping the armrests of his chair, he pulled forward in an attempt to stand. Neither legs nor arms would support his weight. He collapsed back to his mock throne and died as the stuff of life flowed from his open throat to spread crimson through the fabric of his white and gold robes.

A cruel, hard smile moved over Lijena's lips as she watched the last quiver pass from her tormentor's chest. She then turned to the door of the bedchamber to await Velden's guard and her own death. *At least Velden's shade will precede me to Qar's realm of Peyneeha!*

There was no rush through the heavy door—nor even a creak. The portal remained undisturbed.

For minutes that dragged into eternities, Lijena stared and waited. No one, not even the lowest of Velden's servants, poked his head through the doorway. Lijena's heart slowly quieted; her temples gave up their pounding beat.

Quietly, on tiptoe, she moved to the door and pressed an ear to it. Nothing. She drew a steadying breath and inched the door open just enough to peer outside.

The corridor was deserted. In the distance echoed booming voices raised in ribald songs. Velden's men reveled this evening.

The thought she had refused to even consider now

wedged itself into her brain: *escape*. She turned to Velden's motionless form and eyed the corpse, not in revulsion or gloating, but in search of a weapon and clothing.

Bistonia's permanently dethroned Emperor of Thieves carried no weapon, and his blood-soaked robes were of little use. However, his cape would serve her well. Caring not that she touched the flesh of the dead, Lijena unclasped the cape and pushed Velden's body to the floor, then hugged the flowing white velvet about her nakedness as she stepped into the corridor outside.

One of Velden's men weaved in a none too steady stagger down the moss-lit passage of stone. The reek of cheap, sweet wine preceded him. The man's head rose and he stared at Lijena through wine-besotted eyes.

"A wench!" he cried with a halfhearted attempt to throw a greeting arm into the air. "And all mine!"

He stumbled toward her with the grin of a jackass plastered across his face. Lijena tensed: to run would only alert him. It was far better to play the charade he had chosen for her. After all, he was but one man, and a silver dirk dangled in a sheath slung from his waist.

"Come, lover," she urged in her most enticing voice. "Let us go in here where we can be alone."

"Just us?"

"With a man like you, who could want more?" She lured him into her open arms, hands stroking his broad back, sliding downward toward the scabbarded blade and finding it.

"You want to play hard to get?" he asked in a slurred mumble when she deftly avoided his lips as they tried to capture hers.

"No, no longer. You are too much for me to resist. Hold me tightly to chase away the chill."

As his arms encircled her, Lijena stepped forward, the point of the dagger rising between their bodies, then flashing forward. The man gasped, and his eyes rolled to the corridor's ceiling an instant before he collapsed to its floor, never to rise again.

Lijena stood motionless and stared at the unmoving heap at her feet—a crumpled pile of paling flesh that had once been a living man. Hers was the eye of one removed from all around her, as though she stared on a dream that belonged to another.

Tonight she had killed two men, one by accident and the other in cold blood—and she felt nothing, not even the slightest twinge of horror or guilt. There should have been some sensation, some feeling, but there was only a hollow void. She prayed to Yehseen that she might repay Jun for what he had stolen from her in a fashion similiar to the payment she had given his master.

"You present quite a sight," came cold words from the doorway behind her.

Lijena whirled. A piteous little cry escaped her lips.

"It . . . it can't be. I killed you! I saw the last breath flee your chest!"

A laugh that echoed as though rumbling up from some dark, bottomless well answered her from a mouth that did not move! The unholy visage swayed unsteadily as it reached a bloody hand toward her. Its step, however, was solid and determined. "I will teach you to strike the Emperor of Thieves!"

"No! Velden is dead!" Lijena wanted to run, to flee, but her legs betrayed her, suddenly lifeless and feeling as though made from the very stone of this underground hell.

Again its laughter came from unmoving lips. Its eyes, dull and unseeing, glared at her, and blood still trickled in an oozing flow from the ragged wound on its neck. "Aye! For that killing I shall send your soul to Qar's lowest dungeon!"

He stepped again, and again, his arms spreading wide to ensnare the mesmerized woman.

A whimper like that from a frightened child rolled from Lijena's throat. She threw high her arms, not to strike, but to fend away the walking death that came to claim her.

A howl straight from the bowels of Hell reverberated through the passageway. Velden's corpse staggered back and hissed and spat like some giant feline.

The encasing ice about her legs melted, and she ran. Without a glance back at the living, walking man of unliving flesh, she fled.

Down one twisted corridor she ran, and then darted into one that abruptly jutted off to the left. And at the end of it a T junction—and Velden's hideous visage there waiting for her.

"There is no escape...."

She didn't listen to the remainder of the thing's words, but diverted her eyes and lunged into a passage to the right.

How could a man still live when the golden cord of life had been severed? When a man died, he was dead. Qar was too jealous a God not to claim a soul rightfully his! Dead men simply didn't walk.

Yet the fact remained: Velden's corpse did. And it stood before her again, waiting in a four-way junction of the passages honeycombing the ground beneath Bistonia.

*It can't be happening! How can he be here ahead of me?*

How didn't matter; that the gruesome animation of death stood before her did!

"Come to me, my lovely. One embrace is all I ask."

She ducked beneath its outstretched arms and shot into a corridor behind it. And she ran, giving little heed to the fact that this passage narrowed and its walls appeared freshly hewn from stone. Even when darkness enveloped her, she continued to run.

The floor dissolved beneath her feet; she fell!

... Into a flowing river of sewage! A minor river that came but to her waist! She pushed up from the reeking water and stood on unsteady feet. The hint of a smile touched her lips. *Free! I've broken free of Velden's damnable corridors . . . and dead Velden himself! Now all I do is follow the current. . . .*

She turned and froze. *Velden!*

The Emperor of Thieves' ghostly image stood no more than an arm's length ahead of her. It couldn't be—yet it was. And around him was a glow, like the moss of his kingdom . . . sickly and green.

"You can run no longer," those unmoving lips spoke. "Now we embrace."

Not Velden—it couldn't be Velden—the thought penetrated Lijena's numb brain. But some demon bound to Velden, a spirit locked to his flesh.

*Yes! It has to be. The king of thieves could not be assured those who served him would avenge his death— so he found a mage with the power to bind a demon to his own body! An unholy assassin for any who sought to gain his throne!*

Recognition of what she faced brought no comfort. The demon once again animated the dead flesh binding it and reached for her.

She tried to run, only to find her legs once more encased in icy stone and her eyes unable to deny the gaze of those unblinking eyes. Weakly she threw up an arm to fend away the death that came to claim her soul.

A demonic scream tore through Bistonia's sewers— the unholy voice of Hell itself. Velden's glowing form staggered back.

*The dirk . . . silver!*

Lijena reacted without thought. Throwing herself forward, she sank her purloined blade of silver hilt-deep into Velden's lifeless chest.

Its death howl still reverberated through the blackness of the sewers when she realized that she had won. The silver dirk had brought that victory. Whether the silver blade had merely severed the spell that bound the guardian demon to Velden's body or had actually killed the creature, she didn't know or care. All that mattered was that Velden's bulk, its glow now faded, slipped from the knife and sank into the flowing sewage.

Heart still pounding like some jester's bass drum, Lijena peered before her. Ahead lay the darkness of the trackless sewers, and behind . . .

She shivered, imagining Jun donning Velden's crown and giving the command to hunt her down like a *sartha* pursued by hounds, hounds that would find her if she remained here. Besides, she had the current to guide her to freedom.

This guide led her twisting and turning through the sewer system for an hour or two before she heard the sound of falling water. She halted; her mind conjured visions of Bistonia's sewers emptying into some underground river mere feet ahead of her.

This fear she realized but seconds later as she cautiously lifted a foot to test the ground beneath and found none! She scurried back before she lost her balance and went tumbling over the treacherous edge.

*Back . . . have to retrace . . .*

She shook her head. She couldn't go back. Jun and his men lay in that direction, and they would not look kindly on one who had murdered their Emperor. *But what choice do I have?*

Her thoughts swirled and blurred. She needed time to think. There was a way out; there had to be. All she had to do was find it. *But where?*

Trudging to her left, Lijena found a small ledge running just above the sewage and pulled herself onto it. She wrapped Velden's cloak firmly about her and leaned back. She'd rest here for a few moments and give her mind time to sort through the possibilities. She closed her eyes and tried to picture the path she had followed in the darkness. And within mere seconds exhaustion took its toll—she slept.

# chapter 12

LIJENA STIRRED UNEASILY as the chilly wind whipped at her huddled form. She murmured a protest and bundled the sleeping furs closer to her nakedness. The hour was too early and the morn too cold to leave the comfort of . . .

Lijena's eyes snapped open and peered through a cloud of confusion. She had been in her own bed, in her father's house, with her little pet, Zora, curled up next to her.

She glanced down. The brushing insistence against her calf wasn't the cat Zora, nor was it cute and cuddly. A rat with incisors overhanging its lower jaw nuzzled Velden's dirty cape. The rodent eyed her as though sizing up a prospective meal.

"Away!" Lijena shouted. The soiled cape flew open, and she slashed at the creature with the silver dagger still clutched in her hand.

The rat scurried back to glare at her from red-lit eyes filled with hatred. Then it turned and waddled away to vanish into the sluggishly flowing river of Bistonia's sewage.

Lijena's head lifted; she looked to the left, then right. Moisture welled in the corners of her eyes. The security of her home, the comfort of her surroundings had been but a taunting dream. All had evaporated on awakening, leaving her lost amid the dimly lit sewer.

*Light!*

Lijena's pulse raced. When she had fallen asleep, it had been in complete darkness. Now there was light, no matter how dim. And light meant escape!

She scooted from the ledge and slopped ahead. Her imagined abrupt emptying of the sewer into some underground river was just that, imagination. However, the sewer level did drop sharply in one steep step mere yards from where she had spent the night.

Lijena knelt, then swung over the small ledge. It was no more than five feet down, easily managed in the light, but more than enough of a fall to have broken her neck if she had stepped over it last night.

The lower level was but another of the endless maze of sewer tunnels. To her left was a yawning maw of blackness. To the right, less than fifty feet from where she stood—light!

It beamed through the wide openings of a rusted grating, and beyond—the outlines of autumn-browned reeds.

Lijena rushed forward, wrapped fingers around the thick bars, and pressed her head against the rusty metal. The dimness of the light came from the early morning outside and the solid overcast above. Tears of joy trickled down her cheeks as she watched a light flurry of snowflakes fall from those gray clouds into the river Stane, which lay twenty feet beyond the grating.

She pushed against the metal. Nothing. She heaved her full weight against those rusty bars. Nothing. She threw herself into the last barrier between her and freedom. Still the grating refused to budge.

"No!" Her tears of joy threatened to become tears of despair. To have killed two men, dispatched a guardian demon, and found her way this far only to discover mere metal separating her from freedom—surely Raemllyn's Gods could not be that cruel! "No! I *will not* be denied. I won't!"

She stepped back, defiantly planted hands on hips,

and stared at the circular grating. Bistonia's thieves would not leave such an easy access to their underground realm so barricaded. The ten-foot-in-diameter, crisscrossing metal had to be for show, designed to prevent surface dwellers from entering, not thieves.

A pleased smile uplifted the corners of her mouth. There on each side of the grating were quick-release pins, obviously installed by Bistonia's thieves rather than the sewer's builders. She pressed one, then the other. Rust cracked and peeled, metal groaned in protest, and the ponderous grating toppled forward. Lijena stepped into the early light of morning to fill her lungs with fresh, clean, free air.

All the while her gaze took in her surroundings. She stood halfway down the west bank of the Stane. Twenty feet up the angled incline rose the austere gray buildings of Bistonia's business district. She could see the wharves and warehouses that served river barges perhaps half a mile downstream.

*So far from the center of the city,* she thought, realizing that she was not dressed, even for so early an hour, to trek through the streets to the city's northern district and her father's house. Nor was it likely she would find Chesmu Farleigh there returned from Kavindra.

Lijena smiled.

There was one person who could aid her: Amrik Tohon! Her lover, the man she sought as a husband even against her father's wishes, would know what to do, how to handle Jun and the armies of thieves should they seek revenge for Velden's death.

And the Tohon household lay just beyond Porsno Square. If she hurried, she could be there long before the merchants opened their shops for the morning. Hugging Velden's cape about her, she climbed the Stane's bank on legs feeling brisk and strong.

She kept up that brisk pace until she reached Porsno Square. There she halted and pressed into the shadows of an alley. It wasn't merchants but two cutpurses that set her heart apound. Did they merely prepare for a morning's work of relieving the rich of their money pouches — or did they search for her?

Lijena's head jerked back as one of the two nudged the other in the ribs with a sharp elbow and lifted a chin a fraction of an inch in her direction. The recipient of the elbow nodded and raced off as though Qar himself chased his heels.

Lijena had no doubt it was to Jun's ear he ran. Within the hour every cutthroat in the city would be combing the streets for her. Her eyes darted to the left; she could circle the square, keeping to alleys and backways. Such an indirect route would cost her more than an hour. Or she could be bold.

Lijena drew a steadying breath. Bold it would be! There was no time for caution. After all, she was Lijena, daughter of the House of Farleigh. Hers was the blood of Chesmu and his brother Tadzi. And her dagger had killed both man and demon. She stepped from the alley and strode toward the remaining thief.

The cutpurse obviously expected her to flee. When he realized his mistake, it was too late. Lijena's dirk pressed his throat, needle point drawing a drop of crimson.

"Wha-what . . . do you . . . you want?" he stammered as that very point guided him from Porsno Square into an alley.

"I want to send a message to Jun." It took every ounce of courage to speak without her voice breaking.

"Jun? I know of no Jun. I've never heard of any . . . aaggagghhh!"

Lijena's wrist flicked; the dagger's tip traced a red inch below the man's Adam's apple. "Would you prefer your gullet opened from one ugly ear to the other?"

Lijena repressed the urge to do just that, to slice a new mouth beneath the man's unshaven chin. She had never seen his nasty face before, but he, and others like him, had created the cold terror now tightly squeezing about her heart. No man, or woman, had the right to hold such power over another. And for that, and the horror such as he had brought into her life, she wanted to kill.

Lijena held herself in check. She needed this swine for her bold ruse.

"Your new master seeks me." Her voice hissed through clenched teeth. "Tell him to stay his men. I have suffered at his hands and will tolerate no more!"

"Jun's madder'n a stepped-on sewer rat! He don't give a damn about . . . arraagghhh!"

Lijena cut off his words by pressing the dirk's point inward a fraction of an inch.

"Jun *is* a sewer rat! Within the hour others will know how he treated Lijena of the House of Farleigh. His life will be worth less than a rat then!"

She emphasized her words by pressing the dagger a bit deeper, hoping pain would impress the scum and conceal her lie. Were her father in Bistonia, he would see to it that Jun was driven from the sewers—as would Tadzi. In her heart she was certain Amrik would do the same, but something niggled at the back of her mind. She shoved it away and continued:

"Tell Jun this: Velden's death has not sated my claim to vengeance. I'll not be satisfied until his head adorns a pole in the middle of Porsno Square. The full power of the House of Farleigh is arrayed against him. Soon the Harnish Thieves' Guild will enter Bistonia at Tadzi's command. My uncle cherishes the thought of being master of *two* guilds! He has no need for yet another captain of his guards."

The man paled by at least ten hues at the mention of Tadzi's feared name. Lijena's pulse quieted; she had made her point and there was no need to overplay the charade. The uncertainty this sewer rat would plant in

Jun's mind would give Amrik time to gather men, and
her the opportunity to contact her uncle.

Giving the dirk yet another little twist, she spun from
the man and calmly strolled away, Velden's cape flapping in the morning breeze about her ankles. Only when
she turned northward and was safely out of sight did
Lijena release her overly held breath in a whistling sigh
of relief. She smiled broadly with pride—Lijena the Bold
was much more to her liking than Lijena the Slave.

     Amrik Tohon stood with jaw sagging and eyes
asquint. "Lijena?" Her name came out as a question, as
if he couldn't believe that it was truly she beneath the
tangle of disheveled hair and slimy layer of filth.

Lijena smiled and nodded. The strength was suddenly
gone from her. The silver dagger she had wielded so
ably against Velden's guardian demon slipped from her
trembling fingers and fell to the stone steps of the House
of Tohon.

She slumped forward and was caught in strangely
hesitant arms. Then she contented herself with just cling-
ing to Amrik, feeling his arms slowly draw her into their
security. Lijena tried to hold back her tears but failed.
The release of tension was too extreme for her to maintain
any semblance of composure. After all she'd been through,
she had now found a safe haven.

"Whatever happened to you?" Amrik asked. The stocky
young brown-haired man pushed her to arm's length and
stared at her in disbelief. "You look—and smell—as if
you've slept the night in the sewers."

"I have." She started to babble, the story tumbling
out and the words getting in one another's way.

She saw rage darkening in her lover's face, felt the
cording of his muscles as he took her in his arms and
held her. With each recounting of Velden's degradations,
the veins of his neck pushed farther out in bristling anger.

"Let me get my blade!" Amrik's voice came as a feral

growl. "I'll have their black hearts cut from their chest before the day is over! No! Would be too quick! I'll slice their skin away bit by bit before I take their hearts. They shall pay dearly for every moment they dared touch you!"

Moments before, she had yearned for just such a reaction from Amrik. Now all she desired was for him to be near, to hold her, to protect her, and she whispered for him to contain his fury. For a moment he stared at her in disbelief, then saw her tears and felt her trembling. He nodded, acceding to her wishes.

She smiled and hugged him close. He—and she—would have revenge, but it could wait. She urged him into the house. She wanted just to collapse into one of the sumptuous chairs that greeted her, but refrained when Amrik led her toward one, fearing her dirty rags would only ruin the furniture.

"Not here, Amrik darling. The servants' quarters. They're easier to clean if I sit on . . . or touch anything."

She stared at her once elegant hands. The fingernails had been broken into jagged ridges. Cuts remained on her palms as souvenirs of the wine jug she had shattered in Velden's face. Overall her hands' color and texture had gone from porcelain white to blackened burlap.

"Qar take the sofa! I'll buy a new one if needed!" Amrik waved away her protest and settled her onto a comfortable love seat. "You have bidden me stay my wrath against the scum who did this to you, and so I shall. But I will not put aside your comfort!"

Lijena's tears flowed anew. The last time she and Amrik had been on this love seat was the night before her father sent her to Harn. The memory of that brief parting still lingered longingly in her mind. It seemed a desecration to rest on the sofa in her condition.

"Amrik, if I might have some wine and perhaps some cheese and bread . . ." She felt embarrassed at the request, but her stomach had long ago disposed of the sausages she had been fed last night, and they had not made up for the days she had gone without eating.

He nodded. "I'll get some wine."

As he started to rise, she reached out and clutched at his sleeve. Ice touched Lijena's heart. Was she imagining it, or had he recoiled ever so slightly from her? She edged the thought away. She was tired, and her mind played tricks on her.

"I'm sorry. Just don't leave me. Not right away."

"But the wine?"

"Let one of the servants get it, and..." Lijena's voice trailed off.

Amrik himself rather than a servant had answered her pounding on the door. Nor had she seen a servant since entering the Tohon household. With eyebrows raised, she looked at her lover. "Amrik, is anything wrong?"

"Wrong? The woman I love, intend to marry, has been kidnapped by the ruler of Bistonia's thieves, abused and violated, and you wonder if anything is wrong?" His voice roared and scarlet burned in his cheeks.

"No, no. I mean, there aren't any servants. Where are they? And it's cold in here." She shivered, suddenly aware that no fire burned in the great hearth. "Nothing's happened, has it?"

"No," he assured her and shook his head. "Far from it. I gave the servants a holiday. I had completed my packing and was closing the house when you came to the door."

"Packing?" she asked, confused. "You're leaving Bistonia?"

"I *was* going to Harn. I hoped to convince your uncle of my intentions and persuade him to permit our marriage. But you obviously aren't in Harn, and Tadzi probably hasn't the slightest idea where you are. We've no need of his permission now."

Lijena's tears transformed to those of joy. She flung her arms about Amrik's neck and kissed him loudly on the lips. "To hear those words—to know you share the love I hold—almost erases all I've suffered."

Amrik pressed a finger to her lips. "I had drawn myself
a bath. It's still hot, if you wish to wash and rest. While
you prepare, I'll get wine and food. Then tell me all that
has happened."

"A hot bath!" Lijena grinned widely and nodded with
enthusiasm. A bath at that very moment seemed to be
the greatest luxury in all of Raemllyn. "I'll await you in
the bath!"

And so she did, soaking in the warmth that eased the
aches from her bone-weary body. While Amrik sat on
the edge of the sunken marble pool and fed her cheese
and sweetmeats, she recounted all that had occurred since
her father had taken her to Harn.

"Amrik, I love you," she said as she concluded her
woeful tale.

"And I you, my cherished one. We shall never be
apart again. I promise it." Amrik held out a hand and
helped her from the now cooling pool. "The servants are
gone, but if you'll permit me?"

He turned and lifted a towel, which he unfolded and
held out. Lijena stepped into it and let him pat the cling-
ing moisture from her now tingling and clean body. She
sighed with contentment beneath the gentle caresses of
his hands. After the treatment she had endured from
Velden, his men, and his women with their buckets of
icy water, she felt like a pampered member of the royal
family in Kavindra.

"There!" Amrik smiled as he let the towel fall to the
marble floor and took Lijena in his arms and kissed her.
"Now you look like the Lijena I love, and smell like her,
too. Anything else your willing servant can do for you?"

"Oil," she said. "I need body oil. Do it for me, Amrik.
I'd like that very much . . . if you wouldn't mind?"

"Mind? Every man in Bistonia would kill for such an
opportunity, and you ask if I mind?" He grinned as he
spread a fresh cloth on a nearby massage table.

She stretched out atop the linen and sighed anew as his soothing palms spread a thin sheen of oil over her body. Other men might have taken advantage of the situation, but not Amrik. He had listened to her and realized the extent of the abuse she had endured these past days. He recognized it would take time before she would be able once again to make love without being reminded of those abuses. She sensed that in him, just as she sensed he was willing to wait until she could once again be totally his.

"It feels so good," she said almost in a purr as his fingers and palms worked the oils into her skin. "So good . . ."

Her eyes closed and within seconds she drifted into restful sleep, secure in the hands of the man she loved. Nor did she more than moan when those hands lifted her from the table and carried her to the luxurious comfort of a warm, soft feather bed.

"So nice," she sighed, snuggling her head against a satin pillow.

Lips lightly touched her forehead and then her own lips, just before she drifted back into sleep thinking, *Amrik won't allow anything to happen to me. I love him so, and he returns that love. What woman could ask for a better man than Amrik Tohon?*

## chapter *13*

"DUST . . . OVER THAT RIDGE." Davin Anane pointed to a billowing brown cloud that rose from the plains.

Goran One-Eye squinted in the general direction and nodded.

Davin shook his head. Goran was nearsighted in his single eye at the best of times. That the dust column kicked up by the line of wagons rose on the Challing's blind side made his task of seeing especially difficult.

Although how the Challing could see at all beyond the glare of his own clothing amazed the young freebooter. His companion now wore shirt, jerkin, and breeches of eye-blinding scarlet with a makeshift eye patch of the same fiery material. Luck had brought them upon a woodcutter's hut within the forest, and it had taken but a moment's pause in their eastward journey for Goran to exchange the tattered rags Velden had left on his back for the wet garb he found hung outside to dry.

The eye-assaulting clothing had obviously been cut for a man of considerable height and muscles grown thick from the daily struggle of ax against bole. Still, Goran was a giant. The jerkin appeared loose enough, though the Challing popped a button when he attempted to draw it closed, and the fabric of the shirt strained dangerously across the broad expanse of his chest. As for the breeches, they rode at least an inch above the ankles, a situation Goran remedied by tucking the legs into the tops of his boots.

"Might it be them?" asked Goran, peering toward the dust once again. "It's been quite a while since I settled in with a band of Huata."

" 'Settled in' with the Huata?" Davin made no attempt to hide the doubt in his voice. "As long as I've known you, you've said the Huata were no more than filthy, thieving pirates who'd steal their mothers' dowries."

"Aye, that they are. All that and more, in fact." He pointed dramatically to the scarlet patch over his eye. "How do you think I lost this eye?"

"Hmmm, let me think. In Harn, you claimed—"

"It was Huata!" Goran cut him short, warming to his story. "Fourteen summers back it was. I was but a lad then, much as you are, Davin, my friend. Young, callow—"

"Callow!"

"—and the fight! It was over a maiden so fair that the merest glimpse of her beauty set my heart exploding in my chest!" He heaved an overly loud sigh of longing that made his barrel chest quiver. He stared at Davin woefully in his best imitation of a lost puppy. "I loved her, I truly did. And so did her brother."

"Her *brother?*" Davin's eyebrows arched attentively as he prepared himself for yet another intricately twisted tale.

"He was a doughty fighter, the best that Huata band had. Those nomads aren't renowned for their fighting prowess, you know. They turn tail and run at the first sign of danger. Ah, but *these* Huata! They were wanderers selling their philters and potions, and they were warriors, as well."

"Ah, let me guess. This fair maiden had given her own brother a love philter," Davin suggested.

"Nay, it was to *me* she gave the potion. She wanted nothing more of her brother's nocturnal visits. She chose me, and when I became so smitten with her—because of the potion, of course—I lost all my wits." Goran corrected his friend with a flourish of his arms.

"Not hard to do," Davin whispered beneath his breath.

"We fought, her brother and I. And the battle! *Titanic!* We warred all the afternoon, into the night, and through the next morning."

"Your eye fell out from exhaustion."

Davin's own eyes fixed on the distant column of fifteen wagons painted bright and gaudy. He estimated they would intersect the band's path by sundown.

The thought warmed him. Unlike the majority of men and women dwelling in the realms of Raemllyn, Davin held no hatred or fear of the Huata, who were reviled because of hinted dealings with demons and various other spirits of the Dark Kingdoms. Davin had never seen such arcane liaisons among the nomads. Rather, it was the Huata way of life that kindled hatred and jealousy in the breasts of men.

Travel and freedom belonged to the Huata. Those bound to the land, chained to their stores, totally enveloped in their politics, all hated the nomads for that. And at the same time they coveted the Huata freedom. The jealousy only sparked deeper hatred, which led to the Huata being accused of myriad crimes in any city they chanced by, and not always were the crimes their doing.

Davin smiled. Rogues they were—but such magnificent rogues! He had learned many fine tricks from the nomadic bands. He had not become a master thief solely from experience. His mentors had been the Huata's most distinguished thieves and confidence men.

"... almost noon." Goran's continuing yarn wove back into his thoughts. "There we were, eye to eye, knife to knife, our strengths equal. To all, the fight was obviously a draw and would continue until Yehseen's great hunting horn blared to signal the crack of doom. That's when the bastard spat in my eye. He had been chewing *chiin* bark. Poisonous stuff. Blinded me! My eye felt as if a fiery poker had been driven in—all the way to the socket. I naturally yielded. The Huata sorcerer had to remove the entire eye lest the orb become infected and I lose the other."

"How many's that?" Davin grinned at his friend.

"How many what? I have but one eye." Which Goran opened wide and round.

The witch-fire had ebbed low in that orb since his rescue from Velden's torments. Davin doubted not that it would soon flicker and burn with its old accustomed magic, and then . . . A shiver suffused the young thief.

"I meant how many different stories do you have to account for the loss of but a *single* eye?" Davin answered. "This makes nine—no, ten I've heard just since the Harnish Spring Festival!"

"If we are to travel with the Huata, we must practice our skills." A broad grin split the fiery-haired giant's face. "Were you not entertained . . . at least for a few seconds?"

Davin shook his head, though he admitted to himself that Goran was right. When one traveled with the Huata, it was as if one were a permanent member of the band. With every constabulary certain to blame them for any theft while they camped in the neighborhood, the Huata had taken to presenting small shows of legerdemain, juggling, tumbling, and other talents of interest to a rural area.

And the love philters and the fortune-telling . . .

And the thieving . . .

And all who shared their camp were expected to participate in whatever activity was required of them.

"It will be good to return to the bosom of those supporting young Prince Felrad," Goran added. "Being among those dogs yapping the glories of Zarek Yannis

sickens me. 'Tis Bedrich's rightful heir who should sit
on the Velvet Throne in Kavindra!"

Davin chuckled and said, "You are happy to be taken
to *any* bosom, and its politics matter naught!"

"You know me too well, Davin Anane. And I have
come to know you well, also. You can do with a little
diversion among the Huata," Goran replied with a wink
of his patchless eye. "A woman or two will take your
mind off that wench. What was her name? Lilljuns?"

"Lijena." The name came almost inaudibly from
Davin's lips.

"Huh . . . yes . . . whatever." Goran noted not the shadow
that passed over his friend's face. "Two lusty wenches
abounce and awiggle and with full knowledge of all the
Huata love tricks, and you'll forget her."

Davin did not deign to reply. Forgetting the niece of
Lord Tadzi would not be so easily done. Nor would he
soon shed the guilt and shame for what he had done: sold
her to that sewer scum Velden.

He glanced at Goran, then sighed heavily. The price
of a life for a life had been high, but Goran commanded
more than his friendship. There had been the demon in
Lower Raemllyn that Goran fought off while Davin lay
frostbitten and helpless. A single life, no matter how
weakly the flame burned, would have sated the snow
demon. But Goran had refused to abandon his friend and
had risked all.

That only began the long ledger filled with debts he
owed the Challing. Davin admitted that while Goran and
his uncontrollable magicks were oft irritating, as well as
dangerous, he was a staunch companion and one to trust
in a fight—any fight.

*Lijena . . .*

Davin shoved aside thoughts of the frost-tressed beauty
and her prison in Bistonia's sewers. Time had been too
short and his mind too pressed to do other than obey
Velden's command. That the king of thieves had lied so
about Lijena and Tadzi mattered little.

"I tire of this saddle and could use wine and food! And the Huata caravan lies near! Ride, Davin, ride!" Goran cried out in a booming voice as he spurred Orria toward the painted wagons. "Last one to camp has to tend to the animals!"

"I've been tending to *you* long enough. I'm ready for you to curry my horse and feed him and..."

Even as Davin spoke, he urged his steed onward. A sudden spurt of speed carried him alongside Goran. Knee to knee, the pair raced downhill and across the plains toward the Huata.

The fifteen wagons with their gaudy splashes of colors and design were neatly circled about a blazing campfire when Davin and the Challing at last arrived at the Huata caravan. Guards stationed around the perimeter of the camp offered no threat to the pair of rogues, but took their mounts and pointed to the fire, saying, "You are prompt, friends of the Huata. Tymon awaits you."

Davin glanced at Goran and shrugged. While the Huata did not parley with demons, they often knew more than the powers of ordinary men permitted, and were quite secretive about their methods of acquiring that knowledge. How Tymon, leader of this band, could have known it was Goran and he who approached left Davin puzzled. He had seen no scouts, and dusk had cloaked them as they rode toward the caravan.

"Ah, Davin Anane and his mongrel Goran One-Eye, at last you are here!" Tymon rose from where he sat beside the flames, gnawing on a gigantic haunch of roast prairie lizard, to hug the two wayfarers heartily. "I had despaired of either of you being alive."

"Tymon, old cutthroat," growled Goran as he grabbed a flagon of wine from a woman who was passing and slopped it down without pause for breath, "when did we ever give the idea we were unable to take care of ourselves?"

"The Harnish Festival. Who in all of Raemllyn is

stupid enough to steal the entire revenue, then spit in the faces of Zarek Yannis's own guard during the escape?" Tymon, dressed in flowered blouse, black vest, breeches, and boots, waved an arm to the campfire as a signal for his old friends to warm themselves.

"'Twas only the prize money we took. Would that it had been the entire revenue," Goran answered, then squatted and pulled a rib from the roasting lizard that hung spitted over the flames.

"We had to spit in the faces of his guards," said Davin, "because Yannis himself was not there."

Davin cleared his throat, then accurately spit at one of the Huata wagons. He hit a garishly painted character directly in the eye.

"Spit upon Yannis, not upon my wagon. Otherwise I might mistake you for one of the townspeople. They are very provincial in this part of the kingdom." Tymon laughed, unrestrained, from belly, chest, and throat.

"Meaning, I suppose, that they don't let you rob at will." Davin winked as he accepted wine and meat from a black-tressed woman who wore a low-dipping blouse that revealed the lovely expanse of her breasts when she bent to serve him.

"They do protest a mite too strongly," agreed Tymon. "But tell me, Davin, how long will you be with the caravan? We can use skills such as yours." He lounged back, tossed the lizard haunch out into the darkness where the camp's dogs fought for it, then said to Goran, "And I might even be able to find a spot for you, too. How are you as a wildman?"

"What? Wildman? Me!" Goran rose up and roared, long arms snaking out and capturing a passing girl servant. She squealed with delight, and Goran scooped her up and started to carry her off.

"Come back here, oaf," said Davin. "We still have to work out travel arrangements."

"Tymon is fair. You work them out. I have other

matters to tend to." With the girl servant still giggling, Goran departed.

"He never changes." Tymon laughed. "And if he did, I'm not sure I would tolerate him around this camp. He's lazy, strong-willed, a womanizer."

"Are those his good or bad points?" Davin leaned on an elbow and drew a deep breath. There was an aroma to the camp, that of spices and freedom. He smiled; it smelled like home—and he had returned. He'd been too long from the Huata.

"His good ones, of course. Drink, my friend! You look as if the Weight of Cressus is upon you. No mortal should carry that—not without a belly full of wine."

Davin drained his cup and held it up for a refill from a woman standing near with wineskin ready. He downed half of this in one gulp. The coarse dark red wine burned all the way down his gullet, but it did make him feel better. He thought more about his future and less about Lijena's with every mouthful.

"Where are you bound?" Davin asked. "From the general direction, I'd wager on Leticia."

"You'd win that bet. We have to try the more populated spots if we are to make our revenues for the year. Zarek Yannis insists on taxes far too great for our like to pay." Tymon shrugged.

"Since when have you ever bothered with kingdom taxes?"

"Since that vulture Yannis found a mage to cast spells for him. If the collectors find someone unwilling or unable to pay whatever they claim is due, a spell is cast. A demon haunts your tracks, it does, and eventually devours you one joint at a time."

"This sounds like one of Goran's tall tales." Davin shook his head.

"'Tis true. I saw the result with my own eyes. You remember Wukkum the Halt?" Tymon leaned toward Davin with eyes wide.

Davin nodded. The world faded into a nice, fuzzy warmth as the wine flowed into his veins. The fire crackling before him edged away the bite of the chilling air.

"First I saw him, he was minus fully four knuckles on his left hand. A month later he'd lost the entire hand. Two months after that, no right arm. And," Tymon said, his voice dropping to a confidential whisper, "I understand those were not the only joints gone—just the visible ones."

"Considering the way he lived, Wukkum might have had a wasting disease, or the pox," Davin suggested.

Tymon shook his head vigorously.

"I saw! The joints were *gnawed* off."

Davin didn't feel up to arguing with Tymon over the matter. The wine seized him entirely now. He was content to lie back and stare into the flames as they leaped and cavorted.

"You are looking glum," said Tymon after a while. "What fresh mischief have you and Goran One-Eye been involved in? Even Goran looks a little peaked. For him that's unusual. Never have I seen a man so robust."

"Look who I found out in the shadows," came Goran's booming voice. He carried a kicking, struggling woman in his arms.

Davin turned and looked and his heart trebled its pace. His friend carried no girl servant now but Tymon's own daughter, Selene. Like her father, the young woman was tall and lean, with hair the color of a raven's wing and smoldering eyes to match. The turn of her calf, the flare of her hip, and the firmness of the breast that strained against the fabric of the peasant blouse she wore Selene had inherited from her mother. But like Tymon, Davin and she were old friends, though in ways Davin would never share with the father!

"Down with her, Goran," he ordered. "You know how she hates it when you carry her around like a sack of potatoes."

"No potato sack ever squirmed so nicely," said Goran with some satisfaction before setting Selene on the ground beside her father.

"Father, must we put up with such barbarians? They're uncouth and loud, and rumor has it they even *steal*."

Dark eyes moved from Goran to Davin and lingered there. No hint of accusation dwelled in those fiery coals. They caressed and stroked and taunted him, urged him to do more than simply sit.

Davin returned the gaze, feeling familiar stirrings within his core. Again his pulse upped its tempo when the lithe beauty rose and stalked toward him. And she did stalk, rather than walk. With the grace of a sleek panther she moved, her gaze never leaving his as she curled at his side. Davin's arm circled her shoulders and tugged her close. The feel of her, the womanly smell of her, reawoke memories that greeted him like old friends who had been too long from his life.

"What is it troubling you?" asked Tymon, hardly taking note of the reunion between Selene and Davin. "You are not your old self. Nor you, Goran. You appear thinner."

"There's nothing wrong that a few weeks of travel with your band can't cure," said Goran.

"The witchwoman Candra might prove valuable to you," Tymon said with a shrug.

"Candra?" Davin sat up and leaned forward.

Selene's hand crept downward. Davin gently ensnared her wrist and removed the distraction.

"Is Candra with you now?"

"Soon," assured Tymon. "She will be able to help you, no matter what your need."

Whispering so that only Davin could hear, Selene said, "I can supply whatever you need. You shouldn't seek any farther—than my wagon."

"She joins you in Leticia?"

"Who knows the precise location?" said Tymon. "But

she will join us soon. You do have need of her, don't you?"

Davin glanced at Goran, who had discovered another serving wench. This one was much plumper than the first, and the Challing's tastes definitely favored well-fed women. Even as Davin watched, Goran rose and led the woman off into the shadows at the camp's perimeter. If Davin was any judge, Goran had found a companion to last the entire night.

"What do you hear of Prince Felrad?" Tymon asked, also watching Goran's retreat.

"The rumors most concerning me of late have centered on law enforcement activity," said Davin, laughing as Selene's hand worked inside his jerkin and stroked his chest.

"I heard that Felrad is gathering an army in the north-lands." When Davin made no comment, Tymon pushed on. "This is an opportunity for you, Davin."

"I have no desire to be a foot soldier. Where is the glory in dying of starvation or cold or even in being on the receiving end of one of Yannis' lancers' pikes?" Davin shook his head.

The Huata were staunch supporters of the royal family, although never openly, for that would be instant death. Their travels across the face of Upper and Lower Raemllyn provided a perfect intelligence network for Prince Felrad and the lords who rallied to his side—that was, if the prince did indeed live. When the time came, they would raise their swords with Felrad's and strike against the murderous usurper Zarek Yannis.

Felrad's struggle was not Davin's. He cared little whose arse rested on the Velvet Throne. His hate for Zarek Yannis was a private matter that could be settled only when Yannis's heart met the tip of an Anane sword.

"That is not what I meant. With Felrad in far Upper Raemllyn, your heritage demands you join with him," Tymon continued.

"For five years I have heard these rumors of Felrad's great army, the attempt to regain the Velvet Throne, how Yannis will crumble under any sustained attack. For *five years* I have heard it all. The current rumors are no different. They are just the fond wishings of ones like us, who long to see a true king on the throne once again," Davin said in spiritless tones.

"These are true tales, I swear it!"

"Oh? And what of the rumor I heard that Felrad is dead?"

"A foul lie!"

"Or that the usurper holds Felrad in his dungeons? Haven't you just told me Yannis has made a pact with a sorcerer to collect his taxes? Mighty Qar, to collect *taxes*? If I had the use of a mage's spells, I'd have scant need of money." Davin waved away his old friend's rantings of Felrad and his army.

Selene kissed his ear and softly said, "I am all the magic you will need, my love . . . for tonight or a million nights to follow."

"Felrad can use you, Davin. We both know that. You owe it to yourself, to your heritage, to—"

"Damn my heritage! The House of Anane is no more. Berenicis the Blackheart saw to that!" Davin flared.

Tymon rose, leaned forward so that his chest was almost in the fire, and raged at the youth, "You haven't heard all there is! Felrad lives, Davin. He lives, just as you do. And Zarek Yannis *has* used his mage for more than simple extortions." Tymon's face turned ruddy as he spoke. "The usurper fears Felrad will drag him from the throne."

"So?"

"Yannis has unleashed the Faceless Ones."

"Another rumor. You live with rumors, Tymon." Davin uneasily turned, Selene's arm tightening around him in warning. Something about the way Tymon spoke this time was subtly different.

"I have seen them, Davin. With my own eyes, *I have seen the Faceless Ones!* The demon riders are again unleashed upon Raemllyn!"

A shiver ran along Davin's spine as he heard those words. In Harn and in Bistonia he had overheard drunks muttering into their ale about the Faceless Ones, of their spurring their Hell steeds through the night.

"You've *seen* them?"

"I have," Tymon assured him.

"Impossible!" Davin refused to believe that demons from Raemllyn's long-dead past were again unleashed upon the face of the world.

Tymon shook his head and rose. He stared at Davin in silent disgust for several minutes before turning and quietly vanishing into the night.

Davin's thoughts went dark. It was always like this with Tymon. The man thought of himself as a surrogate father, giving out unwanted advice, pushing and shoving Davin in ways he did not wish to travel. Davin heaved a deep sigh and reclined again. Selene remained silent. Her father maintained the fiction of Prince Felrad's return; Davin wondered how often Selene had listened to his ravings.

*But the Faceless Ones . . .*

The ancient legends swirled in Davin's head, made him dizzy. He took another long draught from his cup, emptying it. This time the raw wine brought no real warmth, even to his stomach. The thought of the Faceless Ones chilled him too much.

The demon warriors had been conjured by the black mage Nnamdi a thousand generations lost in history. Nnamdi had ground Raemllyn under his heel and ruled supreme until the Time of the Called, until Kwerin Bloodhawk, First High King of Raemllyn, and his sorcerer Edan, united, summoned magicks and warriors against Nnamdi, destroying the wizard and his demon warriors.

In that great battle the magicks that had bound man

were broken for all time. With every succeeding generation, spells had grown weaker, less effective. To be sure, there had been those mages controlling great powers, but they were as mewling children compared to Nnamdi and Edan.

Davin shuddered at the very idea of the Faceless Ones again aride in Raemllyn. The giants of history, the Kwerin Bloodhawks, the Edans, were gone. No one matched their ability in these relatively tranquil times. If Zarek Yannis had somehow resurrected the demon warriors, he juggled more dangerously than any other ruler had dared for five hundred years—longer!

Felrad could not stand against the Faceless Ones. Davin was not even certain Yannis could. They were juggernauts from a prior era conjured to fight titanic battles.

"You turn so bleak," said Selene. "Do not let my father darken your night this way. Let me brighten it. Let me show you the full brilliance of Selene!"

Her fingers strayed again, and this time Davin Anane did nothing to prevent it. If anything, he welcomed the diversion. He and Selene had always been good for each other, and this night would prove no different, he hoped, for there was much he wanted to forget.

"My mind becomes enfeebled," he said. "I cannot remember which wagon is yours. Can it be that one?"

He pointed. She shook her head and pouted at his faulty memory. "I know. It must be that one."

"No."

"Can it be there?"

"You will take all night checking each wagon. Allow me to show you. Everything!"

Arms around each other, they went to Selene's wagon and the evening of complete sensual pleasure that had always before occurred. But this time he thought of a frosty-haired woman even as he lay in Selene's passionate embrace.

Lijena haunted him still.

# chapter 14

A MUTED BASS RUMBLE like the sound of a distant ... Lijena moaned softly and rolled over in the feather bed, her sleep-cottoned thoughts unable to identify the rumble. Groping fingers crept from beneath the warmth of two thickly piled comforters, found the case of a down pillow, and drew it lower to nestle more securely under her head. She sighed contentedly and snuggled in the cocoon of blanketing.

The deep rumble continued.

*Ansisian, favor me!* she silently prayed to the God of Sleep as she tried to burrow her head into the pillow to escape the sound. She cleared her mind and thought only of sleep's sheltering cradle.

The rumble persisted; her ear and mind were now acutely aware of the annoying sound.

She tossed to her opposite side, and an eyelid lazily opened. The bedroom—she smiled, remembering Amrik carrying her here in his arms—was heavily draped. Not even a faint glow from beneath the rich folds of velvet drapery hinted that the sun ruled the heavens. She had slept long and hard since her flight from Bistonia's sewers. And would have slept longer if it wasn't for the ...

*Voices.* She recognized the source of the rumbling

now. Voices came from beyond the ebony door to the bedroom.

Sleepily Lijena rubbed at her eyes and opened both after several protesting blinks. *Amrik* . . . The smile returned to her face. It was Amrik who was speaking outside—her Amrik—and she was safely tucked away in *his* bed . . . the same bed she hoped they would soon share as husband and wife.

She stretched, rejoicing in the play of her muscles, the luxurious sensation of silk sheets against her flesh, the joy of simply being clean. She was alive, free of Velden and Jun and their kingdom of offal—and the man she loved awaited just outside the door to the bedroom.

A voice boomed loud enough that she distinctly distinguished it as her Amrik's. Then there was silence.

Lijena's brow furrowed while cold sweat prickled over her body. Perhaps she had judged her safety too quickly. Had she detected anger in Amrik's shout—or fear? Had Jun and his army of thieves tracked her to the House of Tohon? Was Amrik in danger? Was she?

With temples apound, she slid from the bed. Her head cocked from side to side, listening. Nothing. Nor did she find Velden's filth-covered cape anywhere in the room. There were the powder-blue robes of a girl servant draped over a nearby chair.

Lijena didn't question the choice of clothing Amrik had obviously placed there for her. After all, the House of Tohon was without a mistress. Instead, she slipped into the coarse fabric and tied it about her middle with a sash of rope.

Her gaze darted about the bedchamber in search of a weapon. She found neither sword nor even a poniard. A slim-necked vase rested on a table beside the door. This she hefted in her right hand as her left eased the door open the width of a single finger joint.

Still she heard nothing.

She pressed an eye to the narrow crack and blinked. Harsh light from lamps scattered along the walls flooded the upper hallway. She barely stifled a startled gasp. She had expected to see sunlight.

*Have I slept the full grains of a dayglass?* She wasn't certain. If the lack of minor aches and pains within her body was any indication, she might have slept even longer.

She blinked again and peered down the hall; there was no one between the bedroom and the staircase that led to the house's ground level. Edging the door wider, Lijena slipped into the hallway and crept to the stairs that swooped downward in an enormous spiral. She cautiously leaned over the ornate banister to peer below.

It wasn't Jun and his army of rag-clothed thieves that Amrik faced but a well-dressed, handsome man. The two sat across from each other in overstuffed chairs beside a blazing fire in the hearth. Each held a half-drained crystal goblet of deep red wine.

A nervous smile of embarrassment and relief erased the drawn concern on Lijena's face. Neither anger nor fear had she heard in her lover's voice; it had simply been raised in a toast to his companion, who now leaned forward. And she fully saw that face.

"No!" The crash of shattering china punctuated Lijena's gasp as the vase slipped from her hand.

Amrik's companion was Davin Anane!

"Lijena!" Amrik Tohon exclaimed. He came up out of his chair as if someone had pricked him with a needle. "Lijena, how long have you . . . uh . . . I didn't expect you to awake so soon."

Regaining his composure, he smiled graciously and held out an arm, inviting her down the spiraling stairs.

Heat flushed Lijena's cheeks. The man beside Amrik now rose and smiled up to her. She had been wrong. It was not that swine from Jyotis at all, though the man might have been Davin Anane's older brother. The two were built similarly, and the faces were almost identical except for the neatly trimmed moustache this man wore and the character lines about the corners of his eyes and mouth, which bespoke at least a decade separating his age from Davin's.

"I'm not . . . appropriately attired for receiving guests," Lijena said hastily to hide her embarrassment as she descended the stairs.

"Darling, I apologize for that common robe, but alas, my closet holds no womanly garb." There was a tightness to Amrik's voice that puzzled Lijena.

"Fear not offending me, my lady." This came from the visitor. "Never has such beauty graced such coarse garments—nor filled them so well."

Lijena wasn't certain whether to accept the man's comment as a compliment or an insult. Nor did she care for the way his dark gaze coursed over the light blue robes she "filled so well." A goosepimply shiver washed over her flesh as though she stood naked before this stranger.

Refusing to be intimidated by his intimate gaze and the hint of a smirk on his narrow mouth, Lijena coolly returned his stare. He was dressed very well; indeed, in finer clothing than Amrik's. Though the wide-collar shirt he wore was simple white, it was woven of the finest of silk, from the Isle of Pthedm off Upper Raemllyn's eastern shores, if Lijena were any judge of fabric.

The heavy winter jacket he wore was basic black, as were his boots and breeches. However, the stitching on that jacket wasn't basic or common. The needlepoint was intricate and flawless. She could only guess at the countless hours that had gone into sewing those multihued, interlocking designs.

In truth, the embroidery had the look of *danne* handicraft, but that would have been prohibitively expensive. Only royalty could afford the embroidery done by the forest spirits trapped by a mage and forced to do one masterwork before being released.

"You recognize the style?" the man asked in a voice an octave below Davin Anane's voice.

"I had the notion it might be *danne* work, but that is only something I've heard of." Even this close to Amrik's visitor, Lijena was struck by his resemblance to the Jyotian brigand who had kidnapped her from Tadzi's guards, then sold her to Velden.

"Ahhh! Not only beauty, but a discriminating eye!" The man grinned, then lifted his goblet to Amrik. "You have chosen well, my friend. I heartily commend your taste."

"*Danne*—it must be worth a king's ransom." Lijena could not contain her awe.

"Indeed," the man said dryly. "Kings have tried to obtain such as this and been unable to do so. I was graced with Jajhana's smile. She placed me in the right place at the right time."

Lijena knew that a small fortune and not the Goddess of Chance had purchased the intricate needlework. She lifted a hand to the jacket, then her fingers hesitated. "May I?"

He nodded, and she lightly touched the interwoven designs with her fingertips.

"It's true! I feel . . . their tears."

The man laughed and shook his head. "That's a myth. But there is great magic locked within the warp and woof of the fabric."

"Darling, would you care for a glass of mulled wine?" cut in Amrik.

The stranger smiled, strong white teeth flashing. He tilted his head, drawing Lijena's attention back to Amrik. She turned and accepted the crystal goblet he held out for her, and sipped. The spicy heated wine ran warm and sweet down her throat.

"My lady, don't tax yourself. Please take my chair by the blaze," said the stranger in the *danne* jacket. "Friend Amrik has briefly told me of your misfortunes in the hope I may aid or give advice. I will be better suited to the task if I hear every detail from you."

Lijena smiled and accepted the chair, her gaze lingering on this stranger as he ordered Amrik to bring a platter of meats and cheeses. She took another sip of the wine and wondered if she had misjudged him because of his resemblance to that blackheart Davin Anane. His genteel good manners and his obvious prosperity hinted at royalty.

Excitement tingled within Lijena's breast. Males of the House of Tohon had been moneylenders for generations, a tradition now carried on by Amrik. It was said that royalty and wealth did not go hand in hand—that members of royal families often traveled incognito to Bistonia to arrange financial matters. Could this man be on just such a mission? Might he be an heir to the throne?

His desire to conceal his true identity would explain why Amrik had not introduced them formally. Wealth in Bistonia did not carry with it ingress to royal functions; Lijena had no idea what any of the men and women in line for the throne looked like, especially now that Zarek Yannis had installed a new lineage.

Her smile grew. *Won't Father be surprised to learn my Amrik is well acquainted with royalty? Well enough to seek this one's advice and aid!*

Those supporters of the Velvet Throne who also had money to lend reputedly did very well. Ofttimes they became landholders of vast estates and sported royal titles.

*Amrik, my darling, you are wonderful! Imagine. Baroness Lijena? Countess Lijena? Or even Duchess! Lady of the Duchy of Tohon!* The enticing possibilities glittered in her head.

"Amrik has spoken well of your courage and fortunate escape from a band of brigands dwelling in the city's sewers. A lucky man, young Amrik Tohon. His fortune and you are so intertwined."

The man's words shattered the mental play of Lijena's first grand entrance to a court ball. She turned to the stranger, again puzzled by the odd way he phrased his compliments. Then Amrik returned, offering her a platter of assorted meats and cheeses. She daintily accepted but one slice each of meat and cheese. Although she could have devoured the entire tray without a pause for breath, she had no intention of offending the sensibilities of Amrik's royal friend by displaying the eating habits of some peasant wench.

As she nibbled ever so slowly at cheese and meat, Amrik took her goblet and refilled it from a decanter on a table behind her. He mulled the spice-laden wine with a glowing iron from the fire and returned the goblet to her hand. Lijena drank rather than sipped to wash down a rather dry bite of cheese. Again the wine ran warm down her throat and into her stomach.

A rush of dizziness assailed her.

"Feeling a bit shaky, my dear?" asked Amrik.

She glanced up with a frown. His tone struck her as odd. It seemed too . . . gloating.

"I think my ordeal has left me weaker than I realized." Lijena leaned back in the chair and placed a hand to her forehead. "The room spins in crazy circles."

"Perhaps you ought to try more of the wine," the royal stranger suggested. "When you are feeling distraught, good hot wine always helps. Try it."

The snap to his words struck Lijena as a command, but seconds passed before she recognized the meaning of what he said. She drained half of the goblet and immediately felt better—for a second or three.

"I'm sor-sorry, but I . . ." She lost her words in the room's topsy-turvy spinning.

"Just sit for a moment. It will pass, I'm sure."

Amrik was right. In less than a minute the spinning stopped and a curious lassitude came over her. Lijena was content to simply sit and let the leaden sensation possess her.

"Is this a satisfactory conclusion to our agreement, Nelek?" Amrik turned to his friend.

"Eminently so," answered the handsome stranger. "I must commend you on the servant's garb. It will make my departure easier than I had anticipated. No guard will suspect a serving wench asleep in her master's carriage."

Lijena struggled to make sense of their words and failed. Her thoughts flowed thick and sluggish like some sugary syrup. Her eyelids grew heavy, and she fought simply to stay awake.

"Nelek?" she asked in a whisper.

"My dear, that is my name. Certainly you know of me. Nearly all of the citizens of Bistonia do." The dark stranger bent low to stare into her eyes.

"And those of Harn and Leticia and most other places in Raemllyn," Amrik Tohon added with a humorless laugh.

"Wh-what is your full name? I...I do wish to know who my b-benefactor is." She managed to force the whispered words over a tongue that refused to obey.

"Her benefactor. That's rich!" Amrik settled into a chair and stared at her, his chin resting on tented fingers.

Lijena had seen this pose before. Amrik always took it before foreclosing on some hapless merchant unable to make the mortgage payment on his home or store.

"I am known by many names," the royal guest replied, "but I am certain you have heard of me under the name Nelek Kahl."

Lijena simply sat and stared at the man. The name seemed familiar; she was sure she had heard it before, in a far-off land, in some distant past.

Then full realization smashed across her consciousness like a tidal wave assaulting a shoreline. "Nelek Kahl the slaver!"

"That is my profession. I am quite good at it, too. But then, I have many able assistants...such as our mutual friend, Amrik Tohon." Kahl inclined his head in the moneylender's direction.

"Amrik..." Words were no longer hers. The thickness of her tongue robbed her of her voice.

Panic railed through her brain only to be caught in the treacle-slow streams of thought. She tried to stand and found that no muscle obeyed her. She did little more than quiver when she tried to rock forward and gain her feet.

"Don't strain yourself, my dear," said Amrik. "The Ansisian's Breath I placed in the wine is very effective. It has had more than ample time to spread through your body."

"Yes," spoke up Kahl. "You are quite paralyzed now, and in only a few minutes you will slip into a deep slumber. It is better that you travel in that fashion. We wouldn't want you waking up at an inopportune moment. There are still many law officers foolishly inclined against slaving."

"Amrik, why?" Somehow she found the strength to force the words over her tongue. "I love you. I... thought... you loved me."

"I do love you, my darling. It's just that I love money more." Amrik shrugged and casually threw out his hands. "And there is an unfortunate incident which requires me to move my headquarters from Bistonia. That meddlesome Lord Lerel has taken it into his head that I've been cheating him. He supplies so many slaves each month and then gets a commission. He claims I have been shorting him. The fool."

"How much have you been shorting him?" Kahl asked in a mild voice.

"Only thirty or forty percent. Call it ten thousand gold bists per month."

Kahl chuckled.

The seed of a thought crept into the back of Lijena's mind, that Kahl probably cheated Amrik of this much — and more.

"I fear that Lerel has made Bistonia much too uncomfortable for me. I called in what loans I could, dismissed the servants, and am now ready to forge outward and seek a new place for my business. It is so lucky you happened along when you did, my dear. You added another thousand silver eagles to my travel budget," Amrik said with another shrug.

"Amrik, bring my carriage around front while I gather my things," Nelek Kahl ordered the younger man. "The night grows old, and I wish to be free of the city before the Ansisian's Breath wears off."

Without question, like some lackey serving a grand master, Amrik pushed from his chair and hastened to do Nelek Kahl's bidding.

"Yes, lovely one, you will serve me well." Kahl knelt and stared into Lijena's eyes once again. "I have a major buyer who yearns for one such as you. A very, very rich man to be certain, but mere riches no longer interest me. It is his power I must tap. Through you—and others, if Yehseen so ordains—I'll do just that, and follow the roots all the way to the Velvet Throne!"

Nelek Kahl hesitated, and his fingers lifted to lightly brush Lijena's cheek. There was a warmth to those fingertips she didn't expect. And his voice held a strange gentleness when he spoke again.

"Rest assured, lovely one, that, compared to the likes of scum such as Velden and Jun, your new master will be kind and with hands of velvet. Nor will you have to long endure his chains of gold. Once you have done as I bid, your life will again be yours and..."

His voice faded, he pursed his lips, and he shook his head. "What care you of my affairs? All that I require is that you do as I bid. Now close your eyes and sleep, for there is much that I must command and little time in which to do it ere that fool Amrik returns. Sleep, lovely one, sleep...sleep...sleep...."

Lijena fought against the lulling sound of his voice, to no avail. Her eyes closed and swirling darkness tugged her downward. Yet before she was swallowed by the yawning maw of unconsciousness, she chiseled two more names in her mind below those of Davin Anane and Jun—the names of Amrik Tohon and Nelek Kahl.

## *chapter* 15

"EVERY TIME I DEPART LETICIA, I wonder what new 'improvements' its leaders will design to make it more of a prison." Tymon shook his head and pointed to new battlements being raised at least a mile from the city's present wall of granite. "And each time I return, they never cease to amaze me. Leticia grows, so yet another barricade is constructed to contain the sprawl. Leticia has no real enemy; why do they continue to build as if they had?"

"Their leaders hold them in rein that way. When there is a threatening enemy to defend against, the populace will ignore the most oppressive measures in the name of security and survival," Davin Anane answered. "And if there is no enemy, well..."

He shrugged and threw up his hands, indicating there was no explanation for such insanity. As he endured the bounce and bone-rattling jars of the Huata wagon, his gaze traced the flat, gray, oppressive walls that hid all hint of the city within, except for a few pointed spires that poked above the battlements and shafted toward a cloudless new winter sky.

"Imaginary enemies are all the better for the leaders. They hold the people in check through fear, and yet no

one need die because of good, honest battle." Goran One-
Eye snorted with disgust, then spat to the ground. "I like
it not."

"Who does?" the Huata leader asked. "But down there
is where our money is. And we do what must be done
to survive in a world ruled by gods who care little for
the lives of those they have created."

"You mean, there is the money you will *steal*," Davin
corrected and chuckled, knowing full well what his old
friend meant.

The people of Leticia had yet to notice the approach
of the nomad band and its gaudily painted caravan. But
when they did, then began the fleecing. The Huata lived
by wits quicker than any city dweller could truly appreciate or conceive—and fingers thrice as fast.

Huata jugglers' skills included more than the abilities
to deftly toss myriad clubs, balls, and plates through the
air. Those limber wrists and fingers were well suited for
lifting money pouches from the belts of men and drawing
open the purses of unsuspecting women.

The pitchmen and their exaltations of the exotic wonders to be discovered within the Huata camp were deliberately calculated to keep the marks mesmerized while
others quietly wove among the assembled crowds to pur-
loin jewelry—and anything else that might be of value.

Scantily clad dancing girls wiggled, jiggled, and
bumped their barely veiled charms through the crowd.
Only a man with the loins of an eunuch had an eye for
anything but the seductive sway of inviting hips, the
lively bounce of beaded and spangled breasts, and the
long, shapely turn of calf and thigh. With desire hotly
coursing in their veins, those men little suspected the
alluring dancers acted as reconnaissance for others with
lighter fingers—and if they did, Davin doubted that they
minded.

Then there were the Huata remedies, for virtually
every sickness and malady known to man. Each could
be had—for a price!

Whether they worked or not was a matter of some dispute, especially among those who had paid handsome sums for the tiny vials. Most often questioned were the love philters purchased by both the young and those who had long lost the blush of youth from their cheeks, yet yearned to recapture passions that were but faded memories of bygone years. To protests of hoax and fraud the Huata merely shrugged, woefully shook their heads, and repeated a saying popular among the nomads, "Not even the gods control love."

"We earn honest money." Tymon protested Davin's insinuation. "The Huata are an honorable people!"

Goran laughed and corrected, "You take good money. How *you* get it is not earning. And there is said to be honor among thieves ... even the Huata."

Tymon eyed the pair of adventurers, sucked at his teeth, and shook his head as though he had no understanding of his friends' un-Huatalike attitudes.

Davin smiled and slapped a hand to the Huata leader's shoulder in sympathy. Tymon would never grasp that selling love philters with scant chance of working or picking the pocket of a merchant too obese with money to care held little challenge for Goran or Davin. All that mattered to them was the risk—the rush of adrenaline when one broke into a building and stole that which was most highly prized, or that which was deemed unstealable. It was the excitement of the stealing—the act itself, not the items taken—that was as addictive as smoking *calokin* buds.

For Tymon and the others in his band, that way lay madness. Why not take what was brought forth eagerly, even offered openly, than risk capture by going after the well guarded? That was the difference. The Huata drifted through the world and attempted to make as few ripples on the ocean of life as possible. Davin and Goran were hurricanes whipping that ocean into frothy frenzy.

"We camp yonder." Selene poked out from the wagon's canvas flap behind Davin. While she pointed with her right hand, her left arm snaked around his waist.

"Mmmmm." He answered the caressing arm first. "So close to the main gate? Is that wise?"

"Why not? It will allow the good citizens to come and see what we have to offer."

Selene wiggled closer and hugged him tightly with both arms, an action that only emphasized her very womanly presence.

"We could all be rich if you ever bottle and sell *that!*" Davin grinned back at her.

"What do you think goes into every love potion?" she asked with a wink. "Those of are my devising, after all."

"I'll take a case."

"When you have the source, why bother with the paltry?" asked Goran, laughing as he ducked Selene's playful swat at his shaggy head.

"Goran," said Davin, his mood suddenly somber. "Tymon says the witchwoman Candra resides somewhere within Leticia. We should seek her out as soon as we finish helping set camp."

"Do you seek an old, dried-up hag when you can have me?" asked Selene with a pout.

Davin squeezed the hands encircling his waist and turned to lightly kiss her lips. "This is private business."

"What business can you have with the likes of her?" Selene arched a thinly plucked eyebrow.

"It would be public business if I told you, my dear," Davin said with all seriousness.

"Huummph!" Selene's arms slid from his waist, and she snorted again as she retreated back into the wagon, jerking the flap closed behind her. She shouted back, "And I will be breaking fast this morn in *private!* If it's food your belly wants, Davin Anane, find it with Candra!"

"Perhaps you will be needing a case of Selene's love potions," Goran said, a broad grin splitting his ruddy face. "Your rude ways have offended the lovely child. How could you be so cold! Hear her weeping tears? My soul shatters at such mournful sounds. I must comfort her!"

Davin reached out and grabbed the Challing by the waist of his red breeches as he tried to crawl into the wagon after Selene. With one tremendous tug, he hauled the giant back to the wagon driver's board.

"Contain your . . . uh . . . sympathy, my friend," Davin said, eyes narrowed in mock threat. "Leticia is but moments away, and there's work to be done."

With a heavy sigh and a longing eye toward the still-closed flap, Goran turned to the road ahead.

The fifteen wagons drew up before Leticia's main gates, then spread in a wide semicircle. Moments later, teams were unhitched and staked out behind the wagons, with fresh hay and water. The wagons themselves were opened and quickly emptied of tightly packed bundles of canvas and poles. First up were the large tents of bright, though slightly soiled, colors. These spacious palaces of color housed the jugglers and dancing girls. Smaller tents came next for the palmists and potion sellers. And last were the broad, eye-catching banners and flags spotted around the camp so that they fluttered in the breeze. And all within a mere two hours!

"This ought to get things started," said Goran, wiping sweat from his brow and casting a disdainful eye on Tymon, who had sat on the driver's seat of a wagon supervising the pitching of the Huata camp. "It's too damned much work for what they make. Better we go into Leticia and find a merchant careless with his shop's revenues."

"Better we go into Leticia and find Candra." Davin glanced at the city with its granite wall stretching thirty feet toward the sky.

Goran fell silent for a moment, then asked, "Do you think this witch can aid me? Will she be able to provide the answers?"

Davin offered no answer; he had no desire to inflame

false hope. The woman's name had come to them by a
devious route, and one that had cost dearly. But Davin
would have willingly paid much, much more if the rumors—hints—about Candra were true. Within her power
might lie the ability to remove the spell binding Goran
to his human body. Once those mortal bonds were severed, the Challing could return to the realm of magicks
that had given him birth.

Davin felt an inward twinge. He would be hard pressed
to find such a staunch companion as Goran One-Eye
among the mere mortals of Raemllyn. But for Goran,
born of changeling ways, to be trapped for eternity in
the body of a man—one man—was the same as being
condemned to the lowest level of Qar's Peyneeha.

"The bazaar will be running well enough soon. And
they hardly need us to help them with their business,"
said Goran, with a tilt of his head to the curious city
dwellers who now wandered into the camp, gawking at
the odd notions and knickknacks for sale. "Soon enough
they'll be lured into tents for shows and palm readings.
Then the serious fleecing will begin!"

"I think you're right." Davin heard the music welling
up from inside the largest of the tents.

He imagined Selene starting her dance. He had no
great desire to stay and watch her pander to the crowds.
While he had no objection to the way she made her living,
Davin had long since decided there was no need for him
to endure the slavering masses of peasants as they ogled
her.

"Into Leticia, then!" he said with a nod to the gates.

The pair made it as far as the entrance to the walled
city without incident. There they were stopped by the
city guard, two self-important younglings barely old
enough to shave. They'd been given this post and the
duty to check out suspicious characters, and they intended to do just that—with enthusiasm and diligence!

"Visas," said the older of the pair. He tipped back a

tall plumed hat sizes too large for his narrow head. It slipped back down and threatened to blind him.

"Since when do citizens of Bistonia require permits to enter our fair sister city of Leticia?" boomed Goran, mustering as much indignation into his voice as possible.

"Those are the regulations. All visitors require visas," the guard answered, still struggling with the wayward hat.

"Show me the regulation. Show me the guidebook that says this!" Goran demanded.

Davin hid a smile behind a cough and a raised hand. If this young soldier could even read, let alone locate the regulation, it would be a miracle.

Playing the charade for all he was worth, Goran drew himself up and puffed out his already substantial chest.

"I am Magister Clump on a visit of state to your Lord . . . uh . . ." Goran faltered.

"Rynatvis." Davin supplied the name of Leticia's ruler for his forgetful friend.

". . . to your Lord Rynatvis." Goran harumphed to cover his momentary lapse of memory. "I am sure Lord Rynatvis will not take kindly to his privates being so bold."

Several citizens nearby tittered at the mention of their ruler's name.

The two soldiers, eyes lacking the confidence that had glittered within them but seconds ago, huddled closely and whispered.

Finally the older of the pair said, "Very well, Magister. I shall personally lead you to Lord Rynatvis's palace."

The redness left Goran's cheeks and his one good eye rolled to Davin, imploring aid.

"You are too kind. But we know the way," Davin said without batting an eye.

"I *insist*." The youth's tone said the matter was not open for further discussion.

Davin and Goran bowed simultaneously and allowed the soldier to lead the way. Within a block they had lost him in a crowd.

"Now that I've properly disposed of that jackanapes, where is this Candra?" demanded Goran. "I am eager to find if she has the power claimed of her."

"Tymon mentioned that her shop was on Rum Street." Davin ignored his friend's braggardly claim.

"A most auspicious-sounding location," Goran said with a loud smack of his lips.

Davin wound his way through the back alleys of Leticia and eventually found the alleyway that was Rum Street and a cul-de-sac with four doorways. Over one hung a weather-bleached skull.

"There," he said, pointing to the skull.

"An ancestor?" asked Goran.

"The witchwoman's quarters."

"Her advertising leaves much to be desired," the redhaired giant muttered.

The fire burning in his single good eye took on the aspect of a conflagration. With the prickle of gooseflesh on the nape of his neck, Davin stepped toward Candra's entry, all too aware of the magicks awakening within his friend.

"Don't just stand there," Goran said impatiently. "Pull the bell rope."

"There isn't one," Davin said with a shrug.

He looked around and saw only a small goat's-head knocker in the middle of the door. Tentatively he lifted and dropped the brass head.

The door boomed as though it had been struck by the fist of a giant. Davin shuffled away in a hasty backstep.

"A simple trick to impress the ignorant," scoffed Goran, lifting the head again and dropping it.

"Then my heart is yet ignorant, for it is very impressed," Davin replied as he eyed the brass goat's head. For such a light weight to produce that thunder meant magicks were woven into its texture. And Davin Anane had no use for the ways of magic.

"Let's go in. We've announced ourselves." Goran pushed the door open.

He entered an incense-smoke-filled hallway barely wide enough to accommodate the Challing's broad shoulders. Davin followed, trying his best to ignore the dim light; in such places he felt trapped like a rat. There might be a dozen bowmen waiting at the far end of the corridor to shoot them down.

Or worse!

Davin shivered at the idea of demons pouring from the simple wooden door at the far end of the hall. He could never drag free his sword in time to fend them off. Nor could he hope to retreat through the . . .

He turned to study a possible escape route and paled at the sight. The door through which he and Goran had entered was gone—vanished as if it had never existed! Only a blank wall spread behind him.

He tugged at Goran's sleeve and informed him of the transformation, but Goran was lost in the quest. He shrugged off Davin's protests.

"Witchery, that's all it is. It impresses the masses. I begin to doubt if this Candra can aid me. What would a card reader know of real sorcery?"

They marched forward and through the only door now in sight. The room beyond was shuttered and hung in dark curtains that killed sound effectively. An array of dried herbs hung on walls cluttered with arcane symbols and pentangles. In the middle of the room, at a small round table, sat an ancient crone of a woman, wizened until she looked like a year-old corpse. Her skeletal hands were spread on the table in front of her, tiny blue sparks dancing from one fingertip to another.

"Enter," she said in a deceptively soft, enticing voice. Davin would have sworn before all the gods that the voice belonged to a woman fifty years younger. "I am

Candra. How may I aid you? A glimpse into the future, mayhaps, or . . ."

The sparking fingertips turned into a light almost too brilliant to bear. Candra's eyes popped open and a look of concern spread over her wrinkled face.

"A Challing!" she said, her eyes fixed on Goran. "A Challing trapped in the body of a man."

"You know what has happened to him, then?" asked Davin.

Candra ignored him, her gaze never leaving the one-eyed giant.

"You wish to free yourself of this mortal husk and return to your own realm," she stated in her young, firm voice. "Tell me everything that occurred. Perhaps, if I study this matter, I may be of assistance."

"This is all simply show, no different from what the Huata put on for their marks," growled Goran.

"Five years it has been," Candra continued. "The mage Roan-Jafar was the one who made you thus."

Davin held his breath when he heard the woman's words. Only he and Goran knew the details, or the sorcerer responsible for Goran's entrapment. Candra somehow saw the facts. Davin's hope soared that she might be able to aid his friend.

"How do you know that?" demanded Goran, still not convinced.

"You killed him with a single knife slash across his throat, from right to left, like this."

One wrinkled hand rose, and a bony finger traced a line across her throat, showing the path taken by Goran's knife almost five years earlier. Where her fingertip touched her flesh, a bright phosphorescent green line remained. It faded to a dark red as she continued, "There is much about this I do not understand."

"Can you help us?" asked Davin.

"I . . . see more. I *feel* more." She closed her eyes and leaned forward, hands clasped tightly in front of her.

Candra began muttering incantations. Davin swallowed hard. Her very words themselves slipped from her mouth, took solid form, and danced about in the air. The words blazed with all the colors of the rainbow, yet he could not read a single one. They were arcane spells, imprecations against demons whose names were best left unuttered, pleas for information from gods who did not take kindly to mortals disturbing them.

"No," she said finally, and her eyes wearily opened. "It was so near, so very, very near, and it is now gone."

Her gaze fixed on Davin. He felt as if she stripped the flesh from his bones and sold his soul into damnation. Then that witch-gaze turned back to Goran, who appeared unaffected by it.

His own firelit eye blazed as brightly as the sun at noontime. Davin felt useless in this, his friend obviously being wrapped up in powerful magicks he could scarce control. And Candra . . . she controlled spells beyond his wildest imaginings!

"I cannot help you regain your freedom, Challing," she said in a voice now heavy with age. "There are powers beyond my ability involved in this. Roan-Jafar was a cruel, evil man, and his magicks were complex."

"There is more," flatly stated Goran. "You know more."

"I am unable to lift the geas on you, but there is one within the walls of Leticia who may be able to show you the way."

Goran stiffened and his lips twisted into an unfamiliar name. "Masur-Kell."

"Yes," said the witchwoman. "Masur-Kell might be of some assistance. But be sure to take a full pouch when you visit him. He is one sorcerer who lusts for gold as much as he does learning of the world."

"He is a man of many weaknesses," said Goran, in a voice unlike his natural one. He appeared to be in a trance, under the control of some unseen force.

"I can be of no more assistance," Candra said with grim finality. Davin thought it sounded as if she had sealed their death warrants.

"How much do we owe you for this?" he managed to ask over a tongue as dry as the deserts of Lower Raemllyn.

"Nothing. I have no need of gold. If you are successful in lifting Roan-Jafer's spell, however, I would know the details. Unlike Masur-Kell, I lust for knowledge alone."

Candra seemed to sink into herself, becoming smaller and weaker even as Davin watched. He took Goran by the arm and led the Challing from the room. Davin blinked in surprise. Simply leaving the witch's room did not take them back into the corridor—the door now opened directly onto Rum Street. They were outside, in a fine drizzle born from lead-heavy clouds over Leticia.

"Are you all right, Goran?" Davin asked in concern. His red-haired friend appeared paler than he ever had, even after the rescue from Velden's torturers.

"Masur-Kell," the Challing mumbled.

Davin shivered. Goran spoke with the voice of a man who had just been sentenced to death.

"Come, we're done with this foul place! What we need is a bowl of mulled wine and a fiery hearth to chase away the chill."

Goran merely nodded and followed after Davin as docile as a mongrel that had been beaten into submission.

# chapter
## 16

"THE HUATA DID WELL LAST NIGHT," said Davin Anane, studying the muddied area around the camp.

The trampled ground gave testimony to the multitude of Leticians who had visited the Huata in spite of the light, misting rain that had fallen through the night— and to the willingness of the human animal to be duped, taken, and enjoy every minute of it.

To be certain, the merchants would rant and whine about the few gold bists and silver eagles lifted from their pouches. But foremost in their minds would be relished memories of the sensuous Huata women and their supple, undulating bodies. The bists were a small enough price for fantasies that would fire their blood on long winter nights spent with wives gone fat and smelling of onion and garlic.

"Surely the compartment beneath the false floor of Tymon's wagon brims with a small fortune," Davin added with a glance at Goran, who sat beside him on the steps of Selene's wagon. "The band will live high when they reach the next city and sell all taken here."

"Bah! What does it matter? The Huata are fools. If Jajhana smiles, Tymon might get a tenth of the true value of his ill-gotten treasure. Not only are the Huata thieves and fools, but they are an ignorant people," grumbled Goran.

The hulking giant sat with his chin perched on a meaty hand. His single eye looked more like a burned-out ember than the witch-fire-lit orb it had been after they visited Candra. Deep lines of worry furrowed his brow, and every few seconds a growl rumbled from his throat.

"We owe Tymon and his band much, as we do all the Huata bands. Scoundrels could not ask for truer friends." Davin glanced at Leticia's high gray walls.

"Nyuria take the Huata! I owe Tymon nothing, or any of these nomadic harlequins!" Goran spat to the ground, then cursed in a tongue totally alien to his companion. "Goran One-Eye owes no debt to any man in this forsaken world you call Raemllyn. May Qar's fiery demon Nyuria take this whole stinking ball of feces!"

Davin Anane sat silent. When Goran descended into these pits of dark depression, it was the best course to take. Nothing lifted the blackness from his mood except time. It was not the Huata that brought the Challing's gloom, but the dead sorcerer Roan-Jafar, who had wrenched Goran from his own mystical realm. The death of that mage at the changeling's own hands had placed a geas on Goran, one that locked him in human form and stranded him here far from his own dimension.

Selene walked from behind the wagon, glanced at Goran, then raised her eyebrows in question at Davin as she proceeded across the camp to chat with three dancers huddled over buckets of soap and water. Davin smiled as the morning light did its best to turn her thin yellow skirt completely transparent. A physical impossibility, of course, but the sunlight did reveal the silhouette of flaring hips, firm thighs, and long, sleek calves.

"Tymon's treasure, Yeheseen's pimpled arse!" Goran growled anew. "If the Huata bastard has a fortune, he hoards it like a miser! Look at his daughter's garb—so threadbare you can see through it! He'll let her freeze to death 'fore parting with a copper. Bah!"

Davin pursed his lips and shook his head. Goran's mood was far worse than he thought. Ordinarily such a titillating glimpse of Selene's alluring charms would have had the red-haired giant twitching like a mink in rut, as it did Davin.

That woman knew more than most learn in a lifetime, and she was only too eager to share her knowledge and skills with him. A man could not ask for more—on occasion. But a lifetime with Selene? That would be suicide for a man such as he.

He smiled and admitted that the reverse was also true. There was a bond between Selene and him, one that united their spirits and passions but would never endure the knots tied by husband and wife. They both drank too deeply of life to be seduced by the false security of the staid and the familiar . . . at least for now.

*But we do love. By Yehseen's potent staff, how we do love! And for now that is enough for the both of us!*

"How can you suffer this dreary existence, my friend?" Goran's complaints wove into Davin's thoughts. "Raemllyn is a dull and colorless land. There are myriad lands beyond—"

"Off your fat backside! I'll stomach no more of your whining and grumbling. Aye, and if you profane the Gods again, they'll reach forth and hurtle you back to the oblivion that spawned your ugly carcass! Now up with you! We've a mage to seek out." Davin stood and pointed to the walled city. "Masur-Kell awaits your bulky presence."

Davin had no real idea what Goran's true form was, nor what the Challing considered a natural existence. He *had seen* Goran, with witch-fire ablaze in his solitary eye, subtly alter his human form. This, the Challing hinted, was a minor talent, a part of the curse that was almost insignificant.

"Bugger the mage, and your pox-ridden gods. Leave

me to my thoughts and what surcease I can find in them."
Goran merely mumbled, head still resting on his palm.

"Aye. . . ." Davin rose and started toward Leticia's
gates. "And I leave you to that hideous lump of fat and
pig-ugliness you jokingly call the body of a man!"

"This clumsy body . . ." Goran spat and looked down
at himself, as if for the first time. "To be free of this
clumsy, awkward body . . . to be a Challing once again!"

While his gloom did not lift, Goran heaved himself
to his feet. "Damn your eyes, Davin Anane. This had
best not take long. Masur-Kell will no more be able to
aid me than Candra could. I feel it."

"The Letician crowds were kind to more than the
Huata yesterday." Davin hefted a bulging pouch. "Think
it will suffice?"

Goran waved his friend away and plodded through
the mud toward the city gates with shoulders slumped
and back bent.

Davin hardly blamed him. There had been many
promises in the past five years, too many promises left
unfulfilled. Perhaps Goran was right in containing his
spirits. But Davin couldn't live that way. He had to
believe that an answer existed, a mage lived somewhere
who was able to counter the spell cast by Roan-Jafar.

They again entered Leticia, this time slipping through
the gates by mingling with a large group of vendors
carting their wares into the city. The guard paid Davin
and Goran scant attention as they helped an oldster with
a balky mule and a cart falling apart under the weight of
onions and potatoes.

"A nuisance," said Goran. "Wonder what they think
they accomplish by such close scrutiny of those entering
their fair city? Hardly enough within these walls to give
a good thief much of a living."

"It's all part of their leader's outlook," Davin answered as they meandered through the maze of streets
with tightly packed buildings rising three stories high on

each side. "Give the appearance of vigilance and the citizenry rests easier."

Goran shook his head in disgust, but his small deception in getting them past the guards was a strong potion. A faint glimmer of devilish light glinted in his eye, and his shoulders and back straightened. He almost swaggered by the time they reached a broad residential avenue bearing the name Two Moons.

"Think this is it?" asked Goran with eyebrows lifted. "Looks too rich for the likes of sorcerers."

"It's the place. Masur-Kell lives here . . . somewhere," Davin said as he peered down the street of cobblestone. "With his tastes for high living, he ought to be easily spotted."

This proved to be the case. Many of the arched entryways were of simple stone. The one leading into the sorcerer's abode had runic figures burned into the rock; the figures writhed and glowed with an inner light that made them seem almost alive.

"His advertising is hardly better than the witch's," Goran grumbled with doubt. He traced a finger over one of the runes.

Davin gasped; the sorcerous fire shot out to swallow Goran's hand . . . his arm . . . his head. Nor did it halt until it completely enveloped the red-maned Challing.

Goran took no notice of it. "Let's not stand here waiting for another of those damnable thundershowers. I want to get done with this as soon as I can."

They entered, Davin twisting so that no part of his body touched the stone entrance. Let Goran tempt the Fates by touching the magicks. He would not play the fool.

His choice ended at Masur-Kell's entry hall. A thick fog of purples and reds boiled within, obscuring all beyond an arm's reach. His skin crawled at the prospect of entering the roiling mists. *Qar's damnation! This strains friendship beyond its limits!*

"Goran, I think that we best be returning to . . ."

He didn't have time to complete his sentence. Goran strode toward the churning fog, which parted, then began to close around the Challing. Sucking in a less than steadying breath, Davin hastened after his friend, the prospect of being left alone within the corridor giving strength to his hesitant legs.

When the fog at last dissipated, they stood in a small windowless room. No arcane relics hung from the walls, nor were there scrawled runes and pentangles. All four walls were simply painted a flat white. Missing, too, were tables and benches ajumble with bat wings, lizard tails, newt eyes, and vials and bottles of foul-smelling potions. There was but one chair in the barren chamber.

In that ornately gilded chair, staring at them down the length of a considerable nose, was Masur-Kell. Old he was, with hair thick and white flowing about the shoulders of his robes.

And those robes! Davin had never seen their like. They looked to be silk. But no silk was ever like this fine cloth. Subtly it shifted hues: first white, then red, then orange, yellow. Shade after shade, it melted through the spectrum into black, then the cycle began anew.

And all the while the wizard's round, watery blue eyes never left the two adventurers. Davin uneasily shifted from foot to foot, wishing he were back in the Huata camp admiring the way the sunlight played through Selene's skirt. He would have willingly left his pouch of bists at Masur-Kell's feet just to be free of that unmoving gaze.

"Why do you come?" the mage finally asked.

"The witchwoman knew without asking," said Goran with no attempt to hide his skepticism.

Davin wanted to kick the Challing. One simply did not take such a tone when addressing a mage—unless one desired to spend one's remaining years as a toad, dining on flies snatched from the air.

"You are a Challing trapped in human form, that much I can see. So?" Masur-Kell shrugged.

"We were led to believe you might be able to lift the geas placed on him." Davin forced himself to speak, not trusting Goran's foul mood. Antagonizing the sorcerer further would net them little but trouble.

Masur-Kell rose, his hue-shifting robes swishing softly as he moved before Goran. Lifting a pale and spotted hand, he rested his palm on the Challing's shoulder.

His response was immediate. "I cannot lift the geas placed upon you by Roan-Jafar," he said.

"But Candra said . . ."

Masur-Kell held up a hand, silencing Davin. "I cannot *fully* lift the geas. It is far too complex a task for any single mage. I can, however, give a potion that will loosen the spell."

"What do I gain from that?" Goran challenged the white-haired wizard with a glare.

Masur-Kell shook his head, then said, "Perhaps nothing. Perhaps you will regain some measure of control over your own magical abilities. Challings in their natural forms possess considerable power."

"But the spell would still bind me to this human form? Pah! What good is this potion?"

"The potion weakens the bond, and in time there might be a more permanent solution." Masur-Kell returned to his gilded chair, waiting silently.

Davin decided the time had come to barter. "We have only a few gold pieces to pay you for this potion, Master."

He tumbled a few coins onto the floor. They vanished even as he looked at them. He took this to mean the payment was not adequate. More were added, and they, too, vanished. Only when fully three quarters of the gold was dropped from the sack did one single gold bist remain.

"This is all the payment I require," said Masur-Kell as if making a magnanimous gesture.

Davin snorted and tried to hide his contempt. The mage probably told all and sundry that he worked for a single gold coin. *What charity on his part!*

"The potion?" asked Davin.

A tiny vial devoid of contents appeared in the air beside Masur-Kell's head and floated there. Droplets of colored liquids formed like raindrops over the opened bottle, then mixed magically to form a clear potion inside.

"Take one drop of this every day at sunrise and at sunset. Do this for one week," Masur-Kell ordered as a cork popped into existence and wedged tightly into the vial's neck.

The wizard nodded, and the vial floated across the room to Goran, who snared it from the air before it dropped to the floor and shattered.

"You are a mighty mage," said Davin, bowing low, then probed, "About the permanent lifting of this curse . . ."

He upended the large pouch and poured forth the remaining gold. Not a single coin hit the floor; all vanished before joining the bist at his feet. He frowned.

It must have satisfied Masur-Kell, however, because the mage said, "A'bre."

"Money was paid for that?" bellowed Goran. "What type of fool do you take us for? A'bre is a mythical city. It doesn't exist, except in the imaginings of fools."

"Goran!" said Davin, out of the side of his mouth. Louder, to Masur-Kell, he said, "My friend is right. A'bre is well known in legend, but all know it lives only in men's minds."

"It exists," said Masur-Kell simply.

"Where?" asked Davin, but he knew there'd be no answer forthcoming. Their bag of gold had vanished and with it any hope of obtaining more specific information. Still he pressed, "Master, we must know more. How can we . . ."

Davin spoke to a signpost outside the mage's house.

"Yehseen's Jewels! How? I didn't even blink my eyes!" He stared about him, to assure his brain that he indeed had been transported onto the Avenue of Two Moons.

"You pressed the bastard too closely, my friend," Goran said with a shake of his head. "Masur-Kell knows no more about A'bre than either you or I. To have to admit that fact would have made him appear a fool—so he gave us the boot!"

Davin glanced at the empty pouch still in his sweating palm. The full impact of all that had happened hit him. Only Goran had been depressed before. Now Davin shared that bleakness. Goran remained in human form, and they were without a copper.

"A'bre," he said wearily. "He tells us to find the opal gates of a myth."

"For centuries men have hunted it," agreed Goran, "but in every legend there is a seed of truth."

"Not in this one. This is a phantasm luring men to their deaths. Sailors crash upon rocky shores thinking they see A'bre. Hunters starve in forests amid ample game as they seek this myth. Explorers combing all of Raemllyn have never once sighted A'bre. And you tell me there is a grain of hope here?" Davin sucked at his teeth in disgust.

"They weren't looking in the right place," said Goran, as if that settled the matter.

Davin shook his head sadly. Disheartened, he glanced at his friend. The potion might help, he thought. At least this visit—and the fleecing—might not have been in vain. If Goran recovered even a fraction of his magical powers, it would be worth losing so much hard-won gold.

"Let's get back to camp. The Huata prepare the finest of breakfasts I have ever eaten," proclaimed Goran.

"Anyone preparing enough food for your boundless appetite you judge as 'finest,'" said Davin, feeling his momentary darkness brighten.

He had been without money before, a multitude of

times. The Huata would provide food and shelter until they could locate a merchant with money pouches ripe for the plucking.

*Why not search for A'bre?* What else did he have to do? Selene held no chain on him or his heart. And the Huata would soon leave Leticia on their way to some other city-state. Their path and his never coincided for more than one encampment. Why not seek out legendary A'bre?

"Aye, let's be going," Davin said with a smile and started to retrace their path through Leticia. "My stomach has been empty far too long."

"By Nyuria's flames, now there's a sight!" Goran whistled in awe. "Aren't they the fine ones in their carriage?"

Davin turned to see a two-passenger carriage with finely worked gold chasing rattle by. Intricate, interlocking patterns on the sides were done in what appeared to be inlays of diamonds and fine *mardak* stones, easily worth thousands of gold bists apiece. Davin's mouth almost watered at the thought of taking a dagger point to that carriage and liberating a few of those fine gems.

"Can't be real," he said. "No one drives about the countryside in a carriage with real jewels encrusting it."

"Not with the likes of us about." Goran chuckled. "I fear you are right, my friend. The gems can't be real, merely cut glass for show."

But Davin's practiced eye said different. Glass did not play with the sunlight like that. These gems were real!

The carriage halted before the house of Masur-Kell, rocking at the curb a moment before a man in an embroidered jacket opened its door and stepped onto the street.

*Danne* work! Davin caught his breath as his jaw sagged. He had seen such a jacket before. *Danne* work it was, a jacket woven by forest sprites. For a man to possess a jacket of *danne* work left no doubt about the carriage's gems; they were real.

"Think we might make a score with yon merchant?"

"Unless my eye deceives me, I think you already have. Look at him, Davin, he might be your older brother!" Goran's gaze moved back and forth between the merchant and his companion. "The resemblance is uncanny."

Davin paid the Challing little mind. His attention had long left the carriage and the man. He now stared at the blonde woman who stepped from the carriage. Nude, except for halter and loincloth fashioned from strings of golden bists, she walked behind the man in the *danne*-work jacket. About her neck was a slim chain of gold that ran downward to golden manacles about her wrists. From wrists to waist ran another chain, and two more streamed down to cuffs of gold about her ankles. The chains of a slave—but unlike any he had ever seen.

"It can't be," Davin muttered to himself.

"What?"

"The woman . . . it's Lijena!" Davin was certain of it, although the woman's downcast gaze never lifted in his direction.

"Who? Oh, the wench you traded for me." Goran stared at the carriage and shook his head. "Velden never rode in such luxury. And if that is her fate, she's certainly improved her lot in life. Would that Velden had treated me to such exquisite tortures."

"You're right," Davin said with an uncertain shake of his head. "It can't be her."

Yet, as he watched the frosty-haired beauty disappear into the mage's house, he knew that impossible as it seemed, that *was* Lijena! And he knew she would never ride away in the carriage that brought her to Masur-Kell.

*chapter*

# 17

"THE CARRIAGE HAS NOT LEFT THE CITY," said Goran One-Eye as he held out his hands and warmed them over the campfire's flames.

"I know," answered Davin, his gaze lifting to Leticia's walls.

"How is that?" Goran's single eye narrowed. "You and Selene spent the night wrapped in each other's arms. *I* slept near the main gate, watching, waiting, doing my duty as a good thief must."

"You have only one eye; I use many," the young adventurer replied and laughed at his friend's puzzled expression. "I asked Tymon to keep watch for me. His men told me our baubled carriage never left Leticia, neither by the main gate nor by any of the dozen lesser ones."

"You mean my nearly freezing to death in the rain was for naught?" Goran threw up his hands and scowled. "You should have told me you planned this."

"You made no mention of desiring to hide in the rain and watch for something that might not appear, either."

The Challing shrugged and did his best imitation of a scolded puppy, which only widened Davin's grin. The changeling in human form had more moods than any

Raemllyn-bred puppy and used them to maneuver and manipulate. *Life without Goran would be a damned sight easier—also a damned sight less interesting!*

Goran stared at the fire's dancing flames. "Then we are of the same mind? We try for the carriage?"

Davin nodded. The lure of those bright gems was too great. Wealth flaunted so openly was just begging to be filched.

"You realize," Goran said, "there are probably magicks woven about the carriage as thick and as tight as a ram's fleece."

"Aye," Davin replied. Such gems had to be guarded magically. "Any suggestions on how we might avoid the spells?"

"I'm wounded to the quick!" Goran dramatically clutched a hand to his chest. "Am I not a Challing? And cannot Challings find ways around simple ward spells?"

Davin looked at Goran to remind him that Roan-Jafar had effectively removed his Challing abilities when the mage confined him to human form. Instead, Davin just sighed.

"By Yehseen's lecherous staff! You doubt my power?" Goran shook his shaggy head and his eye went wide with mock indignation. "Even as I took the first drop of Masur-Kell's potion, the sun rising above the cursedly clouded horizon, I felt a burning pass throughout my miserable body."

Davin stared at his friend. The dancing light in Goran's single eye raged with the intensity of a smith's forge. He had never seen the witch-fire so ablaze or so wild. He shivered. Mere sparks within that solitary orb often forewarned of uncontrollable magical outbursts of indeterminable power and effect.

"And?" urged Davin, with the hope that Masur-Kell's brew had restored the Challing's ability to shape and control his powers. "What new abilities have you gained as a result?"

"None," answered Goran. "But the burning reminded me of the need I have to eat regularly, and that, in turn, brought to mind the jewels so blatantly displayed."

Davin groaned loudly. Goran's logic eluded him. Surely the gods had cursed the last heir of the House of Anane when they interlocked his life with Goran's. No man born of woman was ever meant to endure such frustration!

"Come. Before we plan this deed minstrels will glorify in rhyme, best we find where our *danne*-work-attired merchant is lodged." Goran stood and slapped Davin's back. "And, of course, where he has placed that lovely carriage."

None too certain of the fiery flames still adance in the Challing's eye, Davin rose and walked with him to Leticia's main gate. Witch-fire or not, he wanted to feel the gems encrusting that wondrous carriage, to feel their weight securely in the pouches dangling from his belt!

This time they walked past the guard when a pedestrian mysteriously found fire ants crawling down his back and within his trousers, which created a distracting ruckus.

No one save Davin noticed a hellish blue flame englobe Goran's eye an instant before the poor pedestrian began to hop and shout and slap at insects biting his flesh. The young freebooter shivered, realizing the ants had not come from any soil in either Upper or Lower Raemllyn, but had been drawn from the ether by his Challing companion.

Within the city the pair moved cautiously, asking few questions but learning much from those they did ask. After all, even those jaded by wealth could not ignore a carriage so magnificently adorned. Their path slowly wended through more expensive areas of Leticia until they ended up on an all too familiar street—the Avenue of Two Moons.

"We might have known," said Davin, all hope gone. "He *was* a sorcerer."

"One sorcerer come to visit another? Hardly," said Goran. He stroked his heavy beard as he studied the deserted street in front of Masur-Kell's abode. "Perhaps Masur-Kell weaves the magicks that protect his wealth."

It made sense, but did nothing to lift Davin's spirits. Goran might scoff at the mage's powers; he was not so foolish!

"We'll watch for a while. Perhaps a stroll around the mage's house will provide the fuel to spark my genius!" Goran started toward the sorcerer's haven, then noticed his friend no longer at his side. "Come, Davin, don't be so downcast. You ought to be like me: cheerful, bright in outlook on life. There's plenty to be gained pilfering from the likes of yon merchant."

"What sort of merchant advertises his wealth so blatantly?" asked Davin as he rejoined the Challing.

That was the fallacy of their assumptions: believing the man in the *danne*-work jacket to be a merchant. Only men of power—true power—could afford to be so open with their riches.

And they had ways of making certain the likes of Davin Anane and Goran One-Eye didn't relieve them of their golden burden!

Goran ignored the comment and kept walking, his gaze searching the mage's house and the wall that surrounded its gardens. Davin followed. They had done this often enough, but never with the idea of breaking into a mage's dwelling.

It was difficult enough finding ways around spells purchased and used as wards by simple merchants. Davin had no idea what type of guardian spell a sorcerer might use to protect himself. He wasn't certain he wanted to find out.

"A view of the interior!" Goran pointed to a pine growing near the wall of Masur-Kell's gardens, glanced around, found no others on the street, and scampered up the trunk.

Davin followed to perch on a limb next to his friend.
From the elevated vantage point they saw down into the
inner courtyard of Masur-Kell's estate. A coachman polished the gems and brightwork on the carriage they so
avidly sought to loot, but Davin's eye was drawn elsewhere.

"See?" he said, pointing to a trio of figures off to one
side of the courtyard.

"Masur-Kell," said Goran, his one eye squinting. "The
man in the *danne*-work jacket. And the female in the
carriage. A concubine, perhaps."

Davin's two eyes were sharper by far than his friend's
single one. He saw gold chains glinting in the morning
sun, chains dangling from the woman's wrists and ankles. He was too far away to hear the conversation, but
the gist of it was obvious: the woman was being sold as
a slave.

The Jyotian arms wrapped around the limb to catch
himself before he tumbled head over heels to the cob-
blestones below. "Yehseen!"

The gold-bound woman turned and squarely faced in
his direction. The light was perfect; there were no ob-
structions to his vision.

It was Lijena!

"She's in chains. Lijena's in chains!" He gave voice
to his startled thoughts. He had prayed his eyes had
deceived him yesterday. Now he could no longer deny
the truth.

"Eh?" Goran eyed his human friend. "You mean that
wench actually *is* the one you traded for me? Raemllyn
is an even smaller world than I thought. Velden must
have sold her to the slaver."

"We can't allow her to be sold—not again—and not
to Masur-Kell!"

"Why not?" asked Goran. "We may not like the in-
stitution, but the majority of you humans do or slavery
would not be tolerated. Look at yon peacock and tell me

if he isn't making a fine living off it. He's a merchant, all right. A merchant in human flesh."

Davin didn't hear the logic in the Challing's words. His attention focused on Lijena and her chains. "I am the one responsible for her plight. Without me, she wouldn't be down there."

He shivered at the thought of Lijena forced to share the mage's bed. The stories—rumors—myths—surrounding sorcerers usually told of their perversions, their bizarre tastes, their total scorn of human values and life. They were mortal, but their magicks lifted them above worldly concerns and moral judgments.

"If you hadn't come along, if I hadn't been in the Brass Cock's gambling parlors, Velden would have found someone else stupid enough and cunning enough to snatch her away from her uncle." There was a finality in Goran's voice, and he turned back to the valuables in and on the carriage.

"You're right," Davin said in total agreement—in words, if not in tone. "The sensible thing is to leave her to her fate."

It was that tone which snapped Goran's head around. The Challing glared at his friend, eye aglint with crazy fire.

"Say that again."

Davin drew a heavy breath. "Lijena's destiny is hers alone. We shouldn't get involved."

"Damn it! Nyuria take your arse, Davin Anane!" Goran growled. "How dare you even *think* of rescuing that wench! It's a fool's errand! A *fool's errand!*"

"I know." Davin's eyes shifted back to the courtyard.

"Then, by all the Gods, say it as if you mean it. That tone speaks volumes more than your words. You're going to try to rescue her, aren't you? And you expect me to help you. Isn't that it? Isn't it?" Goran growled on.

"Yes."

He couldn't walk away and leave Lijena, not again.

Before, saving Goran from Velden's tortures had been paramount, but now he could correct the part he had unknowingly played in her misfortunes.

"No, damn you, Davin. No! A thief's life is twisted enough without mock gallantry muddling things!"

"After we get her free, we'll return her to her uncle in Harn."

"Tadzi? Are you completely daft, man! He's the leader of the Thieves' Guild. He'll have our heads on pikes for kidnapping his niece in the first place!"

"We leave Lijena at his gate. There's nothing that says we have to hold her hand all the way to the door."

"Can't you be satisfied with Selene? Now, there's a fine wench. A bit on the skinny side for my tastes, but an active one." Goran stared, total incomprehension in his one eye. "It's madness! Mind what I say, Davin, this Lijena will only cause you worlds of trouble! She has the look..."

Davin's thoughts were elsewhere. He had wronged her. Returning Lijena to Harn and Tadzi hardly righted the damage wrought, but it might assuage his own conscience.

"We'll discuss our plans back at camp. I must talk with Tymon," Davin said as he crawled back to the pine's trunk and carefully picked his way downward.

Goran, still grumbling and cursing, followed.

## chapter

# *18*

"YOU NEED TRANSPORT away from the city," Tymon said, his gaze coolly moving between Davin and Goran. "That will be expensive. Leticia's law bringers are a joke, but the king's soldiers might find this interesting enough to come after us. Zarek Yannis does not like the Huata; he says we are disruptive."

"That's about all he's got right since he stole the throne," Goran growled under his breath.

Tymon ignored the red-haired giant and cleared his throat. "This kidnapping—"

"An un-kidnapping," Davin corrected. "A rescue, if you prefer."

"This kidnapping," the Huata leader went on, as if he hadn't heard Davin's protest, "will bring out the wolves. They'll be yipping and nipping at our heels before we're out of camp."

"Do you know this one in the fine carriage?" asked Goran. "I find it difficult to believe one so laden with jewels is unknown to *me*."

"From your description, that can be only the Prince of Slavers himself, Nelek Kahl." Tymon glanced out the window of his wagon. Apprehension was in his dark eyes.

"Kahl? Aye, of him I have heard. And none of it has been good." Goran's sour expression grew darker.

"What connection does he have with Velden?" asked Davin. "They seem worlds distant. Velden lives in the Bistonian sewers. By Black Qar, I guarantee Kahl does not live there also."

"The connection?" Tymon shrugged. "Who can say?"

"We rescue Lijena," said Davin, getting back to the issue most interesting to him. "We rescue her, get to your wagons, and you will take us to Harn? For what price?"

"High. I have pointed out the problems. We are sure to be searched," Tymon answered.

"You'd hardly want to pull all the contraband you are currently smuggling and replace it with a wench not wanting rescue . . . not without a price . . . a *high* price," Goran grumbled.

"She'll want to be rescued, count on it," said Davin. "But Goran is right about unloading all you are smuggling. That might become a bit sticky."

"Smugglers? Us? You confuse us with others. We are simple entertainers, only traveling to—"

"Spout your lies elsewhere. We all know you smuggle select items. Where did the duty-free *phorra* brandy come from?" Goran interrupted.

"There are a *few* items I carry for personal use which, from time to time, I decide to sell. Only to select friends, mind you," Tymon said with a broad smile.

"How much to aid us?" Davin pressed.

"Five hundred gold pieces," Tymon replied without batting an eye.

"Steep, but fair," said Davin.

"Where are we going to get that much?" asked Goran.

Davin shot him a warning look, trying to stop him from commenting further. Such things were never talked about in the presence of others.

The look was lost on the Challing, who said, "Masur-

Kell took all our gold for the potion."

"You're paupers?" asked Tymon, forehead furrowing. "You can't pay the fare in advance?"

"We'll pay seven hundred when we return with the girl," Davin hastened to assure the Huata leader. "I'm certain we can get that much from the carriage, and still have something left over."

"This is riskier . . . for me," Tymon answered slowly. "I have nothing and still must flee, if you fail."

"Tymon," said Goran. "We will not fail."

Davin's eyes widened in surprise. This was the first hint he had that Goran actually would help him—moreover, that he thought they would be successful.

"Aye," Tymon answered with a nod. "The price is worth the risk. Now to the details of our venture."

Those details took a full three hours to plan, time enough for Goran to haggle Tymon down to six hundred gold pieces for the Huata's part in the rescue. When hands were shaken all around, Tymon departed to prepare for the evening.

Once outside the wagon, Davin restlessly paced through the crowd that wandered the Huata camp in search of glimpses of the future and feminine beauty. All the while his gaze kept returning to Leticia and its high, cold wall of granite. Goran One-Eye after an hour grew bored of the pacing and found a wagon, crawled under it, and soon snored loudly.


"The potion sets me afire," Goran complained. "I cannot tell if it affects me well or ill." He rubbed his belly and stuck out his tongue, eyes rolling down to observe its color.

"If it works as Masur-Kell promised, you ought to feel the effects soon enough. Now what do you see?" Davin softly called to his friend, who once more perched on the pine limb that overlooked Masur-Kell's gardens.

"A single light in a room off from the main entrance.

But there's bad news, my friend." Goran looked down and shook his head. "Very bad news."

Visions of a legion of demons patroling the interior came instantly into Davin's mind. He groaned and leaned heavily against the tree. "Tell me. Don't hold back."

"It's worse than you might think," Goran continued. "The carriage is gone."

"What!"

"Nowhere to be seen. Kahl might be out and about Leticia, but this town probably interests him as much as a sailor wants to see more salt water. I don't think he will be back, if you want my best guess." Goran paused, then added, "There's one last bit of bad news."

"Tell it." After that, Davin was prepared to slink back to camp and forget the whole matter.

"I see that Lijena wench. She's in the room with the light."

"That's not so bad. That's good news!" Davin's mind raced. "Masur-Kell has a goodly amount of gold on hand. He has all we gave him. We might be able to pick up a few trinkets worth Tymon's fee. We get Lijena and what we can carry. That's good news, Goran. What do you find bad about it?"

"Your damned enthusiasm. What can possibly be sensible about tackling a sorcerer to kidnap one of his new toys and rob him blind in the process? Madness."

Goran dropped down from the tree and brushed off his hands on the knees of his breeches.

"How do we get in? Over the wall?" Davin eyed the twelve-foot barrier of stone.

"Not a chance. The mage must realize that is the obvious way to break in. I suggest we simply walk in the front door and see what happens." Goran tilted his head toward the entrance to the house.

"Why not?" Davin had no better scheme, and this was daring enough to give them a measure of surprise. In those moments he could effect Lijena's rescue—for he thought of it as such—and do a bit of looting on the side. With their quickness of wit and foot, they'd be out and away before the sorcerer even realized they had intruded.

At least it sounded good as he mentally rehearsed the rescue.

The runes burned with a deathly pale green light as they stood beside the portal leading into the wizard's home. They looked at each other, then entered.

"See?" said Goran. "Even his protective fog has been put to sleep for the night."

All around them lay only simple flagstone paving. The tunnel of fog they had experienced on their first visit had vanished. This appeared to be no more than the fine home of a prosperous merchant.

Davin walked quickly toward the window illuminated by the yellow light. The silhouette moving from side to side was definitely Lijena's. His heart quickened, then almost stopped in mid-beat when a cracked, ancient voice called to him.

"You, boy. What you doin' in here? This is a private place. Leave and I won't give you the thrashin' you so richly deserve."

Davin turned. A crippled old man, barely able to walk even with the aid of the cane he leaned heavily on, stood facing him. Was this a sample of the guards Masur-Kell sent to protect his grounds? If the old man was lucky, a strong gust of wind wouldn't come up and topple him over like a dried leaf.

"Good sir, evening," greeted Davin. "I come only to speak with the lady in yon room."

"Begone!" shouted the old man.

Davin took another step in the man's direction, intent on silencing him before he awoke the magicks Masur-Kell surely held in reserve.

"I said to leave, you and your Challing thief friend," the old one continued. "Begone with you. Now!"

Davin scowled. How had this nearsighted old man recognized Goran as a Challing? Davin gripped a feeble arm and spun the old man about. "Be quiet, old man, and we will be on our way before you know it."

The man struggled weakly, then swung his cane and rapped Davin smartly on the shin. Pain lanced up the adventurer's leg, but he hung on.

"Let me go, you young ruffian!" the old father wheezed.

The cane jerked up and lashed down again, popping painfully against Davin's leg.

"Qar's demons!" the Jyotian yowled as fire like a white-hot brand shot through muscle to bone. He grasped the old servant by the arms and shook, intent on instilling some sense in the withered man's skull.

"Davin, don't," said Goran in a voice unnaturally low and somber. "He is not—"

"You're right. He's not going to get away with this." Davin shook harder—and found it harder to do.

A scrawny arm beneath his fingers firmed—like a column of steel. The old one's crablike posture straightened.

Something dark and menacing wiggled at the back of Davin's brain: *magic!*

Davin swung his fist at the old man as hard as he could. Straight and true fell that hammer of flesh and bone. It collided with a wall of unyielding brick. Davin howled, unable to confine the pain as he grasped the throbbing, bruised knuckles of his right hand.

The old man smiled—and grew in stature, in power. His cane whistled through the air to land with a meaty thunk on Davin's arm. The Jyotian's entire left side burned as though a flaming lance had skewered his length, then it went numb.

The cane jerked high in the air, ready to deliver its burning anguish anew. Davin didn't wait for the blow. He lashed out with his left leg, found the soft, vulnerable backside of the old one's right knee, and sent him tumbling to the ground.

In the next heartbeat, the Jyotian sat astride his ancient adversary's chest with fingers pressed about his windpipe. Eyes, confused and frail, fluttered open and stared helplessly up at the younger man.

Davin hesitated, holding back, queasy at the prospect of meting out death to one so old. That was his mistake. The manservant's hands encircled his wrists, clamped down, and lifted . . . easily.

"Davin, it's a construct of some sort. Magical. I . . . I sense it. My powers return, and I can sense it. But what *is* this creature?" Goran puzzled.

While Challing idly pondered the magicks aplay, the less than frail old man rolled to the side, pinned his young opponent to the ground, and perched atop Davin's chest. As the Jyotian struggled to free himself, the manservant struck, his fist slamming into the side of the freebooter's head.

Goran called out, "Stop resisting! He feeds off your own strength! Don't fight him."

Davin went limp, and barely dodged a bony fist that descended straight at his nose. He heard a whistle and jerked his head in the opposite direction, just avoiding that damnable cane and the abrupt transformation of his face to bloody jelly.

"Help me!" Davin called as he twisted away from the deadly cane once more. "If I just lie here, he'll ki— . . . Noooooooooo!"

His words were cut short as the ancient man heaved to his feet, bent, scooped the would-be thief from the ground, and hurled him through the air. Halfway across the courtyard, Davin struck the ground in a tumble that ended when he thudded solidly into the brick wall.

Head aspin and eyes blurred, Davin saw the crippled old man turn his attention to Goran. He blinked and swallowed. The old one leaped forward, grasped the

Challing by shirt collar and belt, then tossed him toward the opposite wall.

"Don't resist him," Davin muttered. "Sound advice to give but not to take, eh, Goran?"

Goran hit the ground growling and cursing the names of Raemllyn's Gods. He rolled to his feet with a speed that belied his tremendous size. With a bearlike shake of his shaggy red-maned head, the Challing lifted his gaze to the old man, who stalked forward.

Eye to eye now, they faced each other. In spite of his spinning vision, Davin could see the manservant growing visibly in both size and power. Masur-Kell's servant lifted his cane and swung it in a two-handed grip straight for Goran's left elbow.

The Challing's single eye blazed. Davin threw up his hands to protect his eyes. From between his fingers, he saw a solid column of scintillant red energy surround Goran. The cane hit the magical wall and simply . . . vanished. Davin swallowed again, hard.

Goran reached out to touch the old man, who recoiled for the first time. Too late! The red energy blanketed the Challing like a new skin, glowing and dancing in eye-confusing patterns. Goran's hand grasped his shoulder and firmly clamped there.

The old man's mouth flew wide, lips writhing in anguish, but there was no scream, only horrifying silence. Davin stared on, unable to believe his eyes. The manservant shrank. In an instant he stood as bent and crippled as when Davin first saw him, then he was a mere child . . . an infant . . . then . . .

Nothing. Masur-Kell's servant was, then he wasn't!

"Goran," said Davin, gasping for air. "What . . . how . . . ?"

"I don't know." The Challing in giant's body turned to his friend, shook his head, and grinned sheepishly. "The power came upon me. The burning, just as I feel when I take the potion, came upon me, and I just did what I had to. But how?"

Davin pushed to his feet and nervously looked about. He didn't doubt Goran's sudden preternatural strength had not missed the attention of the mage within the house. "We've work to do. Let's be quick about it!"

"Look!" The Challing turned and brushed his hand against the house's wall. A circular hole, large enough to accommodate a man or a changeling, appeared in the brick. Goran beamed. "I just leaned against the wall."

Davin wasn't listening. Inside, he saw Lijena struggling to open the room's sole door. Her eyes were wide and brimming with panic. Realizing the futility of her effort, she turned and stared in horror as Goran simply burned a new and wider hole in the wall.

"Don't," she pleaded. "Don't harm me. Not like this. Not with the burning again."

"Lijena," called Davin, carefully skirting his red-enveloped friend as he stepped into the room, "I've come for you."

Lijena stared at him, her face clouded. Then the befuddlement vanished, replaced by hate and anger. She lifted hands contorted into taloned weapons.

"Davin Anane! I have longed to see you again. To kill you!"

"Still the same woman charmer of old, eh?" Goran laughed.

"Wait, Lijena. Let me explain. Goran and I have come to take you back to Harn." Davin ducked beneath a raking hand meant to rob him of his eyes.

"Harn?" She paused, looking skeptical.

"I'll explain later. First we've got to get away from here. Surely you prefer your uncle's palace to being a slave here." Davin talked fast, ready to lunge away from the long fingernails she held before her.

Lijena's guard cautiously lowered. She nodded and held out her golden chains to be severed.

Goran dropped to a knee and touched the leg chains first. They crumbled away, transformed to a fine glittering dust. With chest proudly expanded, he stood and tapped a finger atop those on her wrists. Nothing happened. Chains and manacles remained firm and golden.

Goran held out his hand and shook his head. He no longer glowed dangerous and red.

"Lost it. But why? The feel is still the same."

"Lost it? How? Never mind. Come on!" Davin urged, grabbing Lijena by the hand and pulling her after him.

As he reached the sundered wall, he heard the clankings of chains and bars being removed from the door to the room. Davin spun to see the door open.

Masur-Kell stood at the threshold, a scowl shadowing his face. He lifted one hand, finger pointed at Davin. The air around the tip of the finger began to glow and crackle as the mage's magicks came to life.

Davin Anane prepared to die.

# *chapter* 19

THE AIR CRACKLED as sparks flew from Masur-Kell's finger to career in orbit about his extended hand and arm. Even across the room Davin Anane felt the intense heat; beads of sweat prickled his forehead. His eyes darted from side to side, seeking an avenue of escape. There was none.

Power, a hideous power, illuminated Masur-Kell's gloating grin of triumph. "Now you shall pay for violating my sanctuary—pay with your life!"

The wizard's hand flew wide, palm exposed and fingers splayed. Thunder, booming like a thousand storms, shattered the very fabric of the air. Lightning, an actinic bolt of blue-white, exploded from his palm in a sizzling ball of expanding energy.

Not a defiant curse spat into Black Qar's face but a shocked whimper pushed from Davin's lips in shock that, after all the dangers he had faced and escaped, often by a hair breadth, his life would end here, not by the clean bite of honed steel, but by the mere wave of a mage's hand. A simple fireball spell would leave him a smoldering ember on the floor. He steeled himself for the devouring inferno.

It never came!

Rather, Davin saw the ball of flaming death erupt toward him—and stop an inch from the end of his nose.

Beside him, Lijena's terrified scream was transformed into a bewildered gasped "Oh!"

Davin blinked the sting of sweat from his eyes, surprised he still had eyes to blink. The hissing ball of certain death just hovered in the air before his face.

"Qar has no need of your soul, my friend." Goran's voice rolled in a chorus of belly laughs. "At least, not this day."

One nervous glance at the Challing provided an answer to his timely, though unexpected, salvation. Witch-fire danced wildly within Goran's single eye; his power waxed anew. The crimson glow had returned to his body, more intense, almost blurring the features of his face in its fiery glare.

"No!" raged Masur-Kell. "I will not tolerate this! It can't be. I won't—"

Goran's laughter roared. *"Can't be?* Come, come, are you a mage or merely a second-rate trickster? It was your potion, wasn't it? Shall I demonstrate my renewed ability? Here, catch!"

The Challing didn't wait for an answer. He snapped his fingers and pointed at the wide-eyed wizard. Like an obedient performing dog jumping through a hoop, the fireball did a little spinning hop and shot across the room toward Masur-Kell.

The sorcerer's hands flew up, thin, pale fingers weaving a panicked dance. The burning bolt struck, flames leaping forth to swallow their creator in a fiery column.

In a blink of an eye, the consuming inferno died. It left no smoldering ember on the floor. Nor had it even touched the mage, who stood, his body sheathed in glowing blue light, glaring at the Challing.

Goran didn't give his spell-conjuring opponent a chance for a second attack. He opened his extended hand and gave a twist of the wrist. A shaft of red light lanced across the room.

Masur-Kell flicked his right hand ceilingward. The crimson shaft shot up; a hole the width of a man opened in the roof to expose the night's stars. Simultaneously the wizard's left hand pointed fore and little finger at Goran. A blue bolt shot forth, followed by a second bolt from his descending right hand.

Deftly Goran deflected the first and sent it reeling back on its creator. He wasn't quick enough for the second. Blue energy exploded in his face. His crimson coat of magic flickered and darkened to a writhing purple. The Challing stumbled, swayed, and dropped to a knee.

Before Davin's brain accepted the shock of seeing his friend tumble, Goran's shield flared crimson again. Both the Challing's arms jerked up, and a tidal wave of fire rolled across the room.

"Hindered by clumsy flesh and blood I may be," Goran shouted in his booming voice, "but you underestimate me, Masur-Kell. You deal not with a puny human but with a Challing!"

Masur-Kell's arms and hands waved and danced. Then his eyes went wide. The churning wave of fire rolled on, unimpeded by his parry spell, to once more consume him in a flesh-searing column of fire.

"Run!" Goran's head jerked around to Davin and Lijena. "My power can't defeat—only contain! Run! Get out of here!"

"I can't leave you here!" Davin protested, uncertain what he could do to sway the scales in favor of his friend. However, Lijena could escape. She need not die at Masur-Kell's hand. Davin turned to her, waving his arm to the round exit Goran had opened in the wall. "Run! There are Huata waiting outside the main gate! They'll take you to Harn. Run!"

She did—straight to Davin's side. Her hands grasped his longsword and wrenched it from its sheath in one fluid motion. Before the Jyotian comprehended what had happened, Lijena ran toward the dying flicker of crimson flames still covering the unharmed mage. She lashed out, two hands tightly about the sword, and full weight behind a blow aimed directly at Masur-Kell's skull.

Simultaneously Goran unleashed yet another crimson shaft.

Masur-Kell's hands waved to brush aside the new assault from the Challing. It was a mistake. His eyes flew wide as he caught a glint of steel to his side. Magic was one thing, the physical reality of tempered steel was another. The mage was unprepared for the latter.

The crunch of metal meeting bone filled the room, drowning out even the rising hiss of the spell Masur-Kell conjured. The mage dropped face down on the floor.

A fraction of a second later, Lijena's knees buckled, and she crumpled to the floor beside the wizard.

"Unconscious," Davin announced as he knelt and placed two fingers atop her jugular.

"And this one. His shield spell deflected the blade's edge. He took a full blow from the flat. He's bleeding a bit, there'll be a nasty bump, but he'll live."

Davin glanced to see Goran kneeling beside Masur-Kell. Gone were the crimson glow and the witch-fire. His face was pale and haggard, and he staggered as he stood.

"Ohhhhhhhh," Lijena murmured, her eyes fluttering open.

Davin helped her sit, then retrieved his blade and sheathed it. "I know not what made you act, but we live because of your bravery."

"Huh?" Lijena's expression was one of befuddlement.

"Masur-Kell," Davin said, pointing to the mage. "You did that."

"I *killed* him?" Lijena's face contorted strangely, then abruptly relaxed, and she sighed.

"He's no—" Davin began.

"Aye, he's dead. Killed clean and true!" Goran's voice drowned his companion's sentence. The Challing looked at Davin and shook his head, signaling him to remain silent.

Davin raised a questioning eyebrow, but did not press the matter. Instead he helped Lijena to her feet and said, "We tarry here too long. Surely others saw the magic flames and have summoned the city guard."

"Nay," said Goran and firmly shook his head. "Why come this far only to turn and run like a craven? There is treasure aplenty to be had here."

Davin glanced at the unconscious sorcerer. Masur-Kell was only a man, no matter what magicks he used. A blow to the head such as he'd just received would keep him far distant from the world for an hour or more. And hadn't they risked all to come this far? What were another few minutes? City guards would not hasten to the home of a mage. No man with a healthy respect for his own life hastened to where magicks might linger.

Davin looked at Goran, grinned, and nodded his approval. "Get to it, friend."

"You . . . you're going to rob him, too?" Lijena stared at the two in open-mouthed disbelief. "Are you insane?"

"Must be," growled Goran, "to come here like this to rescue an ingrate like you. Here, carry this. You've good arms." The giant looked at her, then winked. "And your legs are nice, too, even if they are a bit scrawny."

Lijena accepted a small gold box Goran scooped from a table set near a wall and shoved into her arms. And while she stared on, still not believing what she saw, the Challing and Davin moved like wraiths throughout the estate, flitting lightly, quietly, taking only the items most easily carried and fenced.

"Here, Davin, here is his treasure trove." The Challing opened a large, unadorned wooden box to reveal thousands of gold bists.

"Too heavy to carry it all," Davin said as he stuffed handfuls of coins into his pockets and pouches.

"Why rob him of that?" She pointed to the gold. "My uncle will reward you handsomely for my return."

"Aye, that he will," said Goran. "A knife in the gut— if we're lucky."

"He doesn't even know that Davin Anane of Jyotis was the one who kidnapped me in the first place," she said, her tone carrying the chill of winter's northern wind.

Davin started to explain the circumstances surrounding her abduction, but one glance at the ice in Lijena's eyes told him the tale would fall on deaf ears. Tadzi might forgive and possibly forget, but Lijena would do neither. She would go with Davin now because he was her only chance to escape Leticia and return to her family. But were the circumstances different, it would be his hide she'd be wanting—sliced from his body while he still lived.

"I can't carry another coin, even if it were made of tin." Goran bulged everywhere, looking as if he had gone on a month-long eating binge.

The "fat" was truly the fat of the land. He had recovered not only the gold paid to Masur-Kell for the potion and the improbable advice to seek out the mythical city of A'bre, but interest on it a hundred times over.

"Thieves," complained Lijena, "you're nothing but thieves!"

"Aye! Remember us when you get back to Harn. You're not likely to meet such a pair of thieves in all of Raemllyn," Goran bragged without shame.

Davin wished his overly enthusiastic friend hadn't said that. Although she said nothing, Lijena's eyes narrowed to mere slits. He had no doubt that she would never forget either of their names. And once she told her tale to Lord Tadzi and her father, they wouldn't either. He would have to give both Harn and Bistonia wide berth for several years.

Still without comment, Lijena followed the two from the mage's house, clutching the gold box in her chained and manacled hands as if her life depended on it.

"Hurry," urged Goran, pointing toward the center of the walled city. "I hear the pad of boots and the clank of armor."

Davin heard, too—guards certainly come to investigate the fiery display that had burned within the mage's home but minutes before. Grabbing Lijena's wrist, he hastened down the Avenue of Two Moons in the opposite direction, toward the city's main gate.

"The gates are never opened before dawn. We can't stay inside the city till then," Lijena protested as she stumbled along behind her kidnapper-rescuer.

"We'll deal with the gates when we get to them," Davin answered and pulled her into an alley on the right.

"Sneak thieves!" She snorted in disgust.

"Aye! But *good* sneak thieves." Goran chuckled as he waddled-ran a step behind her.

Lijena fell silent. Her eyes shifted about, seeking an escape route of her own. She had not forgotten who was responsible for her being taken to Velden and ultimately sold into slavery to Masur-Kell. Her lovely aquamarine eyes burned with hate when they turned toward Davin Anane's back. *If only I had a dagger to thrust into this swine's spine!*

But she had no dagger, nor did she note a route of easy escape. So she ran with Davin before her and his strange one-eyed companion behind.

Their path veered sharply as they approached Leticia's main gates, winding down lightless alleys until they stood in the shadow of Leticia's massive wall of granite three streets from the gates—and hidden from the watchful eyes of soldiers standing guard there. Davin peered toward the top of the wall and whistled. A moment later three ropes dropped down from out of the night.

"The Huata have little respect for city gates," Davin chuckled as he securely tied one of the ropes about Lijena's waist. "Hold tight."

He gave the rope a tug. In the next instant she was hauled upward.

A bundle of sleeping furs struck Davin full in the face. He staggered back and stared at Selene in disbelief. "What the—"

"You've paid good gold for us to care for her, and that's exactly what I intend to do! Find yourself another bed for the night! She sleeps in here with me. She is a *fine lady* and *needs* her rest!" Selene's voice seeped with sarcasm as she slammed the wagon's door in Davin's face.

"You've got such a way with women, Davin." Goran laughed at the confusion on his friend's face. "When in the house of a beautiful woman, only a fool looks at anyone but his hostess."

"What?"

"You paid too much attention to Lijena when you brought her into camp. Selene noticed. She also saw your interest was more than just passing." Goran shook his shaggy head. "You're lucky Selene didn't slit your throat. Huata women are a jealous lot. Did I tell you that it was a Huata wench who took my eye? We had been lovers for several months when my eyes—I had both then— strayed to a tender, young thing of . . ."

Davin sucked at his teeth with disgust and waved his friend to silence. "Come, let's find a soft clump of grass on which to spend the night. We must be ready to move at dawn."

"I'd feel better leaving now," said Goran. "Masur-Kell is not going to be gentle when he wakes! But since we have to spend the night here, I have made other arrangements. Sweet Kayta's bed is far warmer than the ground, and her company more appealing."

Goran started away, but Davin halted him. "Why did you silence me in the mage's house? Why did you want Lijena to think she had killed Masur-Kell?"

"Could you not tell?" Goran replied. "She had no idea that she had struck the old bastard. Someone was manipulating her, whether by spell or hypnotism I know not. She had been given a task . . . to kill the wizard. We had no time to deal with a geas-ridden woman. Better to let her believe the task done."

"Spell . . . to kill Masur-Kell?" Davin stared at his

friend, uncertain he understood. "But why? And who? Nelek Kahl?"

Goran shrugged. "Perhaps. Or Velden? Who cares? The matter is no concern of ours. You have gallantly rescued the wench and may sleep easier. And I have Kayta waiting so that I may sleep easier. In the morn, Davin."

With that, Goran turned and walked to a nearby wagon, leaving Davin standing alone in the night. Cursing to himself, he found a dry, if not soft, spot near the trunk of a nearby *morda* tree. He spread the furs on the ground and slid between them. Within minutes he drifted off to sleep, trying not to think about Selene or the beautiful daughter of Bistonia asleep in her wagon—and failing miserably.

Lijena did not rest, but lay with eyes wide open. She had only feigned sleep to avoid useless conversation with the Huata woman, Selene. Thoughts of blood and murder occupied her mind now. Davin Anane stood at the center of those thoughts. He was the source of all her suffering, and for that he would pay. She had promised herself that.

Lijena rolled to her side and peered down at Selene's recumbent form lying bundled on the floor of the wagon. The slow rise and fall of the Huata woman's breasts confirmed that she truly slept. With infinite caution, Lijena rose and stepped over Selene, moving to an opened chest filled with women's clothing.

The tattered garb of a slave was not suited to the task she had in mind. Lijena selected carefully from Selene's wardrobe, choosing functional clothing. If she were to kill Davin Anane, she didn't want to become entangled in flowing trains at the wrong moment.

A weapon proved more difficult because Selene slept with it near at hand. Necessity turned Lijena into a master thief. She successfully slipped the dagger from under Selene's fingers. Triumphant, she rose and held the naked blade in her hand, her eyes widening at the sleek, shining razor length.

"With this I shall rob you of your life, Davin Anane, even as you have robbed me of my dignity and all I hold dear in the world," she whispered her vow of vengeance.

Slipping from the wagon undetected was another matter. Selene's feet rested against the door. The slightest movement would wake the sleeping Huata woman.

She glanced around and smiled. Another route from the wagon existed. Lijena opened a small window and judged it just large enough to accommodate her slender body. Hands on each side of the frame, she climbed through feet first and dropped to the ground outside.

With her came the small golden box that rested on the windowsill, the same container that she had carried from Masur-Kell's house at Goran One-Eye's demand. Her right hand snaked out to catch the box before it hit the ground—a task she managed, only to have its lid fly open and empty a fine layer of white powder down the front of her stolen blouse.

Carefully snapping the lid back, she quietly replaced the box on the window ledge, then dusted the powder from the blouse. The action—and a slight night breeze— billowed the powder in a cloud. Jasmine incense invaded her nostrils.

Lijena flinched away and held back a sneeze that would surely have awakened Selene. Turning away from the breeze, she brushed the remaining incense from her clothing. Then her attention moved back to Davin Anane.

*Lift the blade . . . plunge . . . quick and hard!* She rehearsed the act over and over in her mind. But first she had to find the horses. She'd need a mount for her flight back to Bistonia. After all, Davin Anane wasn't the only one with whom she had a score to settle.

Amrik Tohon had sold her to the slaver Nelek Kahl. She would deal with Amrik . . . after she was through with the Jyotian pig.

Lijena found the horses behind the wagons. A smile uplifted the corners of her mouth; there among the shaggy Huata stock stood a sleek dapple-gray—her Orria. She quickly cut the mare from the herd and saddled and bridled her. Leaving Orria safely tethered where she could reach her quickly, Lijena went in search of her victim.

The dagger grew heavy in her hand as she crept among the Huata wagons, but her rage mounted. By the time she found Davin in his sleeping furs beneath the *morda,* her need for revenge had become paramount.

—Your lover— came a half-heard whisper.

Lijena spun and lashed out with the dagger. It found only empty air.

She stifled a surprised gasp. No one stirred, not even Davin Anane. She shook her head; her weariness and the late hour toyed with her mind and ears. Lijena turned back to Davin, to measure the distance, to find his heart for the first thrust.

—You want him. You love him. Love him. Love him . . .

Lijena blinked and stared down at the man who had sold her into Velden's cruel hands. *He must die. Die for* . . . Her resolve weakened, her purpose fogged in a misty cloud. How could she so wantonly slay this peacefully sleeping man?

—Go to him. Join him in the furs. Love him. Experience his body next to yours, naked and passionate.

Lijena's will evaporated. The dagger slipped from her nerveless fingers and stuck point down in the ground beside Davin's head. The Jyotian stirred, and his eyes opened.

"Davin," Lijena said listlessly. It was as if she moved in a world suddenly turned viscid. Each movement came as an effort. And the voice whispered seductively to her.

—Love him. He is yours to love. Join him!

"Lijena?" Davin asked, still half-asleep.

"Davin," she said in a monotone. "I want to join you. Join you."

Davin blinked awake, totally confused as she knelt at his side and pressed her lips to his. There had been murder in Lijena's eyes when he left her in Selene's wagon, but now? As her hands began probing, his puzzlement turned to delight. His own hands responded in kind, quickly ridding her of the stolen clothing, then drawing her into the warmth of the sleeping furs.

—You love him.

"I love you, Davin." She repeated the voice's words in an emotionless tone.

Davin didn't question. This is what he had yearned for since first seeing her in the Harnish forest.

—He is brave. Tell him and then talk no more. You know how to keep him silent. Do it all!

"You're brave," she said in response to the mysterious prompting.

Her hands urged him on, and he came to her, his body matching her undulating rhythm, his palms and fingertips speaking works never meant for mere vocal cords. She sighed softly, then her lips and soothing hands were there, taunting, exploring, teasing.

Lijena's body responded with enthusiasm, but her mind was curiously detached. She had been intent on . . . she couldn't remember why she had come to this man of Jyotis. Her concentration focused on the voice within her skull . . .

The voice that spoke now.

—The dagger. Beside you. Take it. Then, when his pleasure peaks—strike!

Davin offered no objection when she rolled him to his back and straddled his waist. He closed his eyes and bathed in the luxurious feel of her.

He didn't see the emotionless mask that shadowed Lijena's face as she reached for the dagger, lifted it high, and thrust for his bared chest.

# chapter
## 20

—KILL! KILL HIM NOW! NOW!

The voice screamed within Lijena's skull, and for Lijena there was no other choice.

The dagger fell, pale light from Raemllyn's two moons glinting along its slender blade as it plunged toward the unsuspecting Davin Anane's chest.

An awkward twist, an unnatural jerk in Lijena's rhythmic undulation brought a sleepy flutter to the Jyotian's eyes—eyes that went round when they but glimpsed the point that arced downward. Davin's hands abandoned the silken warmth of Lijena's flesh and jerked out—too late to stop the deadly descent.

But the dagger did stop: a scant fraction of an inch from his heaving chest.

The point trembled, shook, strained to drive down and pierce his trip-hammering heart. Try as she did, driven as she was by the screaming voice commanding her, Lijena could not break the two hands firmly encircling her wrists: slender, cool hands that belonged to Selene.

Davin's fingers joined the Huata woman's, clamping about Lijena's forearms. Together they tugged and pushed upward.

—Bitch! You have failed! But ere I am through with this frail form, you will serve me again . . . and again.

The voice and the horrid laughter that followed echoed in Lijena's head, then abruptly dissipated.

Her body went flaccid. The hands wrenching at her arms jerked them high, sending the dagger flying from limp fingers into the night's blackness. The hands jerked and shoved, and she tumbled to her side, rolling on the cold ground.

"A fine one you are," Selene spat at Davin. "I should have let her cut out your heart! But I wanted to save that pleasure for myself!"

Selene aimed a well-placed kick that landed with a meaty thud in the Jyotian's side. "Is Selene's passion so cool that it takes *two* women to ease your tension?"

"What in Yehseen's holy—oow!" Davin tried to roll away from Selene's foot and failed. "Damn it, Selene! Stop! My ribs are—"

Her foot lashed out again and found its mark. "It relieves tension. *My* tension! I fall asleep for a moment and find you and this . . . you two-timing whoreson!"

"Wait! I was—" he began—and was cut short by another rib-jarring kick.

"I saw the hate in her eyes for you when you brought her to camp. I feared she would slit your gullet. So when I woke and found her missing . . . Worry, ha! The two of you screwing like *sarthas* in rut! And her about to gut you like the pig you are! What's wrong? Did she find the clumsy gropings Jyotians call lovemaking too coarse for her refined Bistonian tastes?"

Davin didn't even try to avoid Selene's foot this time. He merely groaned as it slammed into his ribs, then began to explain, carefully sidestepping the truth. "Selene, my flower, I thought it was you! I was in a sound sleep and thought you had realized how you misjudged my intentions earlier and had come to make amends. When I recognized my error, I tried to—"

"You weren't trying that hard! You think with your gonads, you miserable son of a—"

Lijena screamed; high-pitched and brimming with horror, her cry rent the camp's silence.

"By the Gods!" Selene's head jerked up and she stared at the blonde.

Lijena screamed again, louder, longer. Her naked body stiffened for an instant and in the next thrashed and writhed. Her eyes were wide but held no sheen. Her arms and legs twitched and jerked as though the muscles beneath the satiny texture of her skin attempted to knot themselves. Her head wrenched from one side to the other while saliva came foaming from her mouth.

"The falling sickness!" Selene stared at Davin. "Get her to my wagon! I'll get my father."

While Davin pushed to his feet and tugged on his breeches, the Huata woman ran for Tymon's wagon.

As suddenly as the fit had started, it ended. Lijena quaked spasmodically one last time, then went flaccid. Her eyes fluttered closed, and her cheek turned to the pillow of Selene's bed. She lay still, deathly still.

"What happened to her?" Selene arched a thin eyebrow and glanced at the three men within the wagon with her.

"Silence, daughter!" Tymon pushed from the trunk on which he sat and placed an ear to Lijena's breast, while he pressed two fingers atop her jugular vein. He sighed heavily when he turned to his companions. "She's alive . . . sleeping."

"Aaaa! I knew this one would be trouble. First she tries to drive a dagger into Davin's heart while tupping him, and now the falling sickness!" Goran shook his head and stared out the wagon's open window. Dawn had long passed and morning's yellow light bathed the camp. "We should have left her with Masur-Kell!"

"Nay, the girl's not suffered a falling sickness fit,"

Tymon said with a shake of his head. "Did you not hear her speak as she writhed?"

"Speak? She growled like some wild animal!" Goran thumbed open the gold box he found on the window ledge. His head jerked back and his nose wrinkled. "Nyuria's arse! This smells like rotten eggs!"

"Eh? Rotten eggs? I noticed the same on the clothes she stole from me." Selene lifted a blouse and skirt from a corner of the wagon and tossed them to Goran.

He sniffed at skirt, then blouse. His head jerked back, and his face squinched sourly. "Aye! 'Tis the same. There seems to be powder or dust . . ."

"If not the falling sickness, then what?" Davin pressed Tymon.

The Huata leader waved him to silence, then took blouse and box from the Challing to examine both carefully. "A trace of powder remains in the box—the same as on the front of this blouse."

He turned to Selene. "Where did you get the box, daughter?"

Selene shrugged. "She brought it with her."

"From the mage?" Tymon glanced at Davin.

But it was Goran who answered. "Aye, I remember giving it to her to carry. It's gold and can be melted down."

"Magicks?" Davin took the blouse and box and studied them. "It looks like the powder some women use to lighten their faces."

"I believe that was the mage's intent," Tymon answered. "Although I suspect it was meant as a gift for another, and not for Tadzi's niece."

"Then magic is aplay!" Davin looked up at the Huata leader.

"I wish we had time to consult with Candra. The old woman might have an insight into what has happened. Look at her." Tymon pointed at Lijena. "She is under some enchantment. That much is clear, but its nature? I cannot say."

"Is it necessarily from the box? Might not Masur-Kell have tracked us down?" Davin asked, trying to ignore the cold dread that crept up his back.

"Would a wizard bother with a coma when he could reduce us all to ash with a single pass of his hand? No, this sprang from the box." Tymon's lips pursed and he turned back to Lijena.

"I can go back into Leticia and find Candra. Perhaps I can bring her out and—"

Davin was silenced by a quick gesture from the Huata leader. The sounds of approaching horses came from outside the wagon, and, above the clop-a-clop, the clank of armor and shield.

"Soldiers! We've delayed our departure too long," said Tymon and motioned to Davin and Goran. "It is time for you two to become Huata."

"But Lijena..." Davin protested.

"She'll be all right for a while. Selene, get Davin something more colorful. Goran's scarlets are bright enough, even for a Huata. The guards will never know the difference." Tymon pushed past Davin and went outside to greet the approaching soldiers.

Seconds later, Davin stepped from the wagon garbed in a Huata blouse of multihued flowers and a matching scarf wrapped about his head. Goran followed him to Tymon's side.

"You seem in a hurry to leave," the Captain of the Guard said to the Huata leader.

The captain was a burly man equal to Goran in both height and width. Nor were the five soldiers with him stripling youths such as those set at Leticia's main gates. All had the hard look of seasoned weaponsmen who long ago had learned to swing their swords first and ask questions later. Their suspicious gazes darted about the camp, alighting on the Huata who were busily loading the wagons.

"We must reach Harn before the week is out, Captain. To do otherwise is to lose out on precious opportunity.

Other Huata head for Harn, also. We must reach that fine city before them," Tymon tried to explain.

"Or lose the chance to fleece innocents of their hard-earned money? Is that it?" The soldier snorted with contempt.

"Captain, we are but honest performers struggling to survive. We give honest entertainment for the few coppers we collect."

Tymon clapped his hands and jugglers performed. Sleight-of-hand tricks distracted a pair of the soldiers, and another wandered after a Huata who seemed to produce gold coins from thin air. The captain, however, gave no indication he found the displays to be the least bit amusing—or distracting.

"What's he do?" the captain demanded, pointing at Goran.

"Perform for the good man," ordered Tymon, unable to cloak his nervousness.

To everyone's surprise but Davin's, Goran took a quick step, performed a cartwheel, a flip, and then a handstand. Such agility in a man so large was remarkable. Then, Goran was not a man but a Challing.

"And this one?" the captain pressed, jabbing a finger at Davin.

Before the Jyotian could reply, Selene jingled and jangled out of her wagon. She wore a full dancer's costume, replete with bells and silken veils that hid little and suggested much.

Davin and the others were quickly forgotten when Selene danced. The soldiers' full attention focused on her. By the time Tymon had forced a few cups of strong wine into the captain, Selene had finished her dance and was perched on the man's knee, her arm around his neck and her lips brushing his ear.

"Well, uh, things appear in order. We received word of, uh, hmmm, work of thieves in the group who assaulted the wizard Masur-Kell last eve. Hmmmm, that's

nice." The man could barely keep his wits about him
with Selene so seductively nuzzling his neck.

"But that cannot be!" protested Tymon, with just
enough indignation to make it ring true.

"No, no, couldn't be," said the captain. He laughed
at some indecent suggestion Selene whispered in his ear.
"But we really must follow our orders. Men! Search the
camp."

Davin silently released a breath held too long and
relaxed. The soldiers making their lackluster searches
would find nothing. The Huata were past masters at con-
cealing what contraband they smuggled.

—Rise.

Lijena moaned and stirred. The voice called her from
a restful dream.

—Rise. The time has come to leave. Let no one stop
you. No one!

She did as commanded without question. For when
the voice spoke, her mind was no longer hers but served
that compelling voice.

She found the clothes she had worn earlier and kicked
them aside. From Selene's wardrobe she selected a heavy
red blouse, black breeches, and a woolen coat. She dressed
quickly, then dropped to her knees. Fingers suddenly as
strong as pry bars slipped between the wooden plank
flooring. With a single convulsive jerk she tore open a
hidden compartment containing a cache of Huata weapons, as well as a small fortune of gold bists. The latter
she left untouched, selecting a sword and a dagger instead. She stood and strapped both about her slender
waist.

She took one step toward the wagon's exit and halted.
A Letician soldier opened the door and stood staring in.

—Let no one stop you!

Coldly, emotionlessly, Lijena whipped her sword from
its sheath and lashed out.

The guard's cry of alarm died in a wet gurgle as his vulnerably exposed throat opened from ear to ear. He stumbled back, then fell, a thick river of blood fountaining from severed arteries.

Davin saw the soldier working his way toward Selene's wagon and moved to intercept him. He also saw the glinting tip of a blade flash from the wagon and trace across the man's throat.

"A trick!" Davin called out. "A trick for our guests! Let me do a trick!"

The diversion might have worked if the soldier had lived. As it was, it only drew unwanted attention. The other guards—and their captain—turned and saw their comrade die.

Swords hissed from scabbards as the guards rushed for the wagon at the captain's command. Davin reacted rather than thought. His own longsword came flashing from its sheath. His wrist flicked. The foremost of the guards cried out and fell face down on the mud, his right hamstring neatly severed.

At the rear of the charging troop, he saw Goran leap to the back of a helmeted soldier, grasp the man's neck in those massive Challing hands, and wrench. There was a loud crack, like that of dry wood snapping, and then there were only four guards with which to contend.

To the left, the Letician captain threw Selene from his lap and freed his sword, fully intent on skewering the lovely bosom he had snuggled against but an instant before.

Davin ducked beneath a wild slash by one of the soldiers, received a nasty nick on his forearm from another's dagger, and managed to thrust just as the captain's arm descended. Flesh raked along the sharp sword edge.

"Aieee!" bellowed the officer, shoving Selene away and turning to face a real adversary.

Davin wanted no protracted battle. He swung his sword around, got a two-handed grip on it, and brought it straight down with every ounce of power he could muster. The blade cut through an upthrust hand, a bony forearm, the shoulder guiding the arm.

Blood sprayed in a shower. The captain spun and tried to run. He got four paces before he toppled onto his face, dead.

Davin pivoted, ready to face a new attack. What he received was an armful of very warm and wiggling Selene. He offered no resistance to the mouth that covered his—one eye revealed that Goran and the Huata men had dispatched the remaining guards.

"He was going to kill . . . You saved me, Davin!" Selene managed between her grateful kisses.

"The least I could do." Davin grinned down at her.

Abruptly she shoved him away. "But that doesn't make up for what . . . what you were doing with that blue-nosed Bistonian bitch! Nothing will ever erase the pain of finding—"

The sound of hooves echoed from behind the wagons.

"More soldiers!" someone cried.

"No!" Davin shook his head and said, "One horse only, and it's moving away from . . . Lijena!"

He raced to the wagon, Selene following closely. The wagon was empty! Davin moved to the side of the wagon and stared after the rider, who spurred the gray mare Orria on in a full run.

"Aye, my friend, that's her riding like the wind," said Goran. The red-haired giant lifted the tip of a bloody sword and pointed with it. "She's going northeast."

Davin glanced at his friend. "But Harn is to the west."

"And Bistonia is to the southwest," finished Goran. "Wherever she rides, it is not to her family."

"Good riddance," spat Selene. "I saw what happened. She cut down the soldier the instant he opened the wagon door. She panicked."

"Panic?" asked Davin. "She was in a coma when we left her. It's Masur-Kell's damnable magicks! They possess her."

"Let her go," Goran said. "She has been nothing but

trouble. The skinny ones are always trouble."

"It might not be that easy," said Tymon as he moved to his daughter's side. "Whatever drives her is of magical birth. Davin, I think you have to find and stop her. You must."

"What is this, old man? A premonition?" demanded Goran. "The world ends unless we find her? Is that it?"

"Not a premonition," Tymon replied. "Just common sense. Your destiny and hers are tied together. They have been ever since Davin traded her for you, Goran One-Eye."

*Lijena's and my destinies are intertwined*. The Huata's words touched something within Davin that he had unconsciously sensed from the very first moment he spotted Lijena riding in the Harnish forest.

Goran glanced at the expression on his friend's face, snorted, and silently went to saddle their horses.

Tymon squeezed Davin's shoulder and said, "It is necessary, my old friend. I feel it. You must find her. How, why, I don't know, but it is necessary."

*Necessary*. Davin didn't question Tymon further. He wasn't certain he wanted to know more. The Huata often knew more than any ordinary man would want to know of the future—or should know. It wasn't because Tymon said it was necessary that he would follow Lijena—it was Lijena herself that drew him.

"Can you deal with this?" Davin nodded to the corpses starting to attract flies in the morning sun.

"We've done it before. This city is no different than a dozen others. Other guards will come, and by the time they finish questioning us about their patrol, they'll think *they* were mistaken, that these poor fools never existed."

Davin watched as the Huata leader turned to tend the burials.

"Davin," Selene said softly. "I'm sorry for all I said last night. She's possessed. You couldn't fight that."

He didn't argue.

"I wish you could stay—for a while longer."

Her meaning was clear, but before he could say anything, she reached up, grabbed him, and pulled his face down to hers for a passionate kiss.

"Return," she whispered huskily. "Return to me!"

Then the Huata woman spun and ran off. Davin Anane heaved a sigh. It was difficult swinging into the saddle and riding off beside Goran. It was always difficult leaving Selene.

Davin turned and looked back at the Huata camp when they reached a small rise. He thought he saw a tiny figure wave, but he couldn't be sure. One day Selene's farewells and greetings would belong to another man.

Davin edged the thought aside. After all, it was a fact he had always accepted. His mind raced after the Bistonian woman who fled before him. Time after time his misadventures had cruelly interwoven into Lijena's life. First she had been Velden's slave, then Masur-Kell's. Now, through no fault of her own, she wore a yoke of magic—though what that yoke might be, Davin could only guess.

He'd find her once again, and when he did, he'd see that she was freed from whatever spell Masur-Kell had placed upon her, and then return her to her family.

*Then I'll be done with her for once and all!*

Davin cursed to himself. The words had a fine ring to them, but somehow felt hollow.

# chapter
# 21

"SHE RIDES LIKE all the demons of Peyneeha are at her heels," Goran complained as he slid from the saddle and led his mount toward a narrow stream.

"Her horse will drop from under her. We'll have her then!" Davin answered with a reassuring smile as his horse drank.

In truth, he worried. They had stopped to rest their mounts several times during the day—had to stop; Lijena did not. The gray she rode should have been dead from exhaustion hours ago. No ordinary horse was bred for such endurance.

But then, Lijena was not astride an ordinary mount; Davin recalled the sleek, dapple-gray mare she called Orria. The horse had come from Lord Tadzi's own stable and had probably cost the price of a hundred ordinary horses. For a high enough price, a man could buy a steed with bloodlines that traced back to Lukiahn, the father of all horses.

*Still she rides the mare like a demon!*

They had not caught sight of Lijena since they had left Tymon's Huata band back at Leticia. If if weren't for the mare's spoor, which Lijena made no attempt to conceal, the two adventurers would have given up the chase after a few hours.

"I'll drop before that mare. She's a desert mount, bred to travel the dunes all day without rest or water," grumbled Goran while he lowered himself belly to the ground and noisily drank from the stream.

Davin squatted beside the water, cupped his hands, and scooped a drink from the clear current. The best he could determine, the stream was a tributary to the river Faor, which meant Lijena no longer rode northeast, but directly north. An easterly course would have taken them across the Faor hours ago. North, however, was not east—she still fled away from Bistonia and Harn.

*What lies to the north? What draws her away from home and family?*

"Davin, what do you make of this?"

Goran's voice intruded on his thoughts. The Challing stood pointing to a patch of dead grass beside the stream. The Jyotian moved beside the withered grass. The grass was ashen rather than winter-fallow.

"I've never seen its like before. Notice the burn marks, almost as if a horse wearing a still-hot shoe seared the ground as it passed." Davin sucked at his teeth and scratched his head in puzzlement.

"Aye, I noted the black marks, but the rest of the grass isn't burned, just dead." Goran cautiously edged around the patch to avoid touching the withered grass.

"Some lack of the soil?" Davin had no idea what caused this. He glanced around and found a trail of the burned hoofprints leading northeast.

"Lijena's trace is over here." Goran tilted his head toward deep impressions of shod hooves. "She's changed directions again . . . riding northeasterly now."

Orria's trail dispelled the ugly notion that had crept into Davin's mind. *Northeasterly!* An even uglier idea came to him.

"Can this be something following her?"

"Some *things!* At least three. Behind her but ahead of us." Goran stroked his matted beard and slowly nodded. "My reading is that the grass is newly dead, no more than an hour or two at the outside. Lijena can't be much farther than that ahead. . . ."

Davin didn't wait for his friend to finish, but swung back into the saddle, ignoring the protesting soreness of thighs and backside. Tymon's warning about the magicks Zarek Yannis had unleashed on Raemllyn wedged into his mind and would not leave. *It can't be! But what other steeds could fire the ground with their hooves?*

"Let's ride. We waste precious time!" Davin urged the Challing back into the saddle, then spurred his mount after Lijena, praying to Yehseen that Tymon was wrong.

Davin coldly eyed the blue-gray of the twilight sky. The Tear of Evening winked just above a stand of *morda* trees they were camped beside, and the Jester rose, barely visible in the south.

The last heir to the House of Anane cursed beneath his breath as he gnawed a bite from a strip of jerked venison and chewed. A whole day they had ridden, and still they had not caught a glimpse of Lijena. And they had lost the trail of the fiery hooves!

Davin stepped across a nameless stream barely wider than his foot and walked to where Goran piled kindling for a fire. "Damnation! It makes no sense! Goran, did my eyes deceive me, or were the last of those tracks smoldering?"

"Smoke came from grass turned to charcoal," Goran assured him. "Then the tracks just vanished—as though the mounts had leaped into the air and taken flight."

"Horses don't fly!" There was a sharp edge to his voice that Goran didn't deserve. *Or do these mounts have wings?* Davin tried to recall the old legends, but remembered no mention of fiery steeds with wings.

"Come and sit. Pacing will do no good." Goran waved an arm to the ground beside him. "We've done all we can this day. Rest is what is needed now."

Davin plopped heavily to the ground and winced.

They had ridden hard, and his hindquarters throbbed in testimony to the distance they had covered. "If it rains tonight, we'll lose—"

"Shhhhhh! Listen!" Goran hushed him.

Davin did and heard the hollow sound of pounding hooves. He jerked around. They came from the north, beyond the *morda* stand. He turned back to the Challing, who nodded, stood, and drew his blade. Davin followed suit, then moved into the trees and up the rise on which they grew.

Goran's quick hand restrained Davin from rushing forward when he saw Lijena crouching by a campfire in the small valley below.

"But Goran, she's—" Davin bit off the words when he saw that she was not alone.

The other riders—the other three—had also overtaken Lijena.

"They're not just a tale to scare the younglings," said Goran.

"The Faceless Ones!"

The three riders reined in and held their snorting mounts just beyond the ring of pale light cast by Lijena's campfire. Their horses pawed the earth, searing the ground wherever they touched; their hooves were afire!

"She's rising to greet them," Goran said in a whisper.

Lijena walked toward the three. As she neared the foremost of the demon riders, he grasped a longsword forged from crystalline flame. It blazed brilliantly as it slid from its dark scabbard, tiny tongues of fire leaping and dancing along its entire length. The Faceless One slashed at the air in front of Lijena. She did not flinch.

The other two drew their swords of crystal fire, then fanned out in a semicircle before the woman.

"We've got to help her. She can't fight them." Davin started forward.

"Stay," said Goran, wrenching his friend back by the belt of his breeches. "What can we do against *their* kind?"

The Challing was right. In the light cast by those Hell-fired swords, Davin saw the heavy cowls pulled forward about their heads. No matter which way they turned, their faces—if they had any at all—remained cloaked in the shadow. But the hands gripping those flaming blades . . . were skeletal!

Lijena's head lifted to the unholy riders, and she spoke.

The Faceless Ones' horses snorted flame and reared, burning hooves pawing at Lijena. She did not move.

"What are they saying?" demanded Goran. "I can almost make out what they say. Almost."

Davin only shook his head. A trick of the wind caused but a snippet to come up the hill to where the pair crouched, watching.

The Faceless One in the center pointed his sword at Lijena and cried, abject fear in the steel-edged voice, "The Blood Fountain!"

Then the rider wheeled his horse and rode hard into the night, his passage marked only by the smoldering hoofprints of his steed. A heartbeat later, the other two howled, turned, and fled.

Davin's hand shook as he sheathed his sword. What could possibly make three of the Faceless Ones flee? What did the fearless fear?

*Lijena? But why?*

"Zarek Yannis truly has loosed them on the world again," said Goran, sinking to the ground. "This usurper king plays a deadly game."

Goran stated the obvious. With the evil of the Faceless Ones again unleashed, powers beyond understanding stalked Raemllyn.

And Lijena had frightened off three of them!

"The Blood Fountain," Davin mused. "What can that mean?"

"I know not," Goran replied. "But there is one who might!"

Davin nodded and glanced back to the campfire below. Lijena was gone!

"There. There she is!" Goran cried, pointing.

Atop a rise Davin saw the silhouette of a woman low against the neck of a straining horse.

"We follow," he said. "We must."

Tymon had been unerringly accurate in saying his and Lijena's destinies were intertwined. Davin Anane feared that not only their personal fates but that of Raemllyn hung in the balance, as well.


### The End


# Book One: *To Demons Bound*
### in the *Swords of Raemllyn* series

# Stories
## ~ of ~
# Swords and Sorcery